Clair Brett

An Heiress by Midnight

Clair Brett

CB publications

86 Riverside Ave.
Lisbon, NH 03585

Editor: Frankie Sutton

Cover design: Heart of Jupiter Publishing

Cover photos:

- Couple: Copyright: Hot Damn Stock Photo
- Medieval sword @mikeaubry | depositphotos.com
- Ghost pirate ship sailing and moon @ plrang | depositphotos.com
- The rocks West Pentire in Cornwall@ flotsam | depositphotos.com

Author photo: BLC Photography

Copyright © 2017 Clair Brett

ISBN: 978-0-9983317-3-7

www.clairbrett.com

Dedication

I am dedicating this book to my husband of 19 years. He has supported me through two pregnancies, three career changes, and all the insecurities that come with being a new author. He is a man in a sea of women in our home, and he has risen to the challenge on more than one occasion. He has also been the one to support us while I go off and try this writer thing, with his blessing. Life is messy and not always pretty, but we have had each other's backs over the years and the struggles make the good stuff all the more better. I love you Brett Jock and thank you.

CHAPTER ONE

Clair Brett

July 12, 1817

"It's about bloody time," grumbled Clive Edward Colcord, Lord of Breakerton. He had traveled the length of the Milton Road looking for a highwayman that he was beginning to think did not exist. Not that he had anything better to do, but he had begun to consider the men who implored him to find the highwayman threatening the area had done so on a lark. His spirits rose knowing he had not been taken for a fool. He could hear the waves beating against the shore, signaling how close he was to the sea. His blood was still boiling from the two gunshots sending his team careening along the moonlit road. It was only just that Clive managed to get a grasp on his walking stick cum saber, but his pistol had been misplaced within the carriage somewhere.

"Step free of the vehicle. I shan't ask again," he heard the impatient braggart demand. Considering the hours Clive was forced to ride the Milton tonight looking for this criminal, he could wait.

The moon still shone brightly, but his foe was crafty and remained in the shadows while the cool briny wind from the ocean stung his face.

"Good evening. Wonderfully bright evening, is it not?" Clive quizzed in his usual jovial manner. The reports of this fiend were woefully vacant of tales of violence. He decided to be at his leisure until the situation called for doing otherwise. He was satisfied when his foe stepped further into the shadows. "How might I be of assistance?"

"I am in need of but two things, and as luck would have it, you can assist me with both," the inky figure answered back in an unusual raspy tone sending Clive's nerves on edge.

"I am at your service." Clive started toward the voice in hopes of better seeing the person who was speaking.

"Stop!" The shadow ordered. "That will be far enough. What I need is for you to leave your coin purse on that rock to your right, and then regain your carriage, instruct your driver to turn around and go back from whence you came."

"If you are playing at being a highwayman, might I ask why you did not instruct me to stand and deliver? I am not accustomed to such employment, but was under the impression it was a requirement of your profession," Clive taunted with humor clear in his voice. His would-be assailant seemed to be taken aback momentarily.

"You, sir, seem to have read your share of penny novels. I would have thought them below your station and gender for that matter."

Clive quite liked a quick wit and it seemed even in these circumstances, he could appreciate it. "Well played, lad," he commended with a bow of his head. "It is quite refreshing to meet one who is so industrious and forward thinking in their craft. I am afraid I will be unable to acquiesce, however." He turned to see what he already knew he would. Paul, his driver, had been instructed to make haste in hiding out of sight. He might like the diversion of hunting dastardly deed doers, but it was no reason to put his people in danger. "As you can see, I am afraid my driver fled. I do believe he is unaccustomed to having someone shoot at him. Not to mention, I quite like where my coin purse is and would rather keep it on my person. Also, I have business ahead on this road, not behind." The din of the waves drowned out the usual night sounds, making this encounter seem even more intimate than he would have thought.

Strange, that.

A stunned silence filled the expanse between them except for the sound of the sea and the wisps of salt air mussing his locks. In the silence, he heard the clean sound of a sword leaving its sheath. Clive, never wanting to be left out, did the same, but continued his attempt at conversation. "Shall I bid you farewell then?" He prodded.

"I am afraid you may not," the voice answered with a deadly tinge to the huskiness. The shadow advanced with a slow stride. One had to be impressed by such confidence, Clive decided. The moon glinted off the highly polished steel. "I will ask only once more. Leave your change purse, then turn tail and take your arse to whence you came."

"I don't believe my arse is any of your concern, but thank you," Clive answered. He was enjoying himself quite a bit, which easily waylaid his annoyance from earlier. If nothing else, this highwayman appeared above the pale where intelligence was concerned. "Did you bring that sword for show or were you planning to use it?" He heckled.

Before he could ready himself for the answer, he was forced to jump out of the way, as the blade hummed past his ear. Along with the humming sound, came the smell of--jasmine? He managed to rally and block the next blow with his own sword making his arm tingle from the reverberation of the swords coming to blows. They volleyed back and forth for several moments.

This highwayman had been trained with the blade. Of that, Clive was sure. He himself had studied at Angelo's Fencing Academy. He felt a pang of homesickness for London, and all his chums that spent time at the prestigious academy. However, he doubted any of them would believe he was at this moment fencing for something more than a free pint. Again, the smell of jasmine skittered across his nose filling his senses. That, mixed with the brine of the ocean was a sensual mix.

Clive shook his head. When had he gotten so depraved that a sword fight became sexually arousing? As he again blocked and parried, he decided he needed to seek out a mistress as soon as he returned home. Either that or call for one of his sisters to come and sign him into Bedlam. When a man began getting sexually aroused during a sword fight--well, let us just say it conjures up all sorts of complications, not to mention many safety hazards. He made a lunge toward his opponent, just missing the braggart's shoulder.

That was when he saw it. At first, he thought, along with his nostrils, his eyes were beginning to falter, but then the moonlight caught and trailed down a distinctly feminine lock of black, curly hair. It lay along the shoulder Clive almost ran through only moments before, trailing along her arm.

A woman.

The damned highwayman was a woman. It all clicked into place. The smell of jasmine, his physical reaction, and the lack of information the other victims, all men, were willing to give.

Unfortunately, his concentration was broken just enough and his jasmine scented thief lunged and made contact. Pain shot down his arm to his fingers, almost forcing him to drop his blade. The litany of expletives was enough to make him blush, but in the shadows, he could see a satisfied cat-like smirk on his opponent. The only woman as of late who could make his loins react was also the one person who could best him in a sword fight. This was not boding well for him in the least.

"I hope you realize my tailor will be less than impressed. This happens to be an original," he said through gritted teeth. The truth was that she had managed to slice him in the meaty upper arm muscle. He could already feel the hot blood covering his left arm, and it hurt like hell.

"I am willing to consider this a warning. Now, toss over your change purse please, then leave, go back and tell your friends not to come this way unless they care to have a similar fate."

She stood silently waiting. He did his best to remain upright as the pain worsened. He was still digesting the fact she was a woman. Angelo would be so disappointed. He eyed her for the tick of a second hand on a watch.

"I would love to do as you have so convincingly asked. However, I am unable to now reach in my waistcoat to procure said item. I am afraid if you truly want my money you will have to gain it yourself. It's on the right side." Clive added to the effect by popping out his right hip. How much did she want his money and how bold was she?

She was out of the darkness enough for him to see her open her mouth then close it again. He could just imagine how lush her lips were. He saw in her eyes the moment she decided to have a go. She took a moment to pull her neckerchief around her nose to hide her appearance and that beautifully full mouth, and then she advanced. He stood still, not attempting a bit of assistance. Not very gentlemanly, but she had just delivered quite a nasty cut to his arm. When she finally wrenched the purse free, Clive's libido reacted and he was grinning despite the pain in his arm. She looked for only a fleeting moment at him. Her eyes were a deep color. The moon was not bright enough to make out the hue, however.

Quickly, she stood back. "Thank you, sir, for your generosity," she said with a flare Clive appreciated.

He inclined his head. "No, thank you. I have never been robbed by one with such a gentle touch. You may have ruined me for my current affair."

She gaped at him for only a moment, and then she was gone. Just like that. In the darkness, he could hear rustling, and then hoof beats leaving the scene. He scanned the darkness for only a moment until Phillip came to the rescue.

"He got ye, my lord! I could see it from where I was! Are ye gonna die on me?" He heard Phillip ask as he ran to assist.

"No, I am afraid you will be stuck with me for a while longer." He chose not to enlighten Phillip on his newfound knowledge. His arm, however, needed some tending. "I would ask that we find our way home post haste."

"Of course, Milord. Jus' hold on."

Once in the carriage, Clive wrapped his cravat around the throbbing under his coat. She did an admirable job, damn it. He tied a knot to secure his expensive makeshift bandage. Adrenaline surged through him, as he could still smell jasmine. He closed his eyes and still heard her voice. Her voice, a raspy, husky, sultry tremor, should have given away her gender. He laid his head against the squabs. When he left for this little assignment, he was intrigued, but now, he was exhilarated. This would prove to be diverting after all.

"Hold on, Milord, we're almost there!" Clive heard Phillip shout. He must have called out in pain, but he didn't remember. Closing his eyes, he hoped his driver was true to his word and he would soon be able to exit this insufferable vehicle. Visions of his assailant were no longer easy to conjure over the pain and queasiness played in his mind.

He laid his head back on the squabs as his prison on wheels continued down the road. He stretched his good arm out to the corner of the bench. His hand slid over something smooth and cool. Clive laughed, which caused him to wince as his shoulders shook and jarred his wound. His pistol had been on the bench all the while. The thought of what he could have done sobered him instantly. Had he put his hand on the firearm earlier, he might well have shot and killed a woman. He wouldn't now be in so much pain bleeding on his favorite London-made waistcoat, but this mystery woman would be dead. Even though she did steal from him and all but cut him to shreds, there was something more to this woman. His jasmine scented highway woman. The magistrate might have put him to finding and stopping a dangerous highwayman, but he now finding a damsel in distress took precedence. The question was whether she would even want a champion. At the end of the day, would he have what it took to be one?

"Oi, this will be exhilarating." He closed his eyes giving into the darkness that engulfed his thoughts and his pain.

"I do not need a surgeon," a very harassed Clive complained the next morning as his housekeeper, butler, and valet fussed over him. As soon as he arrived home the prior night, they had clucked and fretted. It hurt like hell, but he knew it was not life threatening once they staunched the flow of blood. Cook had immediately brought water and linen to clean him up. The bleeding had stopped and he was able to examine his injury. It was a long gash running horizontally along his inner arm. Had it been but a scratch, he would have been thankful, but his little minx of a thief cut him deeply. Therefore, every time he moved his arm, it would begin gushing anew.

"Aye, ye do," grumbled Mrs. St. Syer. "If'n ye don't get that stitched up ye'll bleed out afore ye can heal. May I show 'im up?" She bustled around the bed plumping pillows and smoothing wrinkles from the coverlet.

Could he ever become free of meddling women? "Very well." There was nothing to do but suffer the attentions.

More than an hour later, Clive lay in bed waiting for his brandy. The effects of laudanum were not to his liking. He needed to keep his wits about him, and after years of practice, brandy did not seem to fog his mind as much. He had managed to send word to the magistrate that he had some information about the thief. Just what he was going to offer of all he knew he had yet to decide. It went without saying he could not let the secret of her gender be known. If word got out, several might take a try at apprehending her. That would lead to nothing Clive wished to consider. In fact, any of the men who knew of her gender were unwilling to admit they had been bested by one of the more genteel persuasion. If he could make it appear he believed it to be a man, he might very well be able to keep those men quiet--at least for the moment.

The fire crackled, which was a touch Mrs. St. Syer insisted on. She claimed he might catch a chill. As it was now moving into the summer months, he doubted it greatly. His valet managed to open the window next to his bed and pull the drapes when she wasn't looking in hopes to cool the room a trifle. Lying in the center of the large four-poster bed, he wondered why the room couldn't hold this much heat in the dead of winter.

It had taken much of his remaining energy, but once he managed to throw the last of his well-meaning assailants out of his room and nibbed the lock, he was able to tear his way out of his nightshirt and dressing gown. The saving grace, however, were the drapes, which once covered the window were now a puddle on the floor, allowing in the blessed Scottish breeze. The caress of the heather filled the room and kissed his chest. Goosebumps bristled along his skin and his nipples hardened. The brandy had soothed the worst of the pain, but he could still feel each pucker where the surgeon had put a stitch. Exhaustion pulled on his eyelids while visions of beautiful black hair, luminescent dark eyes, and full rich burgundy lips, drew him down into brandy-hazed dreams.

For the time being.

CHAPTER TWO

"This must be handled!" shouted the buffoon in the corner while his jowls shook.

"It cannot be borne!" Another resounded, slamming his fist on the table.

It had not been three days since his encounter, and to his frustration, his injury had drained much of his energy and it appeared his good temperament. These men, apparently upon hearing of his injury and subsequently his recuperation, if a day and a half could be considered so, deemed to blow into his home like a mighty squall and proceed to interrupt his calm. More frustrating, he was still unsure as to what information he wanted to divulge.

"Well?" The first old codger demanded, looking sullenly at Clive as though this were his fault and thus his problem to fix. Ignoring him, Clive sat comfortably in an overstuffed chair with the offending arm resting in a sling across his chest. He should have felt at a disadvantage for his lack of proper gentlemen's attire. As his clothes were all of the current style, the tightness of a jacket would not do, so he was lounging in his breeches, shirttails, and a waistcoat. To his satisfaction, he didn't feel the slightest bit untoward. He liked to think his father would have behaved the same. He looked around the room. Every eye was on him and waiting.

"Well, sirs, you are correct. There definitely is a thief in our midst." *As good a place to start as any.* He waited while they all nodded and grumbled to each other about the truth of it.

"You, Lord Breakerton, seem to have had the most direct interaction, and was almost killed for your trouble. What have you for intelligence?" Asked the magistrate, another in his majority, but Clive was hoping he had some sense and more importantly, authority over the other doddering fools in his presence.

"I do not have much in the way of plain facts, but I do have some thoughts on the matter." Wincing, he adjusted to sit straighter, pulling on the bandage. His voice now more gravelly than he would like, he continued, "What was it this thief stole from you gentlemen? I purposely had with me a ruby cravat pin, and I wore a very impressive pocket watch complete with fobs. All the thief was interested in was my change purse and for me not to continue along the road."

"Well, yes that's all – th--they demanded of me, but damn it, isn't that enough? My rights were violated! I want justice!" This from the jiggly fellow in the corner of the room. Clive was sure if put to the test, the man wouldn't like puppies, or kittens for that matter.

"Aye, look at you, fer God's sake! That ruffian has injured a Lord of the British realm." Normally, most Scots would cheer that, wouldn't they? Clive thought.

"Yes, well, I am aware of that. However, you gentlemen sent me to investigate so I was not acting as another might. I refused to give. I instigated to see if I would be able to garner the fiend's identity."

"And what say you to that end?" asked the magistrate, with a bit too much enthusiasm. Clive once again looked around the room, thinking and waiting. These were not tolerant men. They demanded order in their existence and this was not giving them order.

"A man-- mid-twenties, long hair." Clive saw the surprise and indignant disbelief on the faces of those having encountered his highway woman. "He is thin, slender almost. At first glance, I could have been sparring with a woman." He hoped he added the correct amount of disgust at the thought, hiding a smile.

"Thin you say?"

"Long hair?" The two men having been relieved of their wealth seemed to grasp the possibility with hope.

Finally, one took the bait offered. "I could see how you might be taken to thinking that it was a woman. Barely any flesh a'tall. I might have thought the same thing had it not been for the voice. Wouldn't you agree, Acton?" He asked the other victim.

"How would you suggest we handle this matter?" The magistrate looked to Clive, the youngest man in the room, for an answer. This was where Clive didn't want to be. If he botched this, people could be hurt. If he was wrong about this woman, she could hurt innocents. However, if he stepped back and let these idiots take the helm, she could be in more danger than Clive felt she already was. This was why he left London, so he would not be put in such a position. Hadn't he proved time and again, he would fall short of accomplishing anything?

"I would suggest you allow me to continue my investigation, beginning with a full recounting from you two." He looked to the corner of the room. "I need not only to know exactly where you were when the thief stopped you, but also, the time of day, day of the week, and day of the month. I am going to try to establish a pattern. We know he isn't attacking people every night so there must be a reason why the three of us were struck when we were or why. I would also use the alternate route to get to Kilbarek Harbor until this is solved. No need endangering anyone else." *Or his damsel in distress.*

"Well, what say you, men? He seems to be invested in this endeavor and Lud knows we all are much too tied up to take on such a task," the magistrate posed to the other two men. They considered it and both grumbled their acquiesces to the proposal. With that, Clive slowly rose out of the chair. Dizziness still plagued him when moving too quickly. He feared more blood was lost than he first thought. "Thank you, gentlemen, for visiting to assure yourselves of my hardy condition." The magistrate rose a bit self-consciously understanding Clive's rub. "If you will excuse me, my butler will see you out. I will be in touch when I have more to offer." He turned on his heels, and as briskly as he could, made his way to the small parlor off the library where after yanking the bell, he promptly threw himself on the couch. He would only rest for a bit. Damn, he hated feeling so useless. It was bad enough he knew the fraud he was, but to show his inability to others was unacceptable. The throbbing in his arm lessened as he relaxed.

"A missive for you," his butler intoned, the vibrations reaching his aching head.

Without bothering to open his eyes, he answered, "I'll read it later. Put it on my desk."

"Yes, sir, you might do that, but I believe it is from your mother."

"What better reason to wait?"

"Ah, because it was sent by a rider, not the post, sir." The ramifications of that news slammed into his relaxed state, shattering it. Clive dropped his foot heavily off the cushion following with the next. Sitting with his shoulders and head on the back of the couch, he extended his good hand for the offending package of velum. The damned letter was so fresh he could still smell her perfume.

"Oh, bloody hell, just what I need." Without opening the missive, he knew it meant a visit was imminent. The sound of crisp vellum being opened and manhandled filled the silence with a long-suffering sigh from Clive to follow.

"Ready my mother's usual room, and have one for Nettie and Mary as well. If this was delivered from my sister's home, which it undoubtedly was, they will be here within a week's time."

"I shall let the staff know. How long are they visiting? Cook will want to be prepared."

"I am sure I do not know that. I promise they will be safely ensconced back in London before winter sets in." If they weren't, he might wander into the wild Scottish winter to freeze to death.

The butler left with his news. Clive moved across the room to the floor length window. The view was of the back garden and path to the folly. In spring, the flowers were just beginning to come into their own and the pops of color drew the eye. His arm began to throb along with his head. Within a few days, he would be able to remove the sling and return to wearing proper attire. His mother and sisters never need know of his injury. As for his nocturnal spying ventures, well, he had spent many years perfecting his stealth. They shouldn't be in his way. Mother was no doubt making the rounds in an attempt to be out of London in the heat, not to mention the Little Season had always pinched a nerve for her.

The one black spot on all this was his sister Nettie. She was a sly one and she wouldn't miss a trick. Hopefully, Mary would keep her busy.

Poor Mary. Clive's heart tightened. He had not seen his fourth sister since he had escorted her to her husband's funeral. She was well out of mourning, but Paul had been the love of her life. Nettie's letters overflowed with concern over Mary's forlorn attitude. She felt Mary was not trying to heal. He would make time to go riding with Mary and see for himself. He might be the youngest child, but he was the head of the family, for what that was worth. He wouldn't let one of his charges be lost to the fates.

Cook needed to be made aware of his mother's favorite dishes so that a trip to the market to acquire the necessary ingredients could be accomplished. He turned and headed to the study to compile a list for the staff. Once done, he would need to ride out to visit his childhood friend, Nicholas. If anyone knew about this highway woman, it would be him. The one glimmer in the fiasco was the fact that his other three sisters would not be in tow as well. One highway woman and three uncontrollable titled women was all, he was certain, one man should have to handle at a time.

CHAPTER THREE

Louissa sat on her bed in the early morning sunlight. It had been three days since the incident and exactly nothing had happened. She had expected the authorities to pound down the front door, or worse, the private army of the new English lord. She had not heard he had an army, but if he did, it was sure to come take her in the dead of night. Nothing. She also expected her uncle to summon her to his study for a very loud dressing down at best and a horrific punishment at worst. Nothing. The unease of it all might cause her to go mad. If the Lord had died, she was certain her uncle would have heard, but if he was not dead, he must be livid and want justice. *Isn't that what all the important men wanted?*

She reached down her bodice to pull out the red ruby locket that had belonged to her mother. If her uncle ever saw the piece of jewelry, he would sell it. It was the only thing she had left. She could remember her mother putting it around her neck and then pulling her up in her lap in front of the looking glass. She would say, "This heart is your family, sweetie. With this heart, you will always be able to prove who you are." She remembered the days following her parents' drowning. She cried day and night. So much so that she had been sick. One morning when she woke, she felt something heavy and cold on her chest. In the night, someone had taken the necklace, which Louissa had assumed went to the bottom of the sea with her mother, and had put it around her neck inside her night rail. Instinctively, Louissa hid it away and never shared with a soul she possessed it. It now shown warmly a red hue that spoke of love and family. She turned it to finger the back where there was an inscription and a divot. At first, she thought it was broken, and that a piece at some point had been broken from it, but Louissa knew differently.

It was where another item would fit to open the locket, but until she found such an item, she would not know. She kissed it, said a prayer to her parents and sent love to her brother before putting it back safe and sound inside her bodice. The small ritual made her feel connected to someone, something, and not so alone in the world.

After taking a long ragged breath, she decided her plan had to move forward faster. She could not control what her uncle, the Laird of Loc Landon did, or more to the point, forced her to do. Not to mention, having no control over a complete stranger who may or may not know her secret. She would need to find the other letters Lady Margaret assured her she had hidden to prove her uncle planned to kill her family. If she was able to find one, there must have been more.

She also needed to find a way to get to a small fishing village south of Eyer's Meade, where she believed her brother to have been raised. If she could just get one person, just one to say they remembered, she would be buoyed and able to continue her search.

Her uncle wouldn't be going out for another few days, so she would have time. Often, when Darius arrived, he would persuade her uncle to ride out and check his operation in the other ports on the Eastern side of Scotland, so she might even have some time alone.

Buffeted by the thought of her uncle leaving for a few days, Louissa stood, brushing off her dress and those feelings of foreboding for that which she could not control yet, and moved about her room tidying and planning. She would have to attend to Bethany, her only friend. She would ask questions about where Louissa had run off. She would have to work on a reliable story for that.

As for getting to that small village, she would need to wait until after her uncle was gone. So, that left looking for the other letters. She exhausted any possibilities of them being in this house. She had searched top to bottom, but it made sense that her uncle was not aware of their existence. If he thought proof of his crimes existed, he would not stop until he was in possession of them. She had also searched her parents' manor, which stood dark and in disrepair since her uncle had it boarded up years ago.

The one place she needed to search was the one place from which she should attempt to stay away. Laird Margaret Colcord of Loc Moore's estate was a dear close friend of her parents and the one who gave her the first letter. Unfortunately, she passed last year. To make matters worse, her British nephew, a certain dusty haired, blue-eyed buck with lazy curls and a wicked smile, held up residence now. Yes, she should stay away from there.

Far away.

She had already almost fileted the poor man, but the heated flush she felt when she remembered him in the moonlight was enough to convince her that it was dangerous. She noticed the room getting warmer and let out an exasperated breath. "Oh, for the love of Cesar," she chided herself, "ye, don't have time dreamin' of men ye'll never have." Ridiculous notions had no place in her current predicament.

Perhaps after-- once her brother was found safe and she was free from her uncle and his plans, well then she would pour some hot tea, butter a scone, and sit down fantasizing about a certain English Lord all afternoon. As for now, other, more pressing matters required her attention.

Going to the slant in the wall above her cot, she counted over seven planks, poked her finger in the knothole in the eighth plank and quietly slid it free. Connected to the inside of the piece of wood hung a rope tied to a nail. The box attached to the other end of the rope popped out of the hole as she pulled the rope up.

The proof was held inside the hand carved box, or what proof she had of her uncle's deeds against her family. She just needed to check one thing, and while her uncle was still eating his morning meal would be as good a time as any. Her time was running out. If she didn't find her bother alive soon, there would be no point in it at all. Quickly, she skimmed the parchment in her hand and there on the page in her father's elegant penmanship it stated that he was beginning to fear his brother was plotting against the family. The document was not enough for a court to see as proof, but it was all she needed. Gently, Louissa refolded it. With remembered touches, she retied and replaced the box in her wall. This one letter was what kept her going, kept her digging.

She fixed her bonnet and checked her one nice gown in the looking glass. "Well, it looks much nicer than black breeches and a mask," she said to no one except herself.

Leaving her room, she turned right to head down the back stairs. If she were quick, there would be biscuits left. Then, she would hurry through the back gate to Bethany's. The vicar's wife was truly the only person Louissa trusted. It was also the only place now where she felt welcome and safe. The safety she knew was an illusion, but it was all she had.

Was it true everything looked better in the light of day? The fear she felt every time Uncle Gareth forced her to get on her horse and guard the Milford road was gone come sunrise, but Louissa still felt the angry finger of blame pointing at her like a beacon of light to a ship. No one could possibly know it was she. They would be doubling their efforts now that she wounded a man. His eyes flashed into her memory. Deep pools of intelligence. She could have sworn he was enjoying himself at least until he was wounded. Men.

Crossing the field, the sharp crunch of the long grass made way to much softer grass as she neared the small church and Bethany's home. She would stop and leave her offering to the poor on her way past the church. Her conscience would then be wiped clean as always. Well, not this time. This time, she had hurt someone. It would take more than a tiny bag of coins to relieve her guilt.

Coming back out of the church, the sun blinding on the warm morning, Louissa saw Bethany taking linens from the line while arguing with Mortomer the cat, over the corner of what looked to be her good table cover.

"Who is winning?" Louissa called with a wide wave as she made her way to the small back garden.

"Oh, that blasted cat is, that's who! Give me that Mortomer!" Bethany's words were softened by the gentle way she picked the fat cat up and placed him behind her. "I hadn't expected to see you this week. Didn't you say your uncle was planning a trip?" She asked going back to folding to protect the other corners from Mortomer's playful paw.

"Yes, well fortunately, Darius has appeared to update Uncle Gareth on his other holdings, so I have heard that he decided to postpone his trip," Louissa answered as truthfully as she was able. Bethany was her friend, but she was also a vicar's wife. She knew that lying to her had to be a sin. She sat on the ground leaning on the stump of a tree, now holding a basket of fresh laundry. Mortomer found his way to her lap and after some adjustment, curled up and began to purr.

"That does sound fortunate for you. I can't see how you are ever able to travel as you do. I would find it exhausting," Bethany commented. "It will also give you ample time to keep searching. Any more luck yet?"

"Shhh! Bethany, I told you, you must keep quiet about my suspicions, please. I never should have told you. It is too dangerous." Louissa looked around, as if someone might be lurking in the bushes.

"Posh, I haven't told a soul! Nicolas doesn't even know. I do think, however, he could better guide you in your hunt. I am ever nervous about your safety."

As am I, Louissa thought.

"The vicar could be of no real help and as for my safety, I am the one who knows how to use a blade. Do not fret over my trivial matter. Truly, I am fine." She had to convince Bethany to leave her husband out of this. She had confided in Bethany when Margaret died, because, well, she needed someone to talk to. It was selfish, she realized now. If Nicholas knew, it would only make him a target of her uncle, which she didn't want. "Where is your husband today? I cannot hear his whistling."

Clair Brett

"Yes, isn't it blessedly quiet?" Bethany chuckled. "I love him dearly, but there is something to be said for silence every now and then." Both women laughed. The vicar had a habit of whistling to himself as he worked. It didn't matter the job either. He could be writing a sermon or tilling the garden. "He has gone riding. A very old friend paid a visit today and asked his help in a private matter. At least that is what I am assuming. Knowing this gentleman, it will have to do with a woman."

"Ah, a rakehell is he?" Louissa asked, not that she thought any man would be anything but. Her question garnered a slight blush from her friend and a twitter of laughter.

"I can only imagine, but as he was not raised here, I cannot say. There." Bethany grabbed the basket from over Louissa's head and headed toward the door. "If the two of you follow me, I might be persuaded to find you each a treat," she called over her shoulder.

"What say you, Mortomer? I am hoping for some cakes. I would bet you are hoping for a nice morsel of fish, so up you go." The cat leapt off her lap and with a shake sauntered toward the door.

The kitchen of the small parsonage was bright and overly warm for such a morning. Many baskets were spread over the worktable and open floor space. Every Wednesday when able, Louissa would assist Bethany with filling baskets for the poor. It was the one social entertainment she was allowed and hated to miss catching up with the local women and children as they delivered them. Not sure how many more of these days she would have, this one would have to be remembered.

An hour later, the baskets were filled and ready to pile on the wagon. The gentleman in question must be very well off and know the life of a clergyman, because he brought a horse for the vicar to ride. His own horse would not be able to keep up with his friend, Louissa assumed. "Louissa, can you go to the barn and get Tilly? I will begin to carry these baskets to the wagon."

Louissa grabbed two baskets to place in the wagon on her way by. The barn was dark and cool, but Tilly whinnied her location. She heard the thunder of hoof beats echo through the old wooden walls as she led the older horse out to the wagon. Even from a distance, she could tell which man was which. The unknown gentleman cut an impressive figure. Considering her future, she was jealous of any woman who might be allowed to give him problems. Her future husband looked more like Tilly than the man galloping toward her, she had been told.

With a snort at her thoughts, she continued hitching Tilly to the wagon, making sure her back was turned against the view.

"Well, good afternoon, gentlemen. I trust you enjoyed yourselves," Bethany called as the men rode up.

"That we did, my dear. I have not had such an exhilarating jaunt in quite some time." Louissa heard one of the riders dismount and walk toward Bethany.

"May I assume you also solved all the world's problems?" She chuckled. Louissa didn't have to see the two of them to know they were kissing. She loved the affection she saw between them. It reminded her of her family and her old life.

"Well, I am not sure about all the problems, but if Parliament calls, we can assist in a good handful," came another unexpectedly familiar voice.

Louissa froze. No, no, no, no, no. She snuck a peek of the other gentleman hoping her every nerve had simply gone into a fit. But, no, it couldn't be that, it had to be him. *All right, he's alive. You didn't kill him.* That was where the good news stopped. What in blazes would she do now? She couldn't be introduced. Even if he didn't recognize her, she would give herself away, and she knew it. The baskets. That was it. She would go and hide until he left. Or, better yet, go after the baskets and just keep going. Turning, she ran as fast as her skirts would allow around the corner of the house and out of sight.

"Bethy, who was that? Have you been hiding all the young impressionable damsels from me?" Clive asked as he watched a streak of skirt, ankle, and long black silky hair disappear behind the house. When he turned back toward his friends, they both looked more confused than he did. He had a suspicion the woman fleeing was fleeing because she recognized him.

"Was that Louissa?" Nicolas quizzed his wife.

"Yes, but I cannot for the life of me begin to know what is in that girl's head," Bethany replied with exasperation. "Skittish as a barn cat," was her only explanation.

"I hope I didn't scare her," Clive responded with concern even though all his instincts were telling him otherwise and to punctuate the fact, both his friends began laughing.

"Louissa might be the one to frighten even the likes of you, but you my friend, would not make her bat an eyelash. Pure steel that one," answered Nicholas in a dismissive tone. "Come, let us go to my study and talk more on that mystery I was telling you about." Nicholas slapped Clive on the shoulder unknowingly eliciting a pain-filled grunt.

"Are you all right?" Bethany asked only to be assured by both men that Clive was just jesting with his old friend about his brute strength. Clive was certain, however, that the woman did not believe one word of the rubbish her husband was trying to throw at her. As the men turned toward the house, Clive leaned toward the corner of the barn. She wasn't there. He knew to his bones, once spooked, his little felon would flee and not hang about.

"I'll be in with some tea and biscuits before I leave with the baskets," Bethany called to them as they entered the house. It was apparent his mystery woman had been helping with baskets for the poor, as there were still many left, yet to be loaded on the wagon.

"Here," Clive handed Nicholas two of the baskets, being careful not to aggravate his injured arm. The men finished filling the wagon to help Bethany after chasing her only labor away. Nicholas didn't complain, just gave Clive an approving smile. Clive suspected Nicholas would naturally help his wife, but never would have suggested such a thing with Clive in attendance. Again, growing up with a gaggle of women made him more inclined to understand the work that women do and appreciate their efforts.

Finally, ensconced in the small, untidy study, he asked the one question that had been taunting him since they got back to the parsonage. "I need to ask, Nicholas, who was that woman? She fits the description."

Nicholas sat behind his well-worn desk, steepling his hands in front of his face. The only sound was the constant ticking of the clock. He was no doubt considering what he could divulge to Clive. They knew each other as children, but not as much since becoming men. This kind of situation was one Clive didn't care for. He knew he wouldn't stand up to too much scrutiny. Eventually, perhaps this very moment someone was going to realize he was an imposter. They would figure out he was not the man his father was, and in fact, was not a worthy man for any lordship. He didn't bend, however, at the intense consideration his friend was making. Finally, Nicholas had made his decision.

"As a man of God, I am beholden to keep knowledge of certain events to myself."

"I am not asking you to break your vows. At least that wasn't my intent, but if that girl is involved, she is well and truly in danger from at least my little gaggle of gentlemen, no telling who else," Clive answered with a grave but respectful tone, he hoped.

With a heavy sigh, Nicholas leaned forward putting his elbows on his desk and began talking. "You might well be the man who can help them both."

"Both who?" All Clive needed was one more body to be responsible for. Hadn't God come across the knowledge that he was bad at this sort of thing?

"Louissa and her brother," Nicholas said with a grave tone. "They have not been afforded the same luxuries most of us were. They lost their parents in an accident when Louissa was eight years old. Her brother was five at the time."

"Losing both parents must have been devastating." Clive knew how the loss of one parent, before he was old enough to remember him could affect your life. Two would have been unbearable he was sure. Bethany's knock stopped the conversation as she bustled in with tea and cakes.

"Thank you, dear. We can pour. You go along and deliver your baskets."

She looked with question at both men, not believing that two men could figure out the teapot, but nodded and kissed her husband, not forgetting to give Clive a quick embrace before leaving, closing the door behind her. Once they each had a cup of tea, with a little something from the bottle in Nicholas' desk and a handful of cakes, Nick continued.

"The two became wards of their only surviving relative. Their uncle, Gareth Adair. He was never a good person and becoming a caregiver didn't bring out his tender feelings. Those children were dragged onto his boat and were carted halfway around the world time and again." Clive could hear the anger in his friend's voice. "At one point, both became ill from a fever and their uncle separated them when her brother took a turn for the worst. Louissa was told a week later that her brother perished."

Clive felt his stomach drop. First to lose her parents, then her only sibling? He couldn't imagine life without even one of his sisters. He had considered it in the past, but that was only when he felt his sanity might be preserved. He figured that was the way of siblings. Clive made to ask Nicholas to continue, but a knock on the door stopped him.

Nicholas moved from around his desk to peer out the window. He excused himself and made his way into the main room. Clive heard the door, then some voices, but couldn't make out the words. Nicholas returned with a stout farmer, hat in hand, following.

"Lord Breakerton, this is Malcolm McSteven. He has a farm

just outside of the village." Clive shook the man's hand and the man bowed. "I am sorry, Breakerton," switching to the more formal name in mixed company, "but I must go to Malcolm's. His mother isn't well, and she is asking that I be at her side."

Clive did not want to end this conversation, but knew the import of his friend to the people in this area. "Of course," he answered.

"Expect a visitor within the next three days. You will get all the answers you need, that is, if I have a promise you will help."

Clive didn't know what he was being asked to do. "You know I will assist if I am able, but I cannot blindly agree without knowing the circumstances."

"Fair enough," Nicholas answered, as he brushed by Clive to grab his hat off the edge of the desk and move back out into the main room. Clive followed with Mr. McSteven following behind impatiently. "I wouldn't expect you to blindly agree to anything. That would be foolhardy and dangerous. You are not that type of man. Your willingness to listen is enough."

The men said their good byes and as McSteven and Nicholas headed north, Clive rode out to the east and home. He now had more questions than answers. Not how he had wanted this meeting to go.

Now he would have to wait for three days at least, before he got any answers at all, and it might not help him even then. Why could one thing in all this not go easily? Who was this other person he was helping? Nicholas said himself that her brother died. Perhaps Nicholas meant helping the family legacy. Also, who was this stranger? His mother and sisters would be in residence soon. Clive was not happy to be waiting on strangers to arrive.

His shoulder pounded from the exertion of riding. Perhaps he should have heeded his valet's warnings about over-doing. Fatigue was getting the better of him, and he decided it best to stop at the stream up ahead to rest and get a drink, than to ride on home and then pass out. Clive slowed his mount and found a suitable stump nearby to help him get off and eventually remount. He dropped the reins to let the horse wander the field, knowing it was a good horse and it would not leave him.

As he made his way to the streams edge, he caught a glimpse of the cause of all his strife as of late. His highway woman. Why Clive started calling her *his* was puzzling, but he pushed that aside and moved ahead. At the moment, she looked nothing of the sort. Sitting with her knees pulled to her chest and her chin resting on them, she looked small, almost child-like. Not being fooled, since he knew how quickly and deadly she could be, he chose not to walk too close when he made himself known.

"Good day, my Lady," Clive said loud enough to be heard, but he hoped not so loud as to scare her. "I don't mean to bother you, but I was hoping to get a drink if you do not mind."

She turned toward his voice and her hair fell from her shoulder down behind her back exposing a high cheekbone and large almond shaped eyes, rimmed with thick lashes. If he hadn't seen any other part of her, he would remember those eyes. He noted she stiffened, but held her composure. Had he not been looking for it, he would not have known she recognized him. Best to play along until he knew the game better.

After a moment, she answered, "Of course, I was just leaving."

"Oh, no please, I will be only a moment." He walked to the edge and knelt a safe distance from her. Safe for her or him, Clive didn't know. The water tasted fresh and clean as Scottish water always did. It was strange how there was a slight flavor that hinted at heather from the moors and pine from the mountains. This drink also tasted sweet as if his companion had dipped her toe. At the thought, he nearly choked on the mouthful. After recovering and coughing some out, he tried to dismiss it. "I guess I should have made sure I hadn't sucked in any rocks in my haste."

To his delight, her face softened and she smiled. Not a laugh or giggle, but a start. "A wise thought," she warmed to the topic.

"You should carve that into a stone and leave it here as a warning to travelers. It could be your legacy."

"Ah, a cheeky one." Clive enjoyed a woman with a sense of humor.

She smiled and he noticed one small dimple dip into her cheek, giving her a mischievous air.

"I am being terribly rude, I am sorry. Lord Breakerton, at your service," Clive, still kneeling bent at the waist in an unsteady, but admirable bow.

"Tis nice to meet you, my Lord." She, however, did not offer her own name in return.

"Were you not just at the vicar's cottage?" Clive asked nonchalantly he hoped.

"No."

"Oh, then I must have you confused. You women all wear such similar clothing, I am sure I just became confused." He would not be getting any information from her this day, and fatigue was tugging at him. He had made an introduction and that would have to be enough. "Can I escort you home, perhaps? I do not like to see a lady such as yourself out alone on the countryside."

"Thank you, but no. I am sure hearing your accent; I have spent more time on this countryside than you, my lord." She rose and made to leave.

"Ah, but you have not yet given me your name, sweet lady. How am I to speak of my morning events if I do not know your name?"

"Just don't tell anyone. I know I don't plan on saying anything of our meeting," she said with an incorrigible grin and turned giving him her back as she walked briskly down the path and out of sight.

"Cheeky." Clive chuckled and made his way back to his mount. He could have engaged more, but then she might have witnessed the scandal that was he, mounting his horse. He was certain it would not end up in an article in the Times as an example of exemplary horsemanship, but then most of those dandies wouldn't be doing it with a sword wound either.

Of one thing he was certain, she was in eminent danger and it didn't appear she had any champions banging down her door. He would wait for this mystery guest to appear, and in the meantime, decide just how fully he was willing to become embroiled in whatever nefarious act was afoot.

CHAPTER FOUR

Louissa entered the house and closed the door as quietly as she could. The walk home was directly in the path of the afternoon sun. The dimness of the entry blinded her as she made her way across the floor. When she set one foot on the first step, he bellowed.

"Louissa! Louissa, is that you lass? Get in here!"

She sighed and redirected herself down the hall. This was not going to be enjoyable. Since she had yet to speak with him about what happened with the errant Lord, she was certain she knew what the topic of conversation would be. When she entered the large study, the smell of cigars and wood smoke filled her nose. To the right, sitting in a heavy wooden chair was one of her uncle's men, Darius. 'Twas bad enough she would have to endure her uncle's anger, but to do it in front of Darius, well, she was certain to need a bath after this. The way he looked at her always made her uncomfortable.

"Yes, Uncle? I hope your day was…"

"Shut up, lass." Gareth Adair, Laird of Loc Landon stopped her words cold. "Do ye know the trouble you have caused me?"

"Uncle, I didn't mean…"

"You what? You didn't mean to slit a Lord limb from limb?" He asked looking over at Darius who nodded at his boss.

Her anger would someday get her killed, but today would not be that day--she hoped. "Uncle, first, I did not slit anyone limb from limb, and secondly, it might be just what you need to warn travelers from the road once and for all."

The noise her uncle made was clear. He wanted to hear none of her excuses. "It wasn't as if you injured a farmer, or even a drunkard. No, the lady of the house chose a Lord, a damned English Lord to battle with."

"I didn't know he was an English Lord at the time, and I only defended myself. He had plenty of warnings."

"According to the accounts circulating in Dunbartan, you nicked him within an inch of his life. They are considering forming a lynch mob," Darius commented with little humor. So, he was here to tattle on her and become a more valuable asset in her uncle's eyes.

She was glad she could assist Darius in his aspirations as a criminal. His parents would be proud, she was certain. Instead of letting her thoughts burst free, she pierced him with a look he knew to be just as dangerous as her uncle's ire. "I swear to ye, Uncle, it was but a scratch. In fact, I am certain I saw him when I was visiting the vicar's wife this morning. He was riding. Not," she afforded Darius another glare, "at death's door."

"Did he see you?" Her uncle boomed shaking the glasses set at the workbench.

"Uncle, I am not dressed as a man. I didn't even speak with him." She may go to hell for lying. At this point, lying might be what tipped the scale for her.

"Darius, have you heard from your reliable sources?" She used the word reliable with as much sarcasm as it was meant to have. "Have they said if they think I am female or male?"

"Nay, most think ye are male. In fact, I have not heard any say you were female. A few mentioned they heard you were slight, but wiry was always included in that," he said. Louissa could tell it pained the man to admit such a thing. She figured Darius would volunteer to deliver her to her uncle's chosen husband if it meant being rid of her sooner.

Ewin Dermit. Hearing his name sent shivers down her back. The man was pure evil. She had never seen his face, but she was sure it would only bring death to her when she did. If she didn't find her brother soon, all her efforts and acknowledgment of listening to her uncle's tirades would be for naught. Dermit had a reputation for outliving his wives.

"Lass, are ye daft? Do you even listen?" Her uncle had come around the table and grabbed her by the shoulders. His shaking brought her out of her thoughts.

"What? Oh, sorry, sorry," she said trying to step out of his manacle grasp, but it was no use. Louissa knew from experience that once her uncle got his hands on you, that was when you stopped fighting. She stood as relaxed and docile as she could, given her desire to run. "I am sorry, Uncle. That was rude. I just feel horrible for bringing more suspicion on to you. What--what can I do?"

Her plea seemed to bring him at least a minimum of comfort. He let her go and she swayed backward a bit, not realizing her feet were not touching the ground. "What I need is for you to do your tasks without bringing attention to yourself. Do you think that is something you can do?"

"Yes, of course, Uncle," she said with her head bowed in supplication.

"For the remainder of the month, I also do not want you traipsing all over the countryside with that vicar's wife." Fear shot through Louissa. If she wasn't able to leave the cottage, she could not continue to look for proof of her brother's life. Thankful now that she had her head down, she tamped down the panic and cleared her expression into dull compliance.

"But, Uncle, if you forbid me to move among the locals, it will surely force many of the women to decide to drop by and check on my health. I think it would be more prudent to allow me my normal routine, so as not to raise suspicion."

Darius, cleared his throat drawing their attention. "I think she has the right of it, Milord, much as it pains me to admit. If'n she doesn't appear as she normally does, those biddies can spell trouble. I've seen it happen afore."

Louissa looked and looked again at Darius, not believing he was siding with her. On principle alone, the man would say it was night when it was clearly day. She narrowed her gaze, but Darius ignored her, all eyes for the Captain.

"Oh, very well, but one more fool hardy thing and I will lock you in the root cellar myself. You might be worth one whole shipment for me, but not worth losing my entire fleet over. I'll kill ye afore Ewin has his wedding night. Now, go!" And just like that, her uncle was done with her.

The bile rose by degrees as she managed to walk from the room and quietly close the door behind her. She could do nothing but run for her room and shut out her uncle's words. If she could not prove her brother was alive and find him, she would not make it to her wedding night. Tears stung her eyes as she fought the need to let them spill onto her cheeks. She decided a long time ago never to afford her uncle the power to produce such emotion. She felt enough fear and anger, but she would not allow him her tears. Those she would reserve for her family that was lost. Her future was planned for her but not yet final, if she had any control.

CHAPTER FIVE

The morning broke chilly. Clive knew this because he felt as if he had raced the dawn throughout the night. He threw back the covers, thankful for the cold rush of air assailing his limbs. As the skin tightened and puckered in goose flesh, he made his way to the fire. There were still coals, but he began by piling some kindling and a peat moss brick or two to coax it into a flame before adding some larger pieces. He rose needing his velvet dressing gown now that he was feeling more himself, instead of the randy fool he had been through the night. He sat in the stuffed chair in front of the fire and watched the flames dance and twirl up the chimney.

After he returned home yesterday, he was on edge, like when one is aware something is off but for the life of them, couldn't place what. He paced and couldn't keep his mind on something for more than a few minutes, before it would drift to large cinnamon eyes framed with deep thick chestnut lashes or waves of long shiny hair the color of rich deep leather. He re-opened the dressing gown to let in the cool air and swore for good measure.

He had eaten alone and tried to savor his dinner knowing his quiet would soon be shattered when his mother and sisters descended, which would be today he was certain. After dinner, he had hoped to find peace in sleep. Sweet oblivion would allow him to think rationally about his role in this charade.

Sweet oblivion like hell.

He spent the entire night tossing and turning, wrestling with erotic images of a woman with those haunting eyes, wearing only the mask, hair wild spilling around her like the flames dancing in the fire. When he would reach for her she would be gone in a swirl of mist, but not before, he could hear her words like a whisper across his bare neck.

Help Me.

Clive reached his hands into his hair and held on pulling slightly. Damn her for her beguiling ways. At that, he laughed at himself. She had no more idea the effect she had on men than his sisters did. Infuriating really, that they could go about their business unaware of their impact, while good, upstanding, otherwise intelligent men paid the price.

Well, there was nothing for it but to jump into the fray. After his discussion with Nicholas yesterday and his second encounter with her at the stream, he was lost. He had to help. It was the right thing to do. That was all, Clive assured himself as he made his way to his writing desk. He had much correspondence which he needed to attend. If he was going to be saving the lives of two strangers, one an enticing woman that affected Clive against his will, not to mention keep his mother and Nettie at arm's length before they caught a whiff of something nefarious, he needed to get his other affairs in order.

Nicholas said he would be sending a visitor to him in the coming days, and then Clive would learn more, but he didn't want to wait. He needed to find out more now. He would have to take care, because if his little gaggle of lairds knew what he was fishing about, they would get suspicious. They were dimwits, the lot, but they were not complete idiots. He would have to continue to feed them with information as well.

Clive spent the better part of two hours dealing with his affairs in England, but had a parcel prepared and sealed by the time his valet entered with his morning tea. "My Lord, you are already awake. Why didn't you ring?" he asked in surprise. Clive took that as a true indicator of how he had allowed himself to get lazy. This little adventure might be what he needed to gain back his resolve. If he was truly their last hope, he could not allow himself to fail anyone again. His father would have known what to do. "My Lord?"

"Oh, yes, sorry old man," Clive answered trying to hide his woolgathering, "woke with the sun and I didn't see a need to bother anyone. I had my work here and decided to get a jump on the day."

"Ah," replied the older gentleman, "your mother is due today." Clive laughed aloud, thankful at least one servant here understood the implications of his mother and two of his sisters visiting.

"Well, yes, and I have some other-- business I am attending to, so I needed to get this wrapped up," he handed the valet the parcel. "Can you see to it that this is on the mail coach today?"

"Absolutely, My Lord." The valet took the parcel and set it next to the tray, exchanging it with a cup of tea for his master.

"I think the blue vest today, with a simple knotted cravat. Nothing too restricting. Mother will take care of that." Both men laughed. Clive continued to enjoy his tea as the valet helped to prepare his master for the day ahead.

Once comfortably ensconced in his study, all necessary paperwork safely on its way to England and a large plate of breakfast fare in front of him, Clive began planning. He needed to speak more to Nicholas, but not at the vicar's house. He would need to get him into a more relaxed environment if he was to get any worthwhile information. Nicholas was a good man, good vicar, and Clive would not do anything to make him betray his vows, but he was certain Nicholas had information Clive would need to help the situation. If he went busting in like some sod it would be devastating and dangerous for everyone involved. Whom was he kidding? It could be dangerous for everyone no matter.

Clive felt the shift in his world, before the dogs' barking heralded the arrival of his family. His heart leapt despite his protests. He did love his mother and sisters, all six of them. He was happy it would not be the whole brood, however. They were troublesome, but then again wasn't family simply a euphemism for troubles? He stepped out of his study in time to see Hector opening the doors and allowing the hounds to bound out the door and down the steps. "Confounded mutts!" Hector complained, "Won't shut up for anything. Going to kill someone with their lack of discipline," he grumbled.

"Ah, Hector, don't you just wish you had the energy they do?" Clive said as he walked up to the elderly servant and clapped him on the shoulder. The servant chose to grumble and made his way out the door to assist as he could.

"Mother!" Clive called as the woman in question disembarked the well-sprung closed carriage with his sister's husband's family seal emblazoned on the door. She looked up and waved as a footman helped her step down. The dogs had calmed to an impatient sitting position whimpering, waiting to greet the guests.

"Breakerton, darling," she said as she stopped and patted each dog on the head. They might appear undisciplined as Hector said, but Clive had made sure to teach them how to treat a lady. Behind his mother, Nettie was next to disembark. He smiled. His hounds and his youngest sister, still older than he by 10 months, had an equal amount of energy and curiosity. He would have to admit she was much prettier than the dogs though. In the past two years, Nettie had blossomed into quite a striking woman with a body that told of more years than the deb out of the schoolroom. Clive was not sure how that made him feel, as the head of the household he would be responsible for seeing her settled, a more difficult task than he was ready to take on, but he and his sister had been like twins as youth and he wasn't sure if he wanted to share her just yet with the world. She took her hat in her hand and waved it, the tassels striking the footman standing next to her. He would have to give him a Guinea for not making any move to protect himself and therefore embarrassing his sister.

Then he watched as his next youngest sister, Mary, left the carriage. A knot in the pit of his stomach formed, one he hadn't felt since he left England and his family home over a year ago. She was gaunt. She had lost more weight than she had before he left. Her skin was pale, leaning toward ashen, and her eyes were dull and dim. She too waved up at Clive, but he could tell the gesture was one of courtesy alone. Once all three women were on solid ground, his mother led the way up the steps to meet him.

The dowager Lady Breakerton enveloped Clive in a hug. She kissed his cheek and placed her gloved palm on his cheek.

"Son, it has been too long that you have kept yourself buried in this wilderness. I have missed you." She pulled back, but instead of letting go completely, she wound her arm with his.

"Hello, Mother. I missed you as well. I have not been buried here."

"Brother." Nettie was next and rose up on her tiptoes to peck him on the cheek as well. "I, however, did not miss you. It has been pleasant without your incessant dictates," she said with the devil in her eyes.

"Well, truth be told, I was hiding from the likes of you dear sister," he shot back and they both laughed.

He sobered quickly, when Nettie stepped aside to pat one of the hounds that seemed to have taken a shine to her, and allowed Mary to extend her greeting. Clive didn't wait, but scooped her up into a strong brotherly hug.

"Mary, darling," he said, "you look well." He knew it was a lie and knew she knew it as well, but there was nothing to be done.

"Thank you, brother, I feel more myself every day," was her automatic answer, but he knew she practiced it. It was not a true estimation of her state. He wrapped his arm around her shoulders protectively and squeezed.

"I am very glad to see you," he said again.

He turned and led the way into the manor. Since he was not set up for formal guests, he led them into his study, library, and great room combination. None of the women commented, all making themselves at home on the overstuffed furniture near the fireplace. If he could keep the conversation steered in the right direction, he might get through the afternoon without having to defend his decision not to yet be with a bride.

"So, Mother, how is Eloise? Is James behaving?" James was his nephew. He loved reading his sister's letters about the trouble the young lad could find to get into.

"Eloise is fine, but I fear James is going to best her," she said with all seriousness.

All three siblings at the same time said, "Never," and then laughed.

"If you will remember, Mother, Eloise often was found dragging me back from some nefarious activity by the ear. I swear to this day that my left is longer than my right because of it. I am sure when the time comes she will have him well in hand."

His mother only shrugged and harrumphed her uncertainty. "He looks just like his father, and that is for sure."

"Were you able to visit Kat?" He asked about his other eldest sister, twins with Eloise. She was also a widow like Mary, but her husband died as an officer in battle. After his death, she chose to occupy the dowager cottage on her husband's family property in North England. He had not seen her since he stopped by on his way north.

"She is doing famously," his mother intoned. "I believe we will all be invited soon to a wedding." He heard the excitement in his mother's voice, and glanced quickly to gauge Mary's reaction, which he noted, was no reaction at all. She sat quietly studying her hands. Guilt again, wound around his gut and squeezed. If he had been a man like his father, she would not be in such a bad way, he chastised himself now, quietly.

"Well, good to hear it," Clive answered hoping to steer the conversation away from marriage. "What of new gossip do you have to share?" he asked.

"Well, you know I do not partake in gossip," his mother said with true insult in her voice. Clive noted the gleam in her eye didn't quite agree with her tone. "I have read in the news prints lately that your friend Renwick is quite happy these days after finding his bride. We still have yet to lay eyes on her or the child." She looked at Clive as if he could control whom Renwick invited to family dinners.

"Yes, he was quite elated to be reunited with Lady Renwick," Clive admitted.

"It is amazing she survived with amnesia for four years, not even knowing who her daughter's father was."

"Yes, amazing," Clive answered, after being the one to reunite his friend and his estranged wife. Amnesia was a better guise for the Ton than the truth that she ran away from the marriage scared of her feelings. If his mother was believing the story, he was sure it would play out well. He wouldn't pass along his own knowledge that Ella was expecting another child. He would let Renwick decide when to announce that.

At a pause in the discussion, Hector bustled in. "My Lord, are the ladies ready to be shown to their rooms?"

"Oh heavens, yes," his mother answered for him and rose. "I would like nothing better than to clean this road dust off and have some tea. Would that be possible?" She asked Hector as she strolled out. "Come girls," she called over her shoulder.

Both girls rose dutifully and turned to follow. Clive reached out to stop Nettie, who hung back. "Mary," Clive questioned, "how is she truly?" The concern made his voice crack.

"She has good days and bad days."

"Are they more good or bad?" he asked already knowing the answer. Nettie didn't voice her concern, but it was evident in her expression. She reached up and pecked Clive again before turning to leave.

"Wait," Clive knew he would regret giving Nettie any information, but it would no doubt be worse once she got a whiff of his dealings with Louissa, not to mention he needed help finding the papers his aunt hid. "I am in need of a favor, but you are the only one to know at the moment."

Nettie regained her seat with interest clear in her eyes. "Of course, what do you need?"

"I need you to help me search the manor for some hidden papers. I am trying to help a local woman and apparently, Aunt Margaret was also helping. I am told she had papers that would help prove this woman's case."

"Will you tell me more?"

"No."

"Where have you looked?" Dropping her inquisition for another time, Clive was sure.

"My chambers and here in the study."

"I will make it a point to begin once I am settled," she agreed then took her leave. Clive wasn't fooled there would be more questions to come, but for now, he would take the reprieve.

The room echoed its silence as he returned to his desk. As much fun as it was to see his sisters and mother, his mind kept drifting to his highway woman. Hopefully, once he moved forward, he would stop seeing flashes of her constantly. He was glad he was the one who was in harm's way this time. He never should have allowed Mary's husband to do something he should have been capable of doing-- just one more thing to prove how not like his father he was. The solicitors had a heyday with him. He would never again ask another person to take on a cause for him. It was supposed to be him doing the protecting, and that was how it would be.

This girl needed his help and he would offer it. She was in danger by the very people that should be caring for her and cherishing her. He would reserve criticism of her brother until he knew his story, but the uncle was beyond his pity. The man needed to be stopped. She had been a victim from the time she lost her parents. Again, a vision of her wearing only a mask danced in his mind. Damn, if he was going to help her, he needed to cool his desire. He would not exploit her vulnerability like every other person in her life. It had been too long since he had found the bed of a woman. He knew of many willing widows and some not widows, but with his mother visiting, well, he hoped that would be enough to cool the flames.

He bent to pen a note to Nicholas asking for an audience at the manor, then one to his friend who may have some information he could share. His dealings often put him in direct contact with men like Louissa's uncle. Working for the Crown of England, Clive considered now, didn't usually put one in the finest drawing rooms of London, but instead along the seedy streets and docks. He was sure there was a metaphor in that thought, but chose not to think that poorly of his country or governments in general. He was much too young to be so bitter.

Finishing both notes, he rose and pulled the bell pull. While he waited for a footman to attend him, he strolled to the window looking out, just in time to see a streak of something, or more specifically someone darting out of the formal gardens and into the field beyond. It was just a glimpse, but he was certain of what he saw. His notes forgotten, when the footman entered only moments later, he instructed him to race out and check the gardens and field. Just as Clive expected, whomever it was had long since made their way back under cover. He checked on his sisters and mother. They were all still in their rooms and hadn't left. None of the servants saw or heard anything strange. He was almost ready to believe he was seeing visions, but then he caught it in the air along the corridor that led to his rooms, a faint scent of lavender and lemons. She had been in his home, his own rooms to be exact. This was an interesting turn of events, as his desire raged on like an inferno.

CHAPTER SIX

It was finally quiet in the manor. Clive's sisters and mother went visiting some friends of his late aunt's this morning after they broke their fast. Only three days after their arrival, his mother felt up to traveling again. They would be gone until sometime tomorrow. He was happy to have them visiting, but didn't like having to curb his need to act on what he was able to find out thus far. There was still no mystery guest, and Nicholas would not be able to visit for another day because of other obligations. What he was able to find out from his staff disturbed him.

Clive made his way to his study where he sat in a comfortable chair to decide his next move. His staff had told him the death of Louissa's parents was never believed to be an accident, and actually, Clive's aunt was bent on proving it, but never got that far. Louissa was a regular guest of the manor when his aunt was still alive. That coupled with his knowledge she had been in the house led him to believe she was looking for something, but he had yet to find anything that would help. His aunt was the untrusting sort and had hidey-holes all over the place. He was certain there were many yet to be discovered. If she had any proof that Louissa's parents did not die natural deaths, she would have it hidden and hidden well. He had started searching his rooms the very night he spied Louissa running from his gardens. Her scent left a trail for him to follow and it went directly to his bedchamber.

Clive tore the room apart looking for anything she might have been looking for. He had considered the possibility that she found what she was seeking, but nothing appeared to have been moved. The next night, he did the same thing, but in reverse order, still with no results. Last night, he moved on to his private parlor, which his aunt had used as a writing room. He looked through every book on the shelves, under the carpets, behind the paintings. Nothing. If he was going to move forward with this before her uncle reached his end game, whatever that was, he needed to do something. He rose from the chair needing to move. That's when he noticed it. On his desk sat a single blank white sealed envelope. He also noticed that the window directly across from his desk was ajar.

"Does anyone bloody use a front door in Scotland?" He scoffed, shaking his head as he swiped the envelope off the desk and ripped it open. No signature, not that he expected someone who would break into his home to leave a calling card with his or her name. The contents of the letter had him shaking with frustration and anger. The note stated there would be a highwayman sighting tonight, which could lead to Louissa's danger because there appeared to be some who were taking matters into their own hands.

"Who are you? And why are you helping me, or more to the point, Louissa?" Clive wondered aloud. How would anyone know I was attempting to deal with Louissa's situation as a helpmate and not an executioner? Most of the county knew he had been put in charge of investigating the situation and stopping it, and probably apprehending said highwayman. Only Nicholas and his valet were aware of the duplicity he planned. Either this was genuine, or he was being lured to a trap. It was time to visit the local vicar for some guidance on the subject. Nicholas was avoiding seeing him, Clive knew, but would not turn him away if he went there.

An hour later, Clive was standing in the study of his childhood friend having a stare down. After many ticks of the clock, Clive broke the silence. "Nicholas, I want to help this woman, but I have a family of my own I have to think of. If I ride out, following the directive in this note and it is a trap, I may very well die myself for no good reason, and leave my mother and sisters alone."

"I know. I am just not sure how I can help. I can't break my…"

"I know you can't break your vows, but do your vows include the requirement to stop evil if you have the means to do so?" Nicholas was silent and looked away. Clive gave him time to consider this and weigh his options.

"I can tell you that an interested party connected with me asked of your involvement. When I assured them you were interested in helping Louissa, he then asked how he might get information to you."

"Fine." Clive would like a name, but knew his friend was not going that far in his generous wealth of information. "Can this person be trusted? Are they also looking out for Louissa or are they working for her uncle?"

"That is a bit more complicated, but I can say you and he are on the same side."

"So, he does work for her uncle, but in a guise of some sort," Clive deduced aloud.

"Breakerton, I cannot promise you that if you go tonight, that you will not be in danger."

"Oh, I am well aware I will be in danger tonight, but if I am not expected and it isn't a trap, the odds lean more directly in my favor," he assured Nicholas. "By the by, I haven't had any mystery visitors come to talk. I have had two incidents of breaking and entering this week, but none wanting a drink and a cozy chair with good conversation."

"Oh, well perhaps he has been held up. I passed the message along."

"Well, I must be going if I am to prepare for this evening. Thank you friend." Clive turned and made it to the door of the study before Nicholas called him back.

"Clive," he waited until Clive turned to face him, "be careful. These men are dangerous. The things they are dealing with are worth a lot of money to them, and they will not hesitate to kill for them."

"I am well aware of the types of men I am dealing with."

"Well, also just remember Louissa has been raised in that environment. She is equally as dangerous when the situation requires it. She wouldn't have survived this long otherwise."

"Of that, my friend, I am painfully aware of as well." He rubbed his arm to punctuate the fact and tipped his hat to the vicar, and then left the cottage to go home and prepare.

After much consideration on his way back to the manor,

Clive felt it prudent to go first as an observer. He would not step in unless it was required. After all, Louissa had handled herself against him. He still was not sure it a good idea to let her know she had a champion. Something told him she would not appreciate that and even take offense. Not that he cared if she cared, he chided himself. He didn't even know her. Deciding his train of thought could only become more pathetic and spiral downward, embarrassingly Clive made his way to the stable and collected the horse he had requested when he went to dress the part. His mount was quiet and as calm as a horse could be. He would go to the field just outside the wooded area where Louissa was known to hide.

Leaving early enough to settle the horse and find a good vantage point, not too close, but close enough that he could see what transpired. It was another hour before Louissa came bounding on her horse out of a copse of trees from way of the field. Clive's breath caught, hoping she did not see his horse, but as she went about dismounting and surveying the area, he relaxed and just watched her. How he could ever have thought her a man was beyond him. Her every movement was feminine. With the breeches and greatcoat, he admitted she was wider than in her day dress, but still even from this distance, he could see the gentle curve of her chin, the fullness of her mouth.

If he didn't stop his randy thoughts, he would be useless if needed. She did not need another man seeing her as a prize or a means to an end. If it were one of his sisters, he would hope a champion would behave in a gentlemanly fashion, so he could expect no less of himself. He was certain it is what his father would have done. Before he had a chance to go down that dark alley way of self-deprecation, he was saved by a carriage bounding at a speed only a fool would take racing passed him on its way to where?

His question was answered soon enough, when only with the mercy of God the pair of horses was reined in to a stop. The sun had set only thirty minutes prior, and the moon had yet to rise to any height making visibility difficult in the dusk. He watched as three men descended from the rig. Like the horses, they were not of the top caliber. Farmers or craftsmen, most like and if their motions were any indication they had been drinking more today than doing their chosen career. He watched while leaning into the brush he was hiding behind to try to hear. His vantage point was safe, but that meant it was far enough that he could not hear, only see.

Louissa had not had an opportunity to remount her horse, but she did have the wherewithal to draw her sword. She stood with the horse behind her, speaking. They spoke back and Clive decided he needed to be closer.

With stealth, he made his way along a mossy path concealing his footfalls. He managed to make it to a spot near where Louissa had ridden out with the horse. As he settled in, he could now hear the conversation.

"I am not interested in ye hide. I jus' needs' yer coin. Then, I'll let ye leave unscathed," she demanded in that husky voice Clive had believed to be male.

"Like ye let that poor English sod go?" The larger of the men slurred.

She nodded, "I gave him the same request. 'Tis not my fault that the English ain't much by the way'a brains." She was laying the accent on much thicker. She was smart. She was connecting with them. Making them feel like she was one of them. All three men laughed and nodded in agreement. "Tis no'a personal thing, gents. I mean ye no ill will. Jus yer coin, tis all."

"Well," the thinner of the three answered, "'tis no'a personal thing against ye, but we," he motioned to his comrades, "must needs ye head t' bring back." At that, the three men advanced slowly. The man in the middle who was shorter than the other two who had a club of some sort. The thin one had a large hatchet, and the largest of the three held a sword, which Clive noted had seen better days. As the group circled each other, the horse sauntered out of the road and meandered to a spot behind the bushes.

Clive froze as the beast worked its way around behind him

and a great snort of air lifted his hair and dampened his neck. Knowing he was at a disadvantage and not wanting to distract Louissa who had her hands quite full, he continued to remain stock-still.

The horse continued sniffing Clive's head and nuzzling his hair until he managed to get his huge nose and muzzle around Clive's shoulder and proceeded to reach out his great tongue and swipe it up along the side of Clive's face leaving a warm, wet trail in its wake. Taking that as a sign of friendship, Clive was a bit more relaxed until he brought his attention back to the scene on the road.

The three men were slowly encircling Louissa. She was able to manage two, but three would be difficult for a prized fighter, let alone a woman playing a role. He was just deciding to step out and become known, when he heard Louissa make a strange sound into the growing darkness. Without hesitation, the horse stepped passed Clive and bolted out, putting itself between her and the interlopers attacking her. This was his chance, he made to rise, but Louissa came barreling through the brush at top speed and crashed into him chest to knees, sending them both to the ground with a muted thud.

CHAPTER SEVEN

Louissa landed hard, but the ground didn't seem to be as hard as she had expected. Recovering by gasping for breath, confusion set in. This bloody path had been made by her as an escape route, and she knew there was no tree in this spot. Her head spun and her knee throbbed. Then in her haze, she heard a commanding, very male, very familiar voice. "Stay here damn it, and stay down!" She saw a man grab her sword and hat that had bounced off in the fall, and fly out of the brush onto the road.

Him.

She lay there draping her arm over the eyes. "Bloody wonderful."

Since he had taken her only weapon, she had no means even to jump in to help and her black hair now spilled around her shoulders giving away her gender. There was nothing for it but for her to slouch down and watch from a distance. She knew he could hold his own. He was good. Almost as good as her. He had been trained; she was sure.

"Ah, change ye mind, ye braggart?" Yelled the larger man.

"Oh, ye thought me leavin'?" Her champion replied, in what was a very good local accent, for a Brit. "I was jus' gettin' ye a little gift." She watched as Clive held out his hand and blew a handful of fine dirt in their faces. They all sputtered and swiped at their eyes, swearing the whole time. Louissa smiled her approval. Before the three could recover, he brandished the sword and ran it along their waists. A knot formed hard and heavy in her stomach. Was he gutting them all right there? She held back a scream, as tears came to her eyes stinging them. Louissa had to cover her own mouth not to let out the cry wanting release.

Instead, as she watched waiting for all three men to fall into their own blood, their breeches one by one dropped to the ground around their ankles. The men were standing with nothing covering their more private parts than their own shirttails. Thankfully, they were turned away from Louissa and their shirts seemed to do an admirable job of covering at least the back part. Joy filled her heart and made the knot in her stomach sail away as butterflies. She did let out a small cry of gratitude before clasping her hand over her mouth again. As the three men scrambled to grab their pants and keep hold of their weapons and their dignity, it was obvious, first to the shorter man, then to the others, that it was an either or situation. They could not fight unless they let go of their breeches and if they did that, well dignity would go by the wayside.

Not to be outdone, Neptune, her horse, rounded the Brit's side and began nipping at each man in turn. It was only a matter of moments before the men gave chase for their carriage. Then they were on their way as quickly, as they had arrived. Before Louissa could get out from behind the brush, her savior was standing in front of her proffering his hand. She accepted it and stepped back onto the road. "There, they should not bother you anymore, at least not tonight," he said looking at her. Louissa tingled with the feel of his intense eyes. The darkness created shadows, but the heat in his stare burned her. The silence stretched.

"It was wholly unnecessary for you to step in as you did, but nonetheless, it was a gallant gesture," she offered him. If she was genuinely grateful, it could encourage him. He was in enough danger right now from her uncle, if he continued this he could be dead.

"A--a gallant gesture?" She held back a giggle at his expression. It was a mix of shock and male cockiness, and a hint of hurt as well. The hurt part tugged at her heart, but it was for his safety. It was not safe-- she was not safe for him to get an interest in. "I-- I just saved your life by all estimations. You are aware of that, are you not?"

"I had the situation quite in hand."

"You were fleeing the area," he pointed out.

"Who's to say I wasn't leading them into a trap in the field that had been set for just such an event?" She rallied. She had been fleeing. After giving the signal noise to her uncle's man, she had hoped she could make the field and get lost in the tall hay. Darius apparently, was slow to respond. "May I have my hat?" The thought of her uncle's men leaving her for dead caught in her throat and she didn't want to think further about the feeling of helplessness she had right now.

The Brit didn't say a word, but stepped into her space sucking the air from the vary woods as he did so. He gently wound her hair up and piled it on her head. He then took her hat from his head and settled it atop the hair. His movements pulled him even closer to her. So close that she could feel the heat of his body against her thin cambric shirt. She looked up into his eyes. The color was hard to decipher in the dark, but she knew they pierced her soul as they read her own eyes. Before she knew better, he lowered his mouth toward hers and wound his once injured arm around her waist, closing what was left of the distance between them. She fleetingly thought his arm was healing nicely if it had such strength, but then realized she put up no fight and had actually leaned into his body a bit more. He paused long enough for her to back away. She knew instinctively he wouldn't force her, but she was lost to the moment.

Louissa popped up on her tiptoes to meet him the rest of the way. As their lips met, her ears filled with a rushing like the waves on the beach as a storm rolled in. His lips pressed with authority, but tenderness did wicked things to all her extremities. Louissa had never been kissed, but she had watched enough sailors greet their wives or lovers when a ship came in to know how it was done. Not one to do anything half way, Louissa wound her hand around his neck and pulled him in to deepen the kiss. She felt more than heard the groan on his lips. The vibration shot to her belly as her knees weakened and she no longer could hold herself up. He had no issue taking her weight and laying it against his body, from knee to chest.

Like an empty vessel, Louissa filled up on the human contact. He surrounded her. She could feel the tears stinging behind her eyes and wondered at why she would be near crying. It was odd as she was always so good at keeping her feelings in check. Pushing the unease aside, she drank in his very breath. It was like a good rum, making her head spin and her body feel light and heavy at the same time. Her hair once again spilled out over her shoulders. He wound his hands into the mess as he cupped her head with both hands and held her to him. Then he was running his hands down her back, rubbing, and sending funny little shivers along her nerves. Her breasts felt hard as they rubbed against his waistcoat and her shirt.

She realized she wanted to be here. For the first time in her recent memory, she wanted to be right where she was. Never had she known such a feeling. It spurred her on, the knowing of its existence. Soon enough she would not be allowed such feelings, so she needed to drink this in. She became more frantic, more desperate to experience.

Louissa slid her shaking hands down along the greatcoat and his arms, finding a way inside. His body was warm and she could feel the hardness of his muscles even through his clothes. She let out a groan that sent her partner into more of a frenzy. That only lasted until she felt him lift her slightly, then set her down and step away.

They stood apart, but close enough to reach out for each other at any moment. Louissa noted he was all but gasping for breath, and even in the darkness, she could see his face was flushed.

For her own part, she too was breathing as if she'd run across the moors. Her hair blew around her as the wind danced in the open space his body left. Her lips felt as heavy as her breasts and she was sure they were swollen. In silence, the two stared off. Louissa would have happily allowed herself to be taken then and there. Hoped for it, craved it, as she had never craved anything before, but instead held strong, not sure the protocol. Her champion for his part looked confused and almost angry, as he appeared lost in his thoughts.

When Louissa thought he might step back into the circle of her arms, noise from the other side of the copse of trees leading to the beach made them both turn.

"My uncle's men," she hissed. "I signaled them earlier." Of course, had her champion not been there, they would be picking up her body to take back to her uncle, because they waited too long. Louissa could not bring herself to be angry however. If they had come when summoned, she would not be here now with him.

"You need to leave," she said stepping up to Breakerton, and shoving him in the direction of the woods from where he came. "If you are caught here, my uncle will have you killed."

When he would have argued, she spat, "Do you not think you have done enough foolish things for one day, my Lord? Perhaps keep one or another for another day, when you are bored with your life."

She saw the anger spark in his eyes. He started to argue, but they could hear the men getting closer. "You need to leave now," she said again, pushing him toward the trees.

At the entrance to the woods, she stopped, and turned to defend the fool. Instead, he grabbed her arm. "We are not through. There is much to discuss." With that, he was gone.

The men burst onto the road, swords held high, looking around for the culprit, Darius leading the charge. "Why did ye call?" he demanded when it was obvious there was no danger at present.

"Hmm, I was asking myself that, as I fended off the three drunkards in the carriage fifteen minutes ago." She was satisfied when Darius looked like a scolded schoolboy.

"Well, you don't look any worse for wear. A little flushed, but mayhap some exertion is good for the soul," he commented dryly. Her cheeks burned from the blush that shone on her face. Thanking the moon for not casting so much light this eve, she mounted her horse and turned the beast so she could see the men standing in the road with nothing to do, but return to the beach.

"I am finished for tonight. I am sore and tired. I trust that you and your men finished up before you bothered to come here, so I assume I am free to go?"

"We are done, yes," was all Darius said. She turned the

horse and raced down the road for home. As she let the horse carry her, her mind went back to the feel of being held in strong arms. She had never thought much about a man's arms, except to know they were stronger than hers were and that it usually was not a good thing.

She was not sure his intentions for following her tonight. She did not want a champion. She could not have it on her conscious when her uncle killed him, or he died doing something foolhardy. She doubted he was fool enough to think himself in love, which was good. She did not want him in love with her. That would be more dangerous than for him to think he could save her, for as long as she knew he could not be in love with her, she might be able to convince herself she would not fall in love with him. But, oh that kiss. She often had felt like the very world she lived in might one day swallow her whole, but she had always feared it. Tonight she knew what it was like to be devoured, and damn it, she liked it very much.

Still caught up in the whir of the moment, Louissa sobered when her uncle's house was ablaze with light when she entered the property.

Damn.

Uncle Gareth must have beat her back. There would be no way to avoid him, if he was of the mind to discuss what just happened.

Louissa brought Neptune to the stable and took her time brushing him and feeding him, but still the house glowed in the moonlight. Deciding that there was nothing to do, but stand before her uncle and answer to his accusations, she lumbered up the lawn into the house. The door had not latched fully when he bellowed.

"Louissa! Now!"

She took in a breath and entered his study. Darius was again in the corner chair, looking…was that worry? A chill slid up her back, tingling the hairs on her neck. She would have to meter her words carefully.

"Uncle, good eve." She made to sit.

"Ye, fool, no sittin' for you. Stand there like the idiot you are." He was standing behind his desk, but Louissa noted she did not feel safer for the large mahogany furniture. She had rarely seen her uncle in such a state and she tried hard not to be the one to put her in such a mood.

"Uncle, I'm..."

"Shut up. Ye, caused me ta lose half the inventory cause of your fool call for help." He leaned over the desk, putting his fisted hands down for support. He was too close.

Louissa knew better than to continue with her explanation. It would only serve to infuriate him more. Instead, she stood, head bent, careful not to make eye contact. The sooner he railed, the sooner he would tire himself out, and she would be allowed to flee to her room, she hoped.

"What in the name of the gods possessed you to call fer help? Darius said you were alone when they raced to the call."

Lord help her, she wanted to remain quiet. Wanted just to let him yell, but something inside, that part of her that still believed her brother to be alive, would not stand down.

"Raced to my call? Is that the word Darius used? Raced? I had been standing by myself alone for more than a quarter of an hour before they showed," she snapped, turning to say it more to Darius than her uncle. "Had I not been able to figure out a way to fend off the fiends, I would well be dead now."

"Ye think ye were worth more than my inventory, do ya?" Gareth asked with contempt thick on his tongue. Louissa's brain signaled for her legs to move, but she forced them to ground.

"How did ye fend off three men?" Darius asked. For the moment, it distracted her uncle thankfully.

"Yes, do tell us." Her uncle agreed.

"Well..." She decided to stick with what happened as she witnessed. "I ran into the woods like I was escaping, then came out with a handful of fine sand. I blew it into their faces, blinding them, and I was able to cut the ties around their breeches. They were forced to flee because they couldn't fight with no pants."

Darius's bark of laughter filled the space jumping Louissa, but gaining a scowl from her uncle.

"Enough!" he shouted and slammed his fist on the table. Both she and Darius sobered. "How in hell do you think I am going to stay in business if you keep calling attention to us? I lost what some would call a fortune tonight, and you think you were clever?"

Louissa held her ground, but noted the heavy paperweight in the shape of siren on the rocks with a wave surrounding her in her uncle's hand. Gareth came around the desk and began pacing in front, leaving no barrier between them.

"Uncle, no—I..."

"I don't need an excuse! Damn it, Lass!"

Pain, sharp and explosive roared outward from Louissa's left eye. The force knocked her off balance and sent her to the floor. The paperweight. Louissa eyed it carefully, but was not quick enough to jerk out of the way, when it suddenly shot from his hand in her direction.

"Jesus, Lass, are ye stupid? Anyone with a brain would well have gotten out of the way."

She sat on the floor, as the room shifted in and out of her vision. With a horrified look, Darius sat at the edge of his chair, which in turn sent more chills to wrack her body and a bolt of nausea so thick, she barely held it back.

"Get ye self outta my sight. Next time ye make me lose money, your pending marriage will not be your worry."

He stepped around her to go back to his desk, and she was forgotten. Louissa forced her legs to move and her arms to boost her up. Her head swam, or perhaps she was back on the ship during a storm. No matter, she saw the door, and willed her body to get her out. Once the door was closed, she made her way to the stairs before a wave of sickness and pain drove her to the floor. Voices came from all sides, but she couldn't open her eyes. She would lose her

Clair Brett

battle with her stomach if she did. Her uncle wasn't one of the voices, she realized, and let the darkness cover her like a warm blanket. No more pain, no more fear, no more uncle. Perfect.

CHAPTER EIGHT

Louissa had always seen her bedchamber as a refuge from her uncle, but the early morning, sunbeams piercing through the unforgiving crack in the window dressings shot into her swollen eyes and burned, sending an ache deep inside her brain to throbbing. The heavy quilt had proven to be as strong as any manacle as she tossed and turned unable to find comfortable purchase on the mattress during the night. She had woken more than once entwined in the bedding, until she gave in and threw it to the floor.

The fire, though burning low now, had most assuredly blazed in the night, bringing the temperatures to unbearable heights. The dreams that kept recurring when she closed her eyes had nothing to do with it.

Hot hands, greedy but gentle, all over her body at the same time. Warm, determined lips covering hers, sending waves of heat as far south as her toes. She would not allow dreams. Figments obviously caused by her pounding head and overly stoked fire played with her emotions.

Cursing the room that once kept out the world at large and just for good measure, she also cursed the world that saw fit to throw her into the paths of unnerving and completely daft men. The floor was not as cool as usual, because she plopped her bare feet onto the blanket which had been tossed there earlier. Even the blasted floor did not do its usual trick of waking her and helping to get moving. Louissa would have liked nothing more than remain curled in her bed dreaming of Lord Breakerton's lips covering hers, and his strong arms holding her when her legs would have given up the battle. She knew, however, she could not allow such fancies. Not if she was planning on seducing the Lord to get better access to his home and therefore allowing her more freedom to search the premises for the proof his aunt had been gathering for her. The plan took root as she fled for home in the moon light. He was affected by her and she would use that to her advantage.

If she were to allow the dreams of last night to continue occupying her thoughts during waking hours, she might well fall into her own trap. Standing, a wave of nausea hit her, sending her back to the edge of the bed. She bent forward and slowly breathed in through her nose and out her mouth until the feeling passed. Perhaps getting moving this morning would have to be a more leisurely activity than she had hoped. She sat on the edge of the mattress and looked at her reflection in the looking glass. It was amazing she could see anything, as her right eye was all but swollen shut and her nose was swollen enough that it caused the bottom of her left eye to pop up into her vision on that side. The bruise was a dark puce color with red, purple, and brown mixing. She had no doubt by the end of day it would be a bright purple stretching across her face like a veil.

She just might have to torch her whole room with its contents, since it all seemed to be working against her. How was she to seduce Lord Breakerton, when she looked like a sideshow boxer who lost his last fight? A knock on her door had her turning her head. Too soon, she realized her mistake as a new round of bile demanded freedom. She lay down on her back and grunted for entrance.

"Och, I thought ye would be a bit queasy this morn," said Mrs. MacDonald, the housekeeper, as she bustled into the room with a foul smelling jar in one hand and a plate with toast in the other. "Let me see ye face, gel," she insisted.

"Nay," recoiled Louissa, "not if ye have a mind to slather me with that vile smelling ointment I won't." She turned away from her guest and the contents of the jar only to have the sunlight force her head back.

"Oi, tha' be one o' the worse ones yet." Mrs. MacDonald tsked as she got a good look. "How many times have I told ye to pay more attention and be more ready to duck out of the way?" She took hold of Louissa's chin and turned her face this way and that inspecting every part of her head for damage.

"My apologies, it never occurred to me that I should step aside when Uncle throws things at me. 'Tis my fault entirely,"

Clair Brett

Louissa spat with annoyance.

"Well, twould work better if someone were to tell the master not to throw things when he is angry, but I am thinking that would not have the desired effect. Mayhap, you could endeavor not to make him angry enough to throw something?" She asked Louissa as she dipped a rag into the salve and began gentle globing it onto the cut at the bridge of her nose and around her eyes. The smell made Louissa's eyes tear and sting, but after an adjustment, her whole face began to feel a bit better and the smell soothed her stomach in a way she would never understand. She chuckled a little at Mrs. MacDonald's suggestion. Both women knew the very knowledge that Louissa lived was enough to send her uncle into a rage as a reminder of his brother and the happy life they had. She would never understand the hatred her uncle had for her father and his family.

"Thank you, now I must rise and get dressed." Louissa tried to pry herself away from Mrs. MacDonald's attentions with no luck.

"And why do you think you need to rise and get dressed? You will be sick for a good bit of the day. You need to rest," the housekeeper spat.

"I have to help Bethany with her luncheon today. I promised," Louissa reminded the woman and again tried to rise. This time, the woman helped by putting a bracing arm behind her back. The wave of sickness was slower to rise and the throbbing in her head seemed deeper and further away than earlier.

"Nonsense, I will deliver the scones for you and you will remain here," she protested.

"I cannot, 'tis the guests that I need to talk with. I will simply explain that a tome fell on me as I was trying to retrieve it from a high shelf in the library," she said, making to rise and thinking twice as she sucked in a breath. "I need to go to this luncheon." She looked at the housekeeper with pleading eyes. If she could go today, she might learn something about Lord Breakerton that she could use, because it was his mother and sisters who were the guests. She was certain his name would come up in conversation, because really he was the only topic any of them had in common. She would learn what she could and possibly gain an invitation to the manor where she would have a reason to meet with him on a more social field and begin her seduction.

"Fine." Was the only answer, but the housekeeper rose and began to gather the only luncheon worthy day dress Louissa owned and helped her with her stockings and boots, as bending caused the entire room to swirl and dip, yet another reason to torch the whole blasted space for raging against her. The once haven looked more like a bright torture box. She decided that until this ordeal was at an end, whatever end it may be, not even her dreams were going to be safe.

Once dressed, she sat at her dressing table. Mrs. MacDonald shoved the piece of toast in her face. "Eat," she demanded as she began combing and piling her hair atop her head. Every brush stroke sent shooting pain to her forehead, but there was nothing to do but endure it, so Louissa did not cry out. Instead, she stared at the toast as a general in an army would stare at the trebuchet aimed at his troops. She knew Mrs. M would not let her leave until she proved she could eat a simple slice of bread without vomiting it up, but Louissa wasn't so sure that would be possible.

"Well, are ye going to will it to disappear, or are ye going to eat it?" she demanded, staring at Louissa from the looking glass.

Louissa swallowed, squared her shoulders, took in a fortifying breath and took a small bite. When that one didn't return with force, she took another and another, until she and Mrs. M were certain she could hold down solid food. To Louissa's relief, she had managed to that point not to lose the contents of her stomach and dearly hoped the trend would continue.

"Here, look at me. If I sweep your hair down to the right and we add your nice hat, you should be able to hide the worst of the bruising."

"Thank you, Mrs. MacDonald. I am sure that will help." It

would have been above reproach for someone to attempt to look under her hair and it did a passable job at hiding her eye that was swollen shut and it also helped to put a shadow over her nose to lessen the look of the swelling there as well.

Before she was ready, Louissa found herself trudging across the field hoping to make the shade of the copse of trees between her house and the road leading to the vicar's house. The hat, which did an admirable job at hiding her bruised nose, did little to shield her eyes from the sun. Since when did the sun shine so brightly in Scotland? At long last, she could see the little cottage. Louissa always entered through the back of the house into the kitchen. She was never so pleased to enter the darkened room, with the smell of tea wafting through the air.

"Good morning," Bethany sing-songed while bustling around the table putting the finishing touches on some dainty looking sandwiches and cookies.

"Morning, I have the scones Mrs. MacDonald made."

"Wonderful, can you put them on that platter over..." Bethany turned to point at the only empty plate, but froze mid-wave when she noticed Louissa's injuries. "Oh, my Lord, Louissa, what in heaven's name happened?" She put down the cakes she was arranging and crossed to examine the damage.

"'Tis not as bad as it looks," Louissa tried to assure her friend.

"What-- How?"

"It was silly really. I was reaching on a shelf for a book of poetry and I must have wiggled the bookshelf. A large heavy tome from a higher shelf fell as I looked up to see what the noise was, and it landed on my nose." She gingerly touched the spot on her nose where the paperweight had found purchase. That would be the last place to heal.

Bethany stepped back and examined Louissa. Beth had seen her with many different bruises, and at first, Louissa was able to explain them away. Now, however, Louissa felt Beth didn't believe, but was too polite to question. Turning toward the scones and the inviting kitchen, Louissa left Bethany staring at her with pity and shock.

"So, when are your guests arriving?" Louissa asked with whimsy in her voice to break the tension of the room. The kitchen was small, but felt like it might fold up and bury her if she didn't lighten the mood.

"Ah, well actually…" Bethany started but she was stopped by the sound of horses' hooves and carriage wheels slowing to a stop. "Now," she amended with a nervous smile as she pulled her apron off and hung it on the hook. She grabbed two of the platters and Louissa scooped up the other two following behind. In the parlor, the women set the food on the small rectangular table by the settee. Fresh flowers around the room sent a fresh scent throughout. Louissa always loved the bright cheery room, but today the brightness still stung her eyes. Bethany scooted back into the kitchen and returned with the tea service just as Mr. Pickard entered to announce their guests.

"Excuse me, Mrs. Allard, may I present Her Ladyship Breakerton, Lady Landsdown, and Lady Breakerton." He bowed, stepping aside as the women breezed through. Bethany set down the tea tray and shuffled to greet her guests. Louissa stood back watching. Lord Breakerton had a strong resemblance to his mother. She wondered if his father was frustrated about that. The elder Lady Breakerton showed her Scottish heritage with her curls of red hair which set off her porcelain skin, still very smooth considering all her children were grown. The younger Lady Breakerton swept in to embrace Bethany. Her expression was warm and welcoming with no underlying show of disdain for those beneath her station. Then Lady Landsdown, one of Breakerton's other sisters who was widowed, followed in half mourning attire. The drab gray of the mourning dress did not lessen her beauty, however, and she too greeted Bethany more as a dear friend than the local vicar's wife.

"Please, come sit, this is my dear friend Louissa," Bethany

introduced as the women entered and headed toward the settee. "I invited her to help even the numbers and perhaps give you more social connections for your future stays." Not that her guests would notice, but Louissa could hear a slight shake to her friend's voice as she made the introductions.

"Oh, my dear, whatever happened to you?" The elder Lady Breakerton asked with surprise. Bethany's eyes widened at the woman's lack of circumspection. Lady Breakerton noted Bethany's expression. "I am sorry. I did not intend to insult you, my dear," she said to Louissa, then turned to Bethany, "or to be uncaring of your guest. It is just that I have enough seasons under my bonnet to forgo some of the ridiculous social nonsense."

"No, 'tis fine really," Louissa assured the whole room. "Tis a freak event I assure you. I was trying to get a collection of poems from a shelf, and I must have jarred the entire cabinet, because I heard a noise and looked up just as a large tome came crashing down upon my nose." Louissa hoped she added just enough embarrassment to the tale. Lady Landsdown and the older Lady Breakerton seemed very sympathetic, but as Louissa caught sight of the younger Lady Breakerton, she felt discomfited, like she knew much more than she should. However, as quick as it was there, it was gone.

"Lady Landsdown, how would you like your tea?" Bethany asked as everyone settled in.

"Please, call me Mary. I prefer to be more informal," the woman corrected with a nervous smile. Both Ladies Breakerton reached over and patted her lap, one on each side.

"And I prefer Nettie, please. No need to bother with formalities when we are in the country. I feel it is much easier to become familiar with a person when such social strictures can be laid aside."

Bethany and Louissa made eye contact. "Unfortunately, I am too aged to be called anything but Lady Breakerton or Mother," the matron of the group said lightening the mood even more. "I am sure it is how the young of our culture are going to change society. I cannot say I disagree with my daughters, but I am too aged to change." Everyone laughed.

The women chatted away, eating sandwiches, scones, and drinking tea. Louissa listened as the sisters Breakerton told Bethany stories she could then use if needed against their brother, who being the only man in the family could stand to be knocked down a peg or two, and if his sisters were not around to do it, the duty must be passed onto someone. Louissa quite liked them--all of them.

This put a crimp in her plans for sure. How would she ever be able to forgive herself for seducing their brother, whom they had an obvious affection for and not make them angry? It was silly, but this was the first time Louissa felt as though she was welcomed into such a little party. Bethany would often invite her, but when it was local women, she was treated with more disdain and tolerance, than kindness and respect. It was no secret that her uncle had a questionable vocation. The fact he had a vocation at all made it bad enough, but common knowledge that bad tidings would befall those who got in his way did not help.

Louissa watched Mary closely. She was still wearing widow's gray. She was still in half mourning, even though her husband had been dead for more than a year, well past the required mourning period. It must have been her one great love, she thought with a sadness that pressed against her chest and filled her throat. She would never get to know such a love, if she didn't find her brother.

Nettie was young, probably closer to her age than Mary was. However, where Louissa was hard edges and strategic plans, Nettie was almost whimsical, with even the look and stature of a pixie. Her coloring was similar to her brother's, and her eyes and nose were the same as her mother and sister, but that was where the resemblance ended. She must only come to her brother's chest when standing, but she seemed to be the one who spoke most ardently about *Clive* needing a strong hand. Louissa had a difficult time considering Lord

Breakerton a man who would bend to such a slight female.

She would most likely never have an opportunity to become friends with these women and she should not become blinded by the thought of a life never meant for her, she decided. She would allow herself to enjoy the moment however. If such a tiny thing as the young Lady Breakerton could commandeer Lord Breakerton's presence and control him, she should have no issues with seducing him to get what she wanted.

His kisses would not be an issue anymore, she thought as the women chatted away, because her reaction was caused from it being her first kiss, and the atmosphere. Therefore, there would be no worries of her being more affected than he was. In fact, now that she considered it, that one kiss would be Lord Breakerton's downfall, because his brand of charm would not have an effect now. The bigger question was if all her efforts would have *any* effect? Would she have the time now that her uncle has moved up his timeline to find the proof and her brother to save her own life?

Louissa instinctively reached for the pendant at her neck. She would not allow the rest of her life to be decided by the man who killed her parents, but dearly hoped her first plan worked.

The remainder of the afternoon flew by with good conversation and a lot of laughter. While Bethany said goodbye to the Ladies Breakerton, Louissa began bringing the trays and tea service into the kitchen. She would stay to help Bethany clean up. She wasn't, after all, interested in going home. She was perfectly content tidying Bethany's quiet little home and soaking in the kindness and love that Bethany always had to offer.

Once the house was tidy, giving Louissa no reason to tarry, she said her farewells and headed back out across the field. She stopped at the stream to delay the inevitable, but told herself this was a quiet and peaceful place to think. The quiet, however, was interrupted by the sound of horse's hooves thundering, so she felt them before seeing a lone rider crest the knoll. Before she had time to realize what was happening, Breakerton was dismounting and at her side.

Without words, or permission, he took her chin in his gloved hand and turned her face to the light. She winced, as the daylight still hurt when forced to look directly up at it. He took his glove off his left hand with his teeth so not to relinquish his hold on her chin. With a feather-light touch, he examined her nose, and then just as gently moved her artfully placed sweep of hair to expose the worst of the injury.

"Jesus, he should be hung for this alone," the hulk of a man growled as he checked around her eye, probing at the delicate bones. When she made to pull away, out of self-preservation, not pain, he would not allow it. "Hold still," he demanded, and bless her, his tone made her stop and let him inspect her.

"Are you quite finished, my lord?" She asked after an inappropriate amount of time. His breath had finally gotten the better of her, washing down her throat and along the swell of her breast. She needed to step back. Needed air between them, that was not warm and sweet from tobacco and apples, carrying the scent of cologne. Fresh Scottish air, cold Scottish air, even Scottish air with the smell of earth would be more satisfactory.

"No, I am not," he said in a clipped tone. "He did this."

It wasn't a question, so she had no reason to give anything for information.

"Louissa, you did not have this last night, and you did not drop a book on your head from a bookshelf. Tell me the truth." The concern in his eyes took her back. She knew there were men who did not subscribe to hitting women, but she couldn't fathom a man who would be so indignant about it.

"I am perfectly well, my Lord," she offered, but knew it wouldn't placate him.

"You are not well. 'Tis looks as if you have a plum for an eye, and your nose, while not broken could very easily be. Now tell me true. Did he hit you?"

"No."

"Louissa…"

She stopped him with a staying hand. "He did not hit me. He has never but slapped me. He was angry about having to shorten his endeavor last night."

"And?"

"He grabbed a paperweight off his desk and threw it. I was too shocked at his action, so I didn't get out of the way in time."

The peaceful stream roared like a raging river in her ears and a bird cried out from a nearby tree, but the look in Breakerton's eyes, turned the tranquil setting into something sinister. Fury burned and sparked a coldness, setting his features to hard planes. His jaw worked as if he was grinding his teeth.

"'Tis truly not something to be worried about." She chuckled meekly hoping to settle his mood. "I must learn to move more quickly, 'tis all. Please do not spend your time on this, my lord." She attempted to turn from him as he grabbed her arm and tugged her into him. She could feel his breathing heavy and labored on her cheek as she felt herself lean into him. His arms pressed heat into her skin where they touched. God help her she closed her one good eye and tried to soak him into her very soul.

"I cannot allow him to get away with this," he said. She could feel every word on the top of her head as his deep voices vibrated the air around them. "No man should have the right or think he has the right to touch a woman."

"My uncle and most of the men he associates with would not prescribe to that I am afraid. Women are possessions to do with as they please."

"I do not consider myself a particularly frugal man, but if I owned such a possession that has value, I certainly would not break it in a fit of anger. When you have such a possession, you give it a place of honor where it will not be harmed, but protected at all cost." He tucked his finger under her chin and lifted her face to see his. "When a man has such a possession, the cost is incalculable and his need to keep it close and safe should outweigh any other emotion."

The planes of his face were still stark and rigid, but his eyes had softened, and for the love of all things saintly, so had his lips. She thought she could feel him pulling her into him more, but she could be leaning instead. For the first time since waking to the sunbeam, her head did not throb. Her breath hitched and with no luck, she tried to take in a breath. Her breasts were so tight against his chest she could not fill her lungs. Perhaps that was what was making her head spin. He was going to kiss her again and she was going to let him.

"You must leave your uncle's house immediately," he said before he dipped his head.

Then, just like that, the moment was gone. "Beg your pardon, my lord?" She asked while she dipped her head down, allowing him to plant an unexpected kiss to her bonnet.

"You need to find someplace else to live, until I can figure out how to get you away from your uncle," he said with annoyance, as he pulled small feathers from his lips.

"I have no place to go, my lord, and at this time that request is both impractical and impossible," she said mourning the moment that passed. It was replaced by a familiar scene-- her being told what to do with no regard for her opinion of the matter.

He straightened his waistcoat and pulled on his gloves in that way men do when trying to ignore someone. "It is decided. I will speak with Nicholas about you staying in their guest room until I have time to dispatch your uncle."

How could it be, Louissa thought, that one moment she was fearing the chance of falling in love with a man, and in the very next breath feeling certain she could dispatch him in a matter of moments? Indignation bubbled to the surface and her head throbbed, knocking on her temple with a 'remember me' rat-a-tat-tat. "My Lord, I will not be staying with anyone. I have things that need to be done at home, and I will not put my friends in danger just because you feel it necessary." She did turn this time and walk away from their tight circle. The air felt different, less charged. She could once again hear the stream and the birds. She was waiting for his deep silky voice to boom like a cannon, demanding to be obeyed.

Instead, she felt him come up behind her. Felt his warmth on her back as he stepped in close. "I will not allow a woman I have put in my safe keeping be treated thusly," he whispered into her neck, sending a shock of awareness down her back.

She turned to face him, taking a step back for comfort. "I am well aware of who and what my uncle is. I have been relying on him for my very life since an early age. I must just keep out of his line of sight for a few days and he will forget I even exist. I am of little consequence to him, if I am not botching up his missions," she assured her would-be savior. "You, on the other hand, will be putting your entire family in danger if you so much as hint at causing a ruckus. My uncle was perfectly within the law when he struck me. I have no legal recourse, and you are well aware of the fact." She had wrapped her arms around herself because talking about her uncle always made her cold. Breakerton stepped forward and pulled her in. Oh, Lord, she was going to be lost if he kept this up.

"You could come stay with me," he declared.

"What?"

"At the manor, come stay with me--and my sisters and mother of course. It would be perfectly respectable. If you are as inconsequential as you say, your uncle would not take note." He looked puffed up like a little boy who just figured out a difficult puzzle. Except that right now, Louissa was anything but inconsequential to her to uncle. She was his ticket to getting him out of debt.

"My apologies, my lord, but I need to be getting home-- my home." She turned and began walking away. She still needed to seduce him, but retreat was of the upmost import at the present time. When all she wanted to do was melt into his strong arms and allow him to hide her away, well that would was not the backbone of a winning sailor. Retreat to fight another day, she thought as she left him standing there.

"My lady," he called and his voice would not allow her to ignore it. She turned to see him tipping his hat and bending in a bow. "My name is Clive and much prefer to hear that cross your lips."

She too tipped her head and curtsied, but turned and continued on her way, because the alternative to run straight into his arms was not to be for Louissa, but oh the thought...

CHAPTER NINE

Impossible woman," Clive grumbled as he mounted and headed for home. He wanted to ride up to Louissa, swing her up on his horse and bring her with him. In his mind, she would not scowl at him with that pout in her lips. He wondered if she would have a wrinkle between her eyes as well when angry. The swelling in her face was too great to see if there was. Hot, immediate anger raged to the surface. When Nettie returned home and told him about the beautiful girl with the injured eye, he knew who it was. He also knew she had not sustained such and injury when he was with her. He urged his horse into a gallop hoping to out run his desire to ride past Louissa, and be at her house with her uncle trussed up as she entered. Instead, he was going home. He had no choice.

He slowed and plotted along considering his options. It wasn't as much the options he disliked, even though many of them were not pleasant, it was the fact he didn't want to choose the wrong one. What if he let her go now? Would her uncle beat her again? If he rode to rescue her, would her uncle kill him and then beat her, and then ruin his family? On the other hand, had his plan gone as he wanted, Louissa would be free from her uncle and safe in his protection. He envisioned Louissa at the stream without a care in the world. No pouting lips, swollen eyes, or even furrows between their depths. She was smiling and the breeze danced in her hair.

Clive groaned. It was a bloody blessing she was not in his protection, because if she were, she would be in danger from him now. Every time they interacted, his desire for her ratcheted up another notch. How was he to protect her when he was no better than her uncle was?

Entering his lands, he knew where he had to go. If he didn't cool his ardor, he would not be able to consider his next move with a clear head. At present, every solution seemed to end with him in bed with her luscious body under his and her gorgeous hair splayed across his pillow. Perhaps his tutors were talking about this when they said he would never be the man his father was. He doubted a man of such character would have such thoughts about a woman he swore to protect. Coming into view was the frog pond. As a child, he used to swim there by the hour. Nettie and he would splash and pretend they were pirates--such an innocent time. Today, his need for a dip was anything but.

The icy water did the trick. As he came up for air after diving in, he was clear headed again. Scanning the grounds as he rubbed back his dripping hair, he saw Mary walking along the fence line by the orchard. She was all but a silhouette in her widow's weeds. Her head was bent, and she looked as melancholy as the scene made Clive feel. He had done this to her. He had taken his options and chosen poorly. Because of his need to always conquer the situation, his beloved sister lost the man she loved.

When he left for Scotland, it was partly to exile himself for his failings, but also he didn't have to be reminded of what he had done to destroy her. In Scotland, he could live a modest, quiet life and be in no position to harm anyone else. "How is that plan working?" he asked out loud. The horse had moved around the pond munching on fresh spring grass, looked up and nickered, but turned back to munching. "Well, no one asked you," Clive replied annoyed at himself and the horse.

His new dilemma was that if he continued in this vein, he might be putting his mother and sisters in danger, but if he didn't, Louissa was guaranteed to meet an unpleasant fate. No matter how many times he turned it over in his mind, it never seemed easier or different. He knew Nettie was on board, which he didn't doubt. She was always up for excitement and never considered the consequences, but his mother and Mary were being dragged along without their knowledge.

He knew that regardless of how many times he had this discussion with himself that he would help Louissa. He couldn't do anything else. He would help her because he hoped when there came a time when he was unable that someone else would step in and help his family. His great fear, however, was that he might not be up for the challenge and cause more harm.

Climbing out of the frigid water, thinking that it would not be the last time he would need a dip in the coming days or weeks, he shook and wrung out his shirt. Next time, he would forgo his coat, waistcoat, and boots. He would need help getting the coat off, of that he was sure. The horse continued grazing in the direction of the stables, so Clive decided to head into the house via the side door and then he would send a boy to attend it. He would need a change of clothes and a drink.

The hallway was dark as his eyes adjusted. The smell from the kitchen made his stomach growl, but he proceeded toward the main hallway to summon Hector. As he rounded the corner, his boots hit the hardness of the marble floor from the gentle spring of the carpeted hall. He caught himself and tried to walk with care instead of purpose. The less noise he made the less of a chance to run into--

"For the love of-- what happened to you?" Lady Breakerton gasped to Clive's right. He stopped hunched slightly with his foot still raised to step. "If that wild mount of yours put you in the pond, I'd be sending him to the tannery."

"No mother, my horse is a perfectly placid creature." He said hoping to pass with niceties and make a quick exit. He had no desire to spend much time with his mother. She always saw more than he wanted and commented more than was comfortable.

"Well, before you die of chills you better be out of those clothes, and then we must talk. I will order some hot tea to help, would you like whiskey to keep away any illness?" She asked him.

"Yes, mother, whiskey would be well received. I foresee that I will be in need of quite a bit." He drawled, resigned to the fact, he would now have to pay an audience to his mother.

"Son, I will not begin to recount the times you drove me to the sherry over the years, so let us not make assumptions about who needs a drink or not," she said over her shoulder as she whisked herself into his study and motioned for the doorman to close the

Clair Brett

door behind her.

Clive decided that in a house filled with women, the only safe place a man had was his bedchamber. Perhaps he could lock himself in and refuse to leave until the women in his life began thinking logically. A vision swirled in his mind of him with a long beard, tattered clothing, sitting alone after years of being in his bedchamber. Shaking his head, he decided it was better to be among the beasts than to let them keep him hidden away.

Once in his chamber, he had to ring for help as his mother had waylaid his plan of getting assistance post haste. He moved to the fire and built it up, then sat on a stool by the hearth and worked at tugging his boots off. The custom-made hessians were trying when dry, but wet made them damn near impossible. As his man Hector entered, he dragged the first boot off, but went over backward off the stool for his attempts.

"Oh, dear milord," the man said as he hurried over to assist Clive in getting up.

"I never liked these boots much anyway," Clive said as he righted himself and accepted a hand in getting on his feet.

"Here, milord, sit in ye chair and I'll get the other."

Clive did as he was instructed and after much tugging, the servant yanked the second boot off, but he too landed with a thump on the floor. "Now, let us see if we can get this coat off without permanently doing damage."

"Did ye fall in the pond or pushed?" asked the man as he turned Clive from side to side looking for the best course of action to extract his master.

"Neither, I jumped in."

"Oh," the man said stopping to examine the Lord of the house. "Oh, was a woman then was it?" he asked a knowing glint in his eye.

"Why is it that they must be so stubborn? I have grown up surrounded by the female of the species, and I admit to still being dumbfounded," Clive said as the man finally picked his course of action and began tugging from the collar and shoulders down his arms, grunting as he heaved.

The man stopped and looked at Clive for another moment, then smiled, "Now, milord, would life be half as fun if they were not contrary? Me self spends most days shakin' me head at me wife's determination to argue about everything, but when she is off visiting relatives for more than a day, I can confess to being lost. 'Tis no fun without, not to mention a man must appreciate a gleam in their eye and color on their cheeks at a good row. Makes a man's blood run hot," he said as he returned to his work, this time tugging from the sleeves.

"Aye to that," Clive said.

"Not speakin' outta turn, but I'm bettin' tha' what got you here in yer chamber wet as trout stuck in ye' fine coat twill be better once ye marry the lass. Then ye won't be needin' cold water. Ye can work it out in more amicable ways."

"It would," Clive admitted, but then added, "but marriage is not the outcome in this tragedy." Finally, his arms broke free from the confines of the coat and both men grunted and staggered from their work. After that, the rest of the clothing came off in short order. Clive went to the fireplace, as Hector got new dry clothing for his master.

"I don't agree, milord. Any man who lets a lass drive him to jumping into a pond during the spring in Scotland, must either be the woman he loves enough to marry, or tis his sister. Did Lady Nettie drive you to it, milord?" He asked as he brushed down a clean dry coat and finished tying a simple knot in his cravat.

"No, this time Nettie is not to blame," he said with an uneasy feeling forming in his stomach. When has a woman ever driven him so to distraction that he must cool his ardor by physical torture?

He continued to turn that question over as he made his way to his study, and his mother. He assumed she would be annoyed at the time he spent, but when he entered she was sitting in one of his stuffed chairs near a fire, she must have had started thinking he would be cold, which he was. One of his hounds sat with his head in her lap and she sat smiling down at the dog, rubbing his head and smoothing the soft fur on his big floppy ear.

"Do not get used to such affection, Brutus, for when mother leaves, you will once again be expected to use the hearth as your pillow." he eyed the dog, but he knew by the dog's tail thap, thapping the floor, he did not feel intimidated in the least.

"Well, I was wondering if you were going to come down clean shaven and dressed for Almack's. It took you long enough," she said, motioning to the teapot and his cup with a generous draught of whiskey already sitting in the bottom. He poured for himself and took a drink, letting the hot liquid with the even hotter burn of the whiskey travel down to that spot in his stomach that had been acting up. Once it warmed him, he decided all might be well with the world. Then his mother spoke.

"Well, are you going to save that poor girl from whatever wretched mess she has herself in?"

Why he thought he was keeping anything from her was beyond him. He really should just stop trying. His life would be much the better for it. "What has Nettie told you?" assuming his sister the source of her information.

"Nothing, that dratted gel keeps telling me it isn't her story to tell," she poked at one of the cakes on the tray set in between them, plucking a chunk and feeding it to the dog. "First, you acting strangely as soon as we arrived, then I noticed your injured arm, and people coming and going in the house like it were a posting in. Really, do any of your acquaintances bother to use doors?"

Clive laughed. He threw his head back and laughed. "You see far too much, Mother," he said after he composed himself. "Perhaps I should employ you as my keeper of security, and I am beginning to wonder if anyone in Scotland knows how to enter a house." He sipped his tea and added more tea and whiskey to his cup.

"Well, when I saw that poor child's eye, and listened to her story about how it came to be, then I saw Nettie's expression, I knew something was afoot." She sighed then and placed a hand on his arm. Again, his mother saw more than Clive would like. "You care for her." Not a question, his mother rarely asked questions.

No point in lying if he cared to have this discussion end before he was in his dotage, "Yes, I do, but it is a complicated matter and she does not care for me."

"MmHm." Was her answer to that.

"Besides, I think this whole situation is well above what I am able to orchestrate," he said looking into his cup, not wanting to admit that and see his mother's face.

"And why would you think that you, Lord Breakerton, would not be capable of protecting a young lady who so obviously needs protecting?" His mother spat, ready to defend him even against himself.

"Mother, it is very complicated and becomes more so by the day. These are people, not pawns on a chessboard. You know full well, I am not..."

"Not what? Not your father?" She all but spat.

"You listen here, my boy. I didn't raise your father. He was fully fleshed and settled into himself long before we were wed, and while I loved him dearly, he was not the paragon you and half the Ton have made him to be."

"Mother, I..."

"Be quiet. It is well past the time you should be listening to me about this. Lord knows you have had your ear bent by every pompous, self-absorbed idiot in a cravat since you were in the school room." Her agitation was so that the dog stepped back and made his way across the room with a hurt expression once he finally found a suitable position. "Your father was a great man, but he was a man. That is the end of it. He had his foibles and plenty of failures. The one thing your father was good at though was protecting what was his."

Clair Brett

Clive sat looking into his once again empty teacup, wishing for more, but he didn't dare reach for it in the middle of his mother's speech. He got the impression she had practiced this for some time. Instead, he set the cup down and stared into the fire listening, hoping to gain some insight into how he could be more like the man. Or at the very least, not as much like what he wasn't.

"I knew," his mother continued without taking a breath, "when you ran for Scotland after Landsdown was killed and Mary was widowed that you felt responsible."

"But, Mother, I was. I sent him to that place, knowing it would be dangerous."

"Did he know the danger?" she asked.

"Well, yes, but that is not my point. I should have considered why I should not have allowed him. I should have thought of Mary, but I did not. I needed to get the job done. I should have gone."

"Well, as much as I liked Landsdown, I have to say I am glad he went instead."

"Mother," Clive chided. After all, this was her son-in-law being discussed.

"I am a mother and I will always want what is best for my children. I will not apologize. I know Landsdown would understand, bless his soul," she added the last as she always did. "You didn't make him go, darling. He chose to go. Mary knows that. She doesn't blame you."

"I carry enough blame for both of us. She shouldn't have to carry blame and grief," he said hanging his head.

"Do you know your father abandoned me in Hyde Park one afternoon when Eloise was but an infant in a stroller?"

"No, I wasn't aware." He couldn't envision the man he had been told about abandoning his young wife and first born child for any reason.

His mother smiled warmly at the memory. "He ran after a street urchin child who had snatched another woman's purse." Her face got a faraway look as she recounted the scene. "We were walking along the promenade. Your father chose not to bring the carriage or his mount. He said he wanted to properly show off his new daughter and start marriage negotiations if need be. As we were walking, there was a woman about the same age as I was walking with a basket of groceries. I remember she was wearing a uniform, so I would assume she worked for one of the inns, or perhaps one of the families in the area. A lad no older than nine came running by us and knocked into her, sending her to the ground. He jumped up like a shot and tore around the corner, just as the woman yelled that she had been robbed." She took a moment to sip her tea and sit back a bit. "Before I knew what he was about, Edward was off after him. I can still remember watching the back of his coat disappear around the corner. I hurried over, helped the woman up, and helped collect her items. We stood by the entrance to the park for over an hour. Just when I thought I would have to find street runners to search for him, he came around the corner. His cravat was askew and his normally meticulous hair was disheveled, but dangling on tiptoes off the end of Edward's arm, was the boy. He handed over the purse and apologized posthaste."

Clive listened to the story. Other than abandoning his wife and child, it sounded like something his father would have done. "Were you angry?"

"Was I angry? A good wife does not show anger," she stated plainly. "I was so angry I could not allow myself the novelty of speech. The blasted fool ran off into the bowels of London alone, leaving his newborn daughter and wife to fend for themselves. I hadn't even brought a chaperone or maid because he assured me there would be no need. But, I will tell you what he did next sent me to a level of righteous anger, I don't think I had experienced before."

"What could he have possibly done to make it worse?" Clive asked, having seen his mother righteously angry and couldn't imagine there was another level to that.

"He informed me that we now had a new house boy, and he

took the little thief home with us."

Clive sat open mouthed and not sure what question to ask first, so he stuck with the obvious one, "Who?"

"Charles. He turned out fine, if I do say so. Both of his parents had died of a fever a year earlier and he was doing what he could not to starve to death. Once bathed, debugged, and fed many times over, he was quite a delight."

Clive shook his head. He had known Charles his whole life and just assumed he came with the house. Now he understood why Charles was always so loyal to the family. He would need to acknowledge him when he returned to London. "So, did father explain why he left you?"

"He did, once I would allow him an audience. It took a few days if I remember correctly. He first admitted that he should not have acted in haste, and he should have asked me if it was quite fine for him to run after the boy. He then said that as an Earl, he had a responsibility to protect those around and below him. He felt that his position, though born into it, was a privilege that came with a heavy price. He felt that as long as he was able, he needed to protect those who could not protect themselves. He also warned me that my life with him would not be boring, but he would need me more than ever to help remind him of that responsibility when he felt like it was too much or that he was not up for the challenge. He was not perfect. He was not fearless. He understood that some things are more important than our comfort and safety."

"Why have you never told me this story before?" Clive asked still trying to envision his father, running after street urchins.

"I felt that you needed to be at a crossroads before the full enormity of it would have any affect. You, darling, are at that point where you are holding back, because you feel a need to keep us safe. You feel that you made a misstep with Landsdown and you are questioning yourself. You have no reason for such. I am well aware you have put your dear father on a throne, which he would say he didn't belong. You can only do as well as you can do. You are not him and I wouldn't want you be just like him. Believe your grandmother made her fair share of mistakes raising him. I am certain I did a perfect job raising you. Now you just need to go out and prove me correct."

"Of course, Mother," he chuckled at her pride.

"Now, as I spoke with Nettie, who was woefully absent of any real information, except that this poor young lady has been living under her uncle's roof since her family died at sea and that her uncle is not a good man."

"That is true. She believes her uncle killed her parents and tried to kill her brother, but he is lost to her right now."

"Terrible. Well, you just need to be aware that this woman has been fending for herself for a very long time and has survived on her own. She is not willingly going accept help, especially from a man. She will have a plan. Be warned you won't like it."

"I am finding that to be all too true, Mother. She is stubborn beyond even what Nettie is capable of."

"Yes, well be advised that a woman when feeling trapped or that she has no recourse will use tactics that could be very dangerous for the wrong sod who falls into her trap."

"Whatever are you talking about, Mother?"

"Oh, dear boy, I would tell you, but I am afraid perhaps you have already fell victim. Just guard your heart, dear. A woman has very few actual weapons at her disposal, but the ones she does have can wreak havoc with a man."

CHAPTER TEN

Clive sat in his study. When he had moved into the old castle that his aunt left him, his first order of business was to convert the massive great hall into his own private sanctuary. Bookshelves lined the walls from floor to ceiling. The large fireplace and hearth had been re-stoned, and heavy plush carpets covered the stone floor giving the room a cozy warmth. He had chairs placed throughout for comfort, and his desk was placed close enough to the fire to stay warm in the winter, but also right next to the three full length windows overlooking the gardens. It had been his haven.

He sighed and took a sip of the brandy sitting next to the letter on his blotter. How could one woman so easily disrupt his safe haven without even have being invited to his home? It seemed he could not step into his study without Louissa being in the very air. Once his mother had finished her tea and her work at making him feel like a naughty nine year old, she had left him in peace to consider what was next.

It was obvious he needed help. He needed to understand this uncle more. To do that he would need to fetch Henry from where ever his hidey-hole was. After sending a boy with a message to Nicholas, Clive was rewarded with an agreement to meet.

Now, Clive sat waiting. Not to be left a contented moment, however, he was delivered a note from the gentlemen of the county demanding an update. It appeared they felt Clive had enough time to recoup from his injuries and they wanted this moving forward. He didn't trust them. Many knew Louissa was a woman, but would not admit it, but they still wanted justice. Justice, Clive knew came at the end of a knotted rope. If he didn't give them something or solve this whole blasted mess, they might go elsewhere. Was this the place where his father would have thrown caution to the wind? Moreover, what exactly would Clive throw into the wind right now? Should he kidnap Louissa and run off into hiding? Perhaps challenge her uncle to a duel?

"I assumed woolgathering was a womanly art," drawled a

voice behind him. Clive turned to see Henry walking out of the shadows and making his way to a chair by the fire. "I helped myself to your brandy, thank you by the way."

"No, please by all means," Clive answered dryly.

"I thought we were agreed you would not summon me again," Henry said, cutting through the drivel. "First, I do not like being summoned, and second, I am a very busy man."

"Yes, well, while you are being a very busy man, your sister is being beaten by your uncle and forced to put herself in harm's way."

That seemed to garner the young man's attention. "Beaten?" he asked with concern and a good bit of justifiable anger.

"Yes, her uncle. It seems he was angry about how his evening went the other night, when Louissa had to fend off three drunken farmers hell bent on stopping the highwayman, and threw something at her and hit her in the face."

Clive's jaw clenched every time he thought of Louissa's eye swollen shut and her nose all purple and cut. It was almost enough to grab his pistol and shoot every man who had ever laid a hand on her, or who didn't rescue her when they had the chance, like her brother.

"What?" Henry asked with all innocence and concern. "I didn't hit her and as much as it eats at me that she is in this situation, there is naught I can do until..."

"Until what? She is dead? Either by the hands of your uncle or the angry residents of this county?" Clive grabbed the letter from his desk and waved it in front of Henry. He grabbed his drink and took a long sip. He needed to keep his voice down and his anger restrained. He took a deep breath before turning back to Henry.

"None of this would need dealing with had you not decided to get involved." Henry took a drink, but Clive caught the worry on his face.

"Had it not been me it would have been someone else. That someone else might not have considered the situation as I did. That someone else might have fought harder that first night. That someone else might not have taken into consideration that Louissa was a woman in danger. That someone else might have taken care of her that night, so you would not have to have dealt with it." Clive hadn't realized he had moved in front of Henry and was leaning on the arms of the chair, pinning him there. His knuckles ached as he finally let go and released his grip on the stuffed arms.

"I love my sister," insisted Henry as he rose as well walking to the window and looking out at the inky blackness of the night.

"Yes, well as one with more sisters than a sane man should have to contend, you are going about it incorrectly."

"You have no ideas about how I am doing anything. I do not have to answer to you, milord."

"Yes, well you do not feel that you have to answer to anyone it seems. Not your uppers, not your dead parents, and especially not your sister who is in dire need of saving. Tell me, what does your soul tell you, or are you able to ignore that as well?" Clive wanted a fight. He was sick of inaction.

When Henry threw himself in Clive's direction, he was ready. He grabbed the younger man and pinned him to the thick stonewall, wedging his forearm into Henry's neck, but Henry didn't back down.

"I am warning you now, Breakerton, as I said before, leave it. You are getting into things you have no business getting into. Your aunt at least understood…"

"My aunt? My aunt was helping you in this fool's endeavor?" Clive asked. He knew his aunt was mixed up in this and wasn't surprised. She always loved a good mystery and if she could find a spot of danger, all the better.

"Let me go," Henry demanded, but Clive held forth. "Let me go and I'll tell you."

Clive grunted, but shoved his body off Henry's extracting a satisfying grunt from his victim. Henry took a moment to rub the tender skin around his neck and move away from the wall and any corners. "Your aunt summoned me, as you did through Nicholas. How she knew I was alive, I was never able to ascertain. Your aunt knew things about every person in the county. When I arrived, she told me that Louissa was trying to find me and was more than willing to put herself in danger to do it."

Henry paused, turning to the door. The large oak door squeaked open and Mary appeared small and willowy against the massive size of the door and room. "Mary, darling, can I help you?" Clive went to her and wrapped his arms around her, placing a kiss on her forehead. His heart rate increased. It was bad enough that his mother knew he was trying to help Louissa, and that he had Nettie searching the manor for what Louissa was looking for. He had no desire to allow poor Mary to be caught up in such things.

"No, I-I heard voices and thought perhaps you and Nettie were talking. I didn't mean to interrupt."

"No, no, you didn't." Clive turned toward Henry and gave him a look that said clearly his villainous intent if he didn't play nice. "I was just talking with a business associate. This is…" Clive paused not sure of how he should introduce him.

"Ewin, Ewin Dermit, Milady," Henry intoned and bent into a gallant bow.

Clive noticed color rising to Mary's cheeks. Given her tendency to such paleness of late, the color shone like a beacon. This could be nothing but intolerable, he thought, and cleared his throat to remind the two he was in the room.

"Very nice to meet you, Mr. Dermit. Do you live near the estate?" She asked coming more fully into the room before Clive could think of a reason otherwise. Instead, he found his way to his desk and dropped into the chair, annoyance tugging at his mood.

"No, I am actually a seaman. I own the Drocet. We are in harbor only for a short time, and then back out to sea I shall go." Clive noted how Henry was more than capable of charming his grieving sister, but completely incapable to having a reasonable conversation with him. He grunted and took a drink.

"What was that brother?" Mary asked.

"Nothing, please carry on." Henry smiled at him, hearing the sarcasm. Mary on the other hand did not.

"I love sailing. My late husband and I took a small trip after our wedding. It was lovely," she said with a sad, but not wholly unhappy expression. Clive had never heard her once speak of Landsdown since his death and to hear her now include the word late caused him to get something stuck in the throat and sting his eyes.

"Oh, I am very sorry to hear of your husband's passing."

"Yes, Lord Landsdown," she said her smile slipping a touch. He doubted Henry noticed, but as her brother and the one responsible, he noted it.

Henry glanced at Clive. He remembered Henry was aware of the situation after bringing it up in their last meeting, but this time Henry's glance was not all knowing and pompous, but almost sympathetic. "He was a very lucky man indeed to have such a loyal and loving wife. Most men would consider themselves kings to have such an accord with their wives."

She blushed prettily again, making Clive uncomfortable and more annoyed than ever. He allowed the pleasantries to continue for only a few minutes before he couldn't take it. After more than two years, Mary had to be affected by this annoyingly arrogant, just out of leading strings young man. He would never understand the female mind, he decided just before he rose. "Mary, I am exceedingly happy you and Mr. Dermit are finding an accord, but we need to finish our business so that I might get him back to his ship."

"Oh, yes, I am so sorry," Mary said rising. As Henry rose, his chair slid back and knocked Clive off balance forcing him to stumble. Good thing he didn't fall, because no one else in the room would have noticed. Henry was too busy bowing over her hand and kissing it, and Mary, too busy looking like a schoolgirl just out of the nursery, all doe eyed and coy. Clive thought he might lose his dinner. That saddened him, because he had quite enjoyed the meal. After this, he might have to strike it from the menu if it would make him think of this.

Mary made her way around to give Clive a peck on the cheek and floated out of the room. Both men watched her leave. As the large door closed behind her, Clive turned a scowl on his guest, who looked as silly as his sister did.

"Your sister is enchanting," Henry said.

"Don't," said Clive.

"Don't what?" Henry asked with mock innocence.

"You are by far not good enough for my sister, and she is not going to have a dalliance with a fool who thinks himself a pirate." Clive was very happy with his declaration, until he looked over to see Henry smiling like the fool he was just accused of being, and not paying any heed to Clive. "Now, back to Louissa. She is in danger and if you won't see…"

"I can see the situation fine, my lord. I am taking steps to deal with the situation. I thank you for bringing the concern of the locals to my attention and will have my men take caution."

"Take caution?" Clive exploded. He had seen how quickly anyone came to help Louissa two nights ago, or how someone stepped in when her uncle beat her. "I am not at all certain who you claim to have protecting her, but to my estimation, the drunks would have at the very least injured her before she could escape, and her uncle could well have done permanent damage in his rage. You will excuse me if I do not hold the same estimation of the success of your men."

Henry had finished his drink and made his way to middle of the room. "Listen well, Breakerton, my sister is my concern, not yours and the more you interfere the more dangerous it becomes for her. As I warned before, you need not to pursue this any further."

"And as I have told you, I do not plan to do any such thing. I have put Louissa under my protection because I do not see those who should be sworn to the deed capable. I will be under your feet if need be, but my main concern is the woman's safety. You might threaten me or my family, but it is family tradition that we take care of those who cannot take care of themselves."

Before Clive could react, Henry was in his face, with a cold calculating look. "I will tell you only once more. I will look after my own and if you continue to get in my way, I will tell my men not to take heed and do what must be done. I do not care to hurt you, but you have no idea what you are messing with."

"Then tell me."

Clive watched the battle rage on Henry's face as he decided what to give up, if anything. After a long moment, he sighed and began pacing.

"I am telling you this, because Nicholas trusts you and your aunt was a true champion of our family. Please be assured, this in no way states my interest in having you under foot."

"Noted."

He eyed Clive for a moment longer, and then began, "I know you have been given the basics of our story. My uncle killed my parents while on a voyage during a storm. He claimed they fell overboard, but he had them thrown."

Henry continued to pace. Clive wanted to ask what proof they had, but feared breaking his thoughts would stop him from talking.

"I too was to be killed, but Cook was not as ruthless as my uncle had thought. Instead, he brought me in a potato sack off the ship and to his family to raise me until which time I could claim my place as heir. I grew up on a coastal farm in the north until I was ten and five. At that time, I boarded a ship as a deckhand and began my training. From there, I rose quickly through the ranks, and in a battle, I managed to win the favor of the captain, who gave me the ship we won, the Dorcet. She has been a good friend since."

He walked to the window and looked out across the gardens. Just as Clive decided he was done, Henry continued. "I have spent the last two years proving myself an asset not only to the Crown, but also the more nefarious sea goers, such as my uncle. I have been in negotiations for months to rescue Louissa, then and only then will it be safe to step up and announce my true identity."

Clive could wait no longer. He had to ask. "What proof do you have that your uncle did kill your parents? I would assume your goal is not only to take back your title, but to have him pay for his actions."

He glanced back into the room with a look of hard resolve on his young face. Clive realized that this man had spent years not having to answer to another person. A situation Clive had dreamed of on many occasions when being chastised by the men tasked to make him a true lord, but now understanding both lives have their undesirable elements. At least Clive had people he could take into confidence and assess matters before acting. Henry had no one to lean on or learn from.

"That was what your aunt was helping us with. I was aware that Louissa had also made contact with her, but your aunt and I both agreed it was not safe to give her enough proof to act, because if she did so while I was at sea, there would be little by way of help I could offer. Your aunt was able to procure letters and log sheets from my father's ship detailing the events from the months before and after my parents' death. She had letters from my mother written to her that my father was beginning to fear for our safety, and was scared they might not make it back to dry land."

"Did you search her out, then knowing she was a friend of your mother?" Clive needed to connect the dots to figure out where he would fit in.

"No, she had been told in a letter that my father had only one ally on the ship that they knew for sure. It was Cook. My mother said they were certain he would do what he could do at the very least to protect us children. When she heard of the deaths, and also of my passing by fever months after, she searched out Cook's family and at that time found me."

"Why didn't she bring you back and call the alarm then?"

Clive asked more to himself than to Henry. His aunt was an eccentric woman, but very clever and wise as well.

"It was decided that I was far too young to defend myself and if my uncle had once tried to kill me, he would again. The law would not have been on your aunt's side and I would have been handed over. She also didn't have proof at that time of foul play. She sent money to help the family that raised me and once Louissa was brought back to the family home, she made an effort to reach out as a concerned neighbor and gentry. My uncle can deal with any annoyance, but your aunt proved to be too much of a conundrum for him, and he never found a way to easily get her out of the picture." Both men laughed at that. Clive knew his aunt would have found a way to solidify herself into Louissa's life if she felt she needed to, even if it meant danger for her.

"Well, where is the proof now?" Clive asked the next logical question. He knew Louissa had already been searching his house, but had obviously come up empty.

"I was away on the coast of America when your aunt passed. We had discussed that she had the papers hidden well, and that when the time came, she would be able to get to them quickly, but that was as far as it went. She was as secretive as she was eccentric."

Nodding his head in agreement, Clive began pacing as well. "I know my aunt has many secret nooks and hidey holes in this old rock pile, but I am not sure where to start." *Not to mention, if they were both working to protect Louissa, neither had the time to search.*

"I have no ideas to help with that. We corresponded primarily through letters. I only visited when I was able and it was safe. Did you not find my letters here?"

Clive had spent the better part of the last year going through his aunt's papers and land holdings, but had not come across even one item of personal exchange. Until now, he had not even realized it. "No, nothing. Now that I think on it, I have not found one piece

Clair Brett

of personal correspondence from or to my aunt in her papers."

Clive knew women. He didn't know how to contend with them, but knew those things that were important to them, and letters from people they cared for were on the top of that list. Unless she was concerned about them being found, she would not have destroyed them. He also had not found any letters from his uncle, which he also found odd. "I know she didn't give it over to Louissa, because I watched your sister from that very window not a month ago fleeing from the side entrance into the gardens. I know she was looking for something, but I am sure she never found it."

"She what?" Henry asked actually surprised. Clive realized he knew more about Louissa's character than her own brother did.

"She is brave, bordering on reckless. I am not sure what your image of her is, but you should reconsider the constitution of any woman able to dress as a highwayman and take on carriages at night alone," Clive pointed out. He was getting the impression that Henry had the two ideals of his sister separated in his mind in such a way that he could not connect the two.

"Yes, I suppose you are right. I just never thought…"

"Never thought she was in any real danger? That she was just like every other young lady in the country? I would be willing to bet your sister could better handle a pistol than an embroidery needle, my boy."

"I--I just thought--I suppose it was easier not to think about it." He sat heavily in the chair closest to him and put his head in his hand. The ramifications of his actions, those of a young man with no adult guidance seemed to weigh heavy on him at that moment. Clive took pity and filled his glass setting it next to the man's elbow. He then took the seat closest to him.

"I know you are doing what you can, but you need to realize that your sister also has been surviving for just as many years. She has protected herself and her parents' memory, all the while trying to find you and regain your family name right under your uncle's nose. You have had the luxury of anonymity. Louissa has had to use subterfuge and cunning all the while having the fear of exposure."

Henry was silent. Clive didn't blame him. It had been Clive's burden since birth to see to his sisters. He was certain they would not see it that way, but still he understood the burden. Henry was only now realizing his sister was not what he expected.

"I'm not going away. You know that."

"I am becoming aware, yes," Henry acknowledged.

"My sister is going to begin searching for the missing papers. We all spent time here as children and know the grounds and building well."

"I must ask…"

"I am not yet sure of my intentions with Louissa, but I refuse to leave her in harm's way while I sort it out." Clive shifted in his seat uneasy with admitting his weakness.

Henry sat silent for some time. He was a man used to being alone. If he hoped to gain back his sister and his title, he would have to get used to help and criticism. Clive knew better than most. His first lesson would be that his sister would not stand for any amount of controlling efforts on his part. Clive actually felt a pang of pity for the boy. That just might be his biggest challenge in life.

"Now that we have the niceties out of the way, what is our next move?" Clive asked.

"If you are correct and the proof is still on the property somewhere, it needs to be a priority. I am not able to protect Louissa, because my uncle doesn't know me as his nephew, I would be found out."

"I have made it my priority to protect Louissa from herself if need be, at great expense to myself I have determined."

"I have been told there is a very fine line between bravery and stupidity," Henry pointed out. Both men laughed.

Clive stood, walking to his desk. "I still do not know what business you are involved, but I will protect her above all else. Even if it means exposing you, if it comes to that."

Henry didn't answer. He got to his feet, nodded, and left by where he came. Clive was certain his, Louissa, and his family's lives could very well be in as much danger from Henry as from the uncle, but it was a risk he had to take. At least he felt a margin of comfort that Henry's men were not going to come looking to kill him. Yet.

CHAPTER ELEVEN

Louissa had made great strides in avoiding her uncle as of late, so as she padded down the stairs to appear from his summons, she couldn't figure out what he might want.

"Well, 'tis about time, gel," her uncle complained, not even bothering to look up and see her breathing hard.

"My apologies, Uncle. What is it you need?" Not bothering to argue about the fact, she made it to his study in record time, after hearing him bellow from the foot of the stairs. She was certain there was no bellowing going on at the Ladies Breakerton estate.

"Ye 'ave been invited to Breakerton's for a luncheon. What do you know about this?" He quizzed, assuming it was a conspiracy of some sort against him, she assumed.

"Nothing, I know nothing of it. I met the Ladies Breakerton and Lady Landsdown at Bethany's when she invited them for tea a few days ago. 'Tis all," She assured her uncle. They had mentioned having her visit, but had assumed that was just politeness, "I have no intention of attending, Uncle. I promise…"

"Nonsense, ye be going. I want to know what his lairdship knows if anything, and what his plans are for the community. 'Tis a perfect way to get inside and find out," he reasoned while still not acknowledging her.

"But, Uncle I…"

"Ye what? Ye, cannae even handle a luncheon without botching it? Is that what ye are saying?" He looked up at last with annoyance and the beginnings of anger.

"No, I just assumed you would not want me to socialize so, and wanted to assure you I had no desire."

And that I in no way plan on bringing you back any information which would help you. Her words tasted sweet on her tongue, but she wisely swallowed them and agreed to give a full accounting when she returned. Louissa returned to her room to change into a more appropriate gown for a luncheon at an English Lord's home. She doubted anything she had would be appropriate.

Two hours later, Louissa was introduced in the large sun

filled parlor of the Ladies Breakerton and Lady Landsdown. Nettie jumped up and embraced her warmly, while Mary and her mother stood and nodded with warm smiles.

"I was certain you would come, but Breakerton said he didn't think you would," Nettie prattled on.

"Thank you for the invitation. We get so few new people in the area, that it is always enjoyable when I meet a new family. I do have to say I was surprised at your invite," Louissa admitted, as they all found their seats again, and got comfortable.

"My dear," Lady Breakerton explained, "we like all sorts of people and I have always felt a well-rounded social group is the only way for one to stretch themselves into more complex individuals."

"What my mother is trying to say," Nettie explained, "is that she cannot tolerate the pompousness of many of the Ton's members and finds the company of people who are more involved with living than how their lives look to others is refreshing."

"Well said, my dear," Lady Breakerton acknowledged her daughter.

After the niceties were finished, the women settled into a discussion about the local area and Her Ladyship had many stories of growing up visiting the area. A few even included Louissa's father and mother.

"I am terribly sorry for your loss, dear." Lady Breakerton leaned forward and patted Louissa on the hand. "Your parents were lovely people and what happened was such a tragedy."

"Thank you. I miss them a great deal still to this day."

Just as Louissa feared, Her Ladyship would begin talking about her brother being lost as well, which always happened with these conversations, as Breakerton walked in. Louissa felt the air being sucked out of the space before she heard his baritone vibrate from the doorway behind her.

"Good day, ladies," he said by way of a general greeting as he entered, then bent to kiss his mother's cheek. "Mother, you look ravishing as always. It must be this clean Scottish air."

When he turned to greet Louissa, her body seized. He was everything a British Earl should be. He had just come from riding and his riding breeches were a light brown, like a fawn just after they lose their spots. His tall hessian boots were not shiny as would be expected in London, she assumed. They wore road dust on the toes and mud splatter up the front. He was so close, she could smell the briny air on him, but could not bring herself to raise her glance to his face. He waited until she knew if she didn't make eye contact she would appear rude or half-witted. She wasn't able to rule out the latter all together.

"Good day, Miss, I trust you had a pleasant walk over," drawing her eyes to his. The rest of him was not as untidy as his boots, but even dressed in the casual country fashion, he made an impressive display. His jacket was bottle green with gold binding around the seams. Under that was a white shirt and cravat with a simple knot. He had chosen to leave off a waistcoat, as she was certain all the layers would be over warm on a day such as this. It made her stop on her visual trip up to his face to ponder what he would look like in just his shirtsleeves. As she made her way up and found his eyes, they were piercing her with intensity and made her cheeks burn more than they already were from her thoughts.

"Good day, my lord." She made to stand, but was waved back down.

"Nonsense, who needs to stand on protocol? We are in the country." He held out his hand waiting for hers. With reluctance, she proffered her hand and he took it with a gentle touch and brought it to his lips. She was certain the whole of the room stopped breathing. She waited for his mother to scold them both for improper behavior, but he set her hand back on her skirts and made his way around the table. He was having to get even closer rubbing his knee on hers as he passed by to find a seat next to Nettie, who gave him a look of annoyance such as a sister should.

Just then, the butler announced luncheon. "Shall we?" Lady

Breakerton rose and led the way to the patio where a simple table had been set with fine china. The contrast created a comforting scene. Once everyone was seated, being a round table there was no need for proper placement and she got the feeling this family wouldn't be hindered by such. Louissa, the coward she was, placed herself between Breakerton's sisters. If she were to play out her plan of seduction, she would need to find some courage, but right now was not that time.

The meal was served, the fare delicious, but simple country food. She wondered if this was what Lady Breakerton preferred, or if she was eating as her son preferred, since it was his home. The conversation was meant to include, not exclude their guest.

"Miss Louissa, how goes the crops in the area this year? My brother tells me it has been unseasonably dry thus far, damaging some of the more demanding of species," Mary asked in her quiet way. Louissa noted Clive's reaction to his sister engaging in conversation, as if he did not experience it near enough.

"I am afraid, with my uncle being more seafaring minded, I only know what I hear from neighbors, but yes, I do believe the dry weather is not helping the growing at all," Louissa responded as best she could.

"My farmers have lost two whole fields for grazing and a field of potatoes. I hadn't much hope for that crop. The soil was not to my liking, but felt it was the only crop option for that," Clive went on to discuss. "Why, Mary, have you read any reports to the contrary?"

"No, what I have been reading is equivalent to what I have heard in the area. I wonder if such should be of more concern, is all."

Louissa decided she much liked Lady Mary. She didn't speak often, but when she did, everyone in ear's reach should listen.

"Well," Nettie entered the fray, "I think that Parliament is not at all concerned with such matters, they are more concerned with their own pocketbooks."

Clair Brett

"Enough," Lady Breakerton intoned. "I am certain poor Miss Louissa does not care to hear about Parliament's lack of concern for the lowly farmer. I know this, my dear, because I am tired of it." Louissa fought back a grin at the look on Nettie's face, but Mary quickly changed the subject to something more benign, which left Lord Breakerton the one to be uneasy in his seat.

"Miss Louissa, if I recall our last conversation, I promised you the grand tour of the estate when you visited next," Clive interrupted his sister in mid-description of the dress she was preparing for the summer ball they were planning. Clive looked both surprised and resigned at the talk of hosting a ball, which made Louissa more endeared than she cared to be.

"You did, my lord, but I am currently here to visit your mother and sisters. It would be rude to leave their company to wander the estate," she said, not wanting to seem too eager.

"Nonsense," Lady Breakerton reassured her. "It is near time for me to go work on correspondence that I have been neglecting. The girls also have letters to pen to their sisters as well." A point to which both women agreed and encouraged her to enjoy the tour, as the grounds were lovely in full bloom.

Louissa took one last sip of her tea wishing it had a little something in it to give her some courage. She would be putting her acting to the test, since she was probably more familiar with the house and grounds than Breakerton himself. As Breakerton offered his hand to assist her standing, she felt a tingle of excitement travel through his hand into her gloved fingers and up her arm, raising the fine hairs along her neck.

The women assured her they would be available before she left to say goodbye, and bent to finishing their luncheon.

Already outside on the veranda, she followed Breakerton into the main hall leading back to the entrance. They walked in silence next to each other, but when the hall way split, she felt his warm, large hand splay across the dip in her back to turn her in the correct direction.

To her chagrin, she stumbled on the carpet edge, but caught herself before she needed saving. She only felt his hand flex a bit, but as a gentleman should, he never made mention of her near miss and they continued along unheeded.

"So," once in the hall, Breakerton stopped and turned to her. "What would you care to see first? We can begin in the gallery, which many guests have said is one of the best in all of Scotland. We have tapestries and portraits dating back to the time of Robert the Bruce, or we could begin in the solarium which is awash with fragrance this time of year."

Louissa knew there would be little fear of being caught in the gallery, as it was certain not to be frequented by the family or staff. "I would love to see the gallery. I am a lover of history," she added to make her choice of pure innocence.

"Very well." He bent in a slight bow and offered his arm. She couldn't help but smile at his gallant pose and expression. Her stomach fluttered as he took her offered arm and tucked it snug to his side while cradling her hand in his. It would not do to fall into her own snare she thought to herself, as they ascended the grand staircase, which was obviously not original to the original castle construction. She decided it would help her not think about how solid and comforting his side was against her arm if she was to try to recount what his aunt had told her many times about the history of the building. She wondered if her partner was as familiar with its history.

Breakerton must have noticed her attention to the staircase. "It does seem out of place, doesn't it? It was not original to the castle. One of my ancestors decided to make a grand entrance indeed and had it built. My aunt always thought it a travesty, I think was the term she used."

Louissa smiled because that was exactly what the woman used to say every time she passed by it. "Yes, I believe that was the term she used."

"Ah, yes, you were familiar with my aunt. You could

probably give me a tour of my own home." He conceded with humor coloring his voice.

"No, my lord. I am certain twill be very interesting hearing your rendition of the history," she assured him. She knew as yet, she never leaned into his aunt as she spoke, but he drew her into his aura with his voice. She could feel the pull.

"Well, in that case, I will confide that Nettie and I found the eyesore of great use when wanting to slide down the banister."

"You didn't?" she asked. She had memories of her brother and her having grand adventures, so was not surprised, but the Lord standing before her didn't appear to be the banister sliding type.

"Oh, we did." He leaned in so his cheek almost brushed hers. "Nettie was much better than I, but I will deny it to my death, so do not bother to tell her. I would not give her the satisfaction."

Louissa had stopped climbing the steps when he leaned in. She got the feeling her feet would no longer follow her direction anyway. Then, to hear such a confession with quite a playful tone… If she didn't get to her seduction soon and get it over with, she was going to…well, she didn't want to consider that.

"Which way would you like me to take you to the gallery?" He asked.

"Whichever way you prefer, my lord, but if you also wanted to tour the grounds, I would suggest the more direct route, for time purposes," Louissa suggested, thinking the fresh air might help calm her rattled nerves.

"Of course, this way, my dear." As he topped the stairs, he turned her to the left. The term of endearment, did nothing to harden her resolve. Either he was a world-class manipulator or she was in serious danger; a danger she was ill equipped to manage.

The hallway stretched east and they passed several closed doors leading to guest rooms and suites. Many, Louissa remembered wandering in. It felt as if it was just yesterday she was a regular day guest. The house was open to her, so she had a place to escape.

"Ah, here we are," Clive pulled her out of her memory as they entered the large room that the hall spilled into. The room would lie directly over the grand hall and was as big with ceilings as high. Each wall facing south and north had a bank of large windows flooding the room with natural light during the day. Any solid wall space left was filled with portraits and tapestries. A walk through Breakerton's family on his father's side. In the middle was a freestanding wall with portraits hanging on both sides and easels dotted the corners and empty areas of the room around some benches and chairs for sitting and reading, or drawing. She followed Clive around the room listening to him recount stories he could only have heard from his aunt. Louissa thought about how much he reminded her of the woman. His smile, when genuine, would reach his eyes and make the gold flecks brighter. The curl in his hair, if left to grow, would be the envy of every woman in the land. She smiled at her own thought and was caught.

"What?" He asked, catching her eye as she glanced up.

"Nothing, I was just thinking of something."

"Ah, so I have bored you to the point where you have gone within yourself, so not to perish at my feet?" He asked with mock distress. She laughed, as was his goal, she was sure.

"No, I was thinking about your aunt and how she loved this room. As it is obvious you do as well." Louissa meandered through the easels and furniture as she spoke, not wanting to be so close, but knowing she needed to act on her plan. She turned back toward him with intent footfalls. "You are quite like her in many ways."

"Yes, so I have been told. I assure you I am very different from my aunt in some very fundamental ways," he said with an edge sending a wave of unease and anticipation through her. Emboldened, she continued toward him and didn't stop until her slippered toes bumped his boots.

"Of that, my lord, I am aware." She hoped she added enough of a dip in the tenor of her voice as she had watched countless women do in port when the men came ashore. For effect, she assured herself, she reached out and laid her hand on his arm. His height required she look up at him and he bent his head to see her face. They were mere inches from each other.

Tis now or never.

She pushed up on her tiptoes and just brushed her lips against his. She would have left it at that innocent encounter, but he reached his arm around her waist and tugged her into him, lowering his head to take her mouth more fully with his own. Louissa's head began to swim. She could taste the tea on his lips with a hint of honey from the scones. She gave in and leaned more into his solid frame, giving herself to the kiss. His lips were soft, yet demanding. Gentle, yet unyielding. She liked this. The gods help her; she liked it. At what point Breakerton took over the seduction, she wasn't sure, but she was definitely no longer at the reins, and this beast was being whipped into a frenzy. Like the ship when her uncle would allow full sails, she felt pulled into the strength of his embrace. He had his arm around her in such a way that she was unable to be an equal participant. She did not have the use of her arms, which were held at her waist, so all she could do was tip or turn her head, and lean into his body with hers. He noted her frustration and the movement of her nose showing that he had tickled her when his whiskers shushed by the corners of her mouth. He broke the kiss, but kept his forehead touching hers.

"My darling, this is one realm, where it really is customary that you allow the gentleman to act first," he said through raspy breaths just as heavy as her own, and his eyes were dark pools that shimmered with gold flecks, much darker than earlier in the day.

"Have I angered you? 'Twas not my intent, I couldn't help myself, my lord," she said hoping to sound embarrassed and apologetic.

He reached up and brushed away a stray curl caught in her eyelash. The tender act brought tears to her eyes and she blinked them back hoping he would attribute it to his removal of the curl. No man since her father had been able to make her cherished, but

Breakerton did. She was certain that was not his intent, but she guessed when one has gone for so long with little affection that a kind gesture could feel like an intimate moment. She cleared her throat and stepped back out of his embrace and away from the emotions swirling there. Again, she noted he was affected as much as she was, so her plan could work. She did have to agree that it was more perilous than she thought, but if she could fortify her resolve, it could--

A painting just to the left of Breakerton's ear caught her eye. She had not noticed it over much before, but just now, as the light glinted off the frame, it stuck away from the wall more than the others did. The painting was of Breakerton's great grandfather's ship with full sails. It was the only painting with any nod to the once seafaring past of the family and just the place Breakerton's aunt would leave valuable information for her to find. Her breath caught.

"What is it?" Breakerton asked turning toward her stare, "'Tis a spider? Let me…"

"No, it was a bird fluttering past the window. Quite pretty, but alas, as birds do, it has flown by onto its destination," she said, turning him toward the door and away from the painting. She would need to come back, but the question was when? She would need to find out their social engagements and try to sneak in. Perhaps the proof she needed was just waiting for a time when her guard was down to make itself seen. If luck but would shine on her this one time, she wouldn't have to continue her plans for seduction. Which was just as well, because she wasn't any longer so sure she could control the situation to her satisfaction with his man. "I have not seen the rose gardens in full bloom in so long, please, can we stroll out there next?" she asked to change the subject.

"Of course, darling, anything you wish," he replied patting her hand in an affectionate way that melted the resolve that was left and had her smiling like a giddy school girl. This was not going to do. Not at all.

The fresh air was a relief as the two made their way into the rose garden, but not as much as she would have liked. His kisses were amazing, but if not for his gentleness, she was sure she could hold against the surge of physical wanting. She felt adrift now. Never in her recent memories had any man been so kind, and tender toward her.

"What is that?" He pulled her out of her heavy thoughts.

"Pardon, my lord?"

"That necklace, it is very unique. Does it hold special sentiment for you?" Clive turned and wound his finger inside the long chain around her neck to pull the small vial and heart shaped locket up for inspection. Louissa's breath caught. She was too close to let her plans out. She knew his sense of protecting the weak would not allow her to have such an item at easy reach.

"Oh, that. 'Tis a vial my mother gave me. She said it was filled with mermaid tears and that as long as I wore it I would be protected," she explained, plucking it from his fingers and settling it back into the bodice of her dress. She would make an all right playwright, she thought as she considered the story she weaved from nothing, so get his mind away from the vial of poison. If her plan went well, 'twould not matter because she could destroy it, and if her plan failed--well it would not matter then either, because she would be dead.

"Is it working for you?" He asked falling back into step and giving her space to breathe once again.

"Well, I suppose Mother never thought my life would have taken such a detour from her plans for me. Perhaps, if I had married and had a family by now, they would be working marvelously."

They walked in silence for a bit until the smell of roses assailed their senses. Clive spoke first.

"Funny, how as a boy I always associated the smell of roses to grand adventures and sword fights with my sisters. This must be why. I cannot count the number of times our adventures led us here. It seems it was a perfect hideaway for young souls."

She tipped her head up to get a better look at his face and

she immediately regretted it. His expression was soft with gentle lines that crinkled around his eyes and mouth when he smiled. Such fond memories of a happy childhood. It made her heartsick for her brother while at the same time, warm compassion and something else she couldn't explain for the man in front of her welled to the surface. Without knowledge of her own actions, she watched as her hand lifted and cupped his cheek and jaw. She should pull it back, she knew, but was unable to make her limbs do her bidding. It appeared they had a different agenda.

He reached up and covered her hand with his own, leaning his head into her palm and closing his eyes.

Oh for Lord's sake, don't close your eyes.

She watched mesmerized by the emotion playing on his face. She managed to pull her hand away, but the heat of his cheek and firmness of his jaw went with her.

"We are not visible from the house out here," he stated, as if she should know why that was of import. For the life of her, she could not think. His eyes bored into her own, making thought impossible. "You chose a very useful destination for our tour, my lady," he continued as he dipped his head down and took her lips with his own. Louissa knew at that moment, she would never again smell roses without the taste of his lips on hers, and his hand firm on her back pulling her to him. And *the gods help her*, she went willingly. He took a step back to absorb her weight. Damn if she didn't want to suck him in. Take in all his optimism, all his happy memories. Her head swam with sensations. She couldn't even begin to decide where to feel first. Her lips, where he was relentlessly plying, shaping, and parting at will, or his one hand that held her fast at the nape of the neck, not that he needed to hold her, or the hand at the base of her back, very close to her bottom where he kept their bodies connected in a most delicious and intimate way. Yes, she wanted it, him, and everything he had to offer. She could almost be lost and forget...

She managed to drag her head back from his penetrating

kisses. Both of them were all but panting. Louissa took a step back. He affected her in a way she had no real defense against, but as her brain cleared and she noted the strained look on Clive's face, she realized he was similarly affected. She must remember her purpose, she reminded herself. With satisfaction, she acknowledged her plan of seduction was working. It was working on them both.

"Oh, dear, what time is it?" She asked with concern.

"It is half, three," he answered looking at his watch hanging from the chain on his waistcoat.

"Heavens, I must be going. My uncle gave strict instructions to be home by four O'clock. If I do not leave at once I will not make it." She had to give an excuse for leaving so quickly. Her instincts told her leaving at this point was best to keep his interest peaked. "I, ah, thank you, my lord, for the luncheon and the tour." She curtsied, but could not make eye contact. She felt her cheeks burning and knew it was not the tour of the gardens, but the tour of her more sensitive places that she was considering. He knew as well.

"You are most welcome, my lady. I hope we are otherwise occupied more in the near future. Any time you wish for a tour, I will drop all that I am doing and accommodate your requests," he said with a grin, and something else in his voice, that sent shivers dancing down her spine and desire pooling in her belly.

She turned and made haste to the path, leading home. As she walked, she felt more herself. If she had luck on her side she could return, and possibly get into the gallery to see if that painting had any hidey-holes, and perhaps further her seduction. She decided her afternoon amorous endeavors were going to be the most pleasant thing that happened all day. Considering she was headed back to her uncle, she was sure of it.

CHAPTER TWELVE

He watched Louissa scurry from the garden toward home. He sensed her excuse for fleeing was just that, but he knew her fear of her uncle was real. Every person in this district had a healthy fear of Gareth Adair; fool and scholar, pauper and wealthy landowner, they all would avert their eyes and stammer when asked about him. All Clive knew was his name and all that Louissa's brother had shared.

Clive continued on to the stables to check on the horses and collect the dogs for the night. Even though his mother claimed that she preferred for them not to sleep in the main house, it was Clive's home and he would have the dogs with him. He also wanted to find Eric, a trusted employee and after his one dip into the match making pool, a trusted friend. He was certain he would never match make again, but the result had been favorable, and connecting with Eric had proved helpful. If there were additional information to be had on this uncle, Eric would know.

After speaking with Eric and commandeering the dogs, Clive went to the house with the younger of the two hounds nipping at his heels all the way.

"Oh, for God's sake, please tell me you didn't force that lovely girl to wallow in the stables with those, those…"

"Dogs? They are dogs, Mother, not rabid hell hounds come to rid the world of all that is holy. Just dogs." Clive wasn't sure when his mother began pretending to dislike dogs, but was certain it had been long enough for her to make it part of her very being. "And no, I did not bring Louissa to the stables. She had to leave, forgetting another appointment for her uncle. While I was almost to the stables when I said my farewell, I continued along on my own."

The younger dog, Margret, after his late aunt, could not sense Lady Breakerton's faked unease and bounded up to her with the enthusiasm her namesake had in her own life and endeavors. Lady Breakerton gave the dog a dubious stare, but did not shriek or swat at the puppy as it pawed at and yipped at her skirt. "Why did you not offer the carriage to the gel?" His mother forged on.

"Because, I knew she would not accept it. She is of the independent nature in case you hadn't noticed," Clive answered. He moved to the decanter and filled a healthy amount of brandy into a glass. After what Eric confirmed, he deserved a drink-- at least one.

His mother settled in on the settee and took up her needlework, but had a telltale smile on her lips. "Yes, dear, I am well aware that she is her own person. I quite like her."

"I am glad you approve of Mary and Nettie's choice of acquaintance here in Scotland. It will be good for them to mingle socially while here."

His mother did not even pretend, which would have been the polite thing to do, that she could see through him. "And you as well. I am certain you are not immune to her. After all, my son, you are not daft, nor dead."

"Mother, I am not at all interested in adding one more independent woman to a group of already insufferably independent women in my life."

"Of course, dear," was his mother's only answer, which caused Clive to take a longer drink of his brandy than was prudent.

He attempted to change the subject. "I will not be in residence most of the day tomorrow. I am certain anything you need can be cared for by the staff. They have been told to take care of your needs."

"Fine dear. We will be perfectly taken care of I am sure. I hope you are stepping in to protect that poor girl from whatever issues she is trying to handle on her own." His mother never looked up from her needlework.

Clive just stared at her. She never missed a thing, and it was high time Clive stopped trying to hide things. In fact, it would probably make his life much easier if he were not worrying about shielding her from things she would see regardless. "I am attempting that, Mother, but she is not—well, she is not a willing participant in my attempts to help or protect her. Unfortunately, it is not something as simple as having a talk with her guardian."

"I am sure 'tis not," was her answer.

Clive needed to have some alone time and think on what to do next. He was really at a standstill until all of his inquires came back, but he knew he was still looking for something in the house, and he now had a place to look, so he downed the remainder of his drink and bid his mother goodbye.

"I will probably take a tray in the morning, so I will not be in the dining room to see you off. Good luck, my dear," she said as he bent to kiss her cheek.

One sharp word had the dogs following him out of the room, but instead of going directly to his chamber, he made his way to the gallery and the painting that put the flush to Louissa's cheeks earlier. Thinking of his aunt, it was clear now that they, including Louissa, had been looking in the wrong place.

The painting was beautiful and called to anyone who loved the sea. Clive held a candle above him, giving him more light around the edge, and sure enough, the entire frame set apart from the wall. Not enough for the unsuspecting viewer of art, but for a person looking for hidden spots, it was unmistakable. He had no doubt his lovely burden would be making a midnight stop to burgle the contents, but he was determined to, for once, have more information than another in this farce. Upon further observation, he found the painting's frame to be hinged on one side. Once swung away from the wall, the locked box stared out at him from a hole very crudely chiseled in the thick stone wall of the room. If the hole was crudely made, it was not haphazardly sized. He had a bugger of a time, but managed to wiggle the heavy box out of its nesting place. He had no idea which of the myriad of keys that his aunt had left him would open this, and knowing his aunt, it was not with the others. He would need the key because he knew his aunt, and understood that she could very well have rigged the bloody thing to do something to destroy the contents if not opened properly.

Clive and his entourage of canine companions made their way back to his chamber. He smiled, wishing he could see her face when she came back and found the space behind the painting empty. As he passed one of the many flower vases that his mother's arrival seemed to conjure, he had an idea. In a moment, he was back at the painting, placing a single rose in the space. A silent nod to the fact he knew of her many uninvited visits and to the fact he was aware of her need to find some information. He told himself that was all, but couldn't shake that desire to have her stomp her way down the hall, enter his bedchamber and demand the contents. After the kiss they shared in the folly earlier, he would not turn her away, for if her passion tasted half as sweet-- Clive stopped himself and turned back to his room. He had to curb his desire for this woman, at least until she was no longer in danger from her uncle, the local authorities, her brother, or anyone else. The woman seemed to be in danger from every quarter. Yes, he needed not to be the one that put her in danger either. For if he let himself have the thoughts he was having, she would be in danger of losing the very thing right now making her valuable and keeping her alive-- her virtue.

His room glowed with the flickering from the fire and the candles already lit waiting for him. The dogs found their places, the older ones curled on the rug at the hearth and Margret on his bed, right in the middle. Clive paid no heed as he went to his writing desk and took out the large metal ring with all the keys from each lock in the house. He examined the lock on the box, then each key, and just as he assumed, none appeared to fit. He sat at the desk perplexed. Now, where could a key such as the one needed to open the box be hidden? Then he remembered as a boy sitting under this very writing desk while his aunt spoke to him about spies, battles, and such. He was on the floor in seconds scooting his now adult male frame into a spot meant for a woman's legs and a chair. Once down, he lay there gazing up at the desk bottom. It was dark and there was no way to get light into the cramped space, so he closed his eyes and glided his hand over the smooth wood surface, until he

Clair Brett

felt it. A small hair-like crack in the otherwise solid piece, then his hand connected with the other side, again just a hairline crack. With gentle tension, he pressed up on the piece of wood and slid it back until he felt it slide out of his way, and with a thud, a metal object dropped out and landed on his forehead, and then slid to the dark floor.

Clive shimmied out of the tight space and groped around on his hands and knees until he came up with the key. He remembered the day he found the secret compartment. His aunt was not angry, but simply said that to protect one's loved ones, sometimes secrets had to be kept and protected. She said just because a box is locked doesn't make it secure if everyone knows where the key is. He really needed to do some research on who exactly his aunt was. He was sure he would be shocked and amazed. As he made to get up, the two older dogs noticed him on the floor and ambled over for the rare playtime. Before he could right himself, Clive was being licked and pawed.

"Down Zeus, for God's sake, if Hector walked in here now, I would never hear the end." The dog sat back, but bounced caused by his tail wagging so violently. The youngest of the group sat on the bed and barked with excitement. As Clive managed to right himself, he thought it was telling that his nights had been reduced to wrestling on the floor of his bedchamber with one of his hounds, while the others watched on with excitement. Not exactly how he would like his evenings to go.

Louissa, naked and twisted in his sheets came as a vision so blasted strong it almost toppled him over. He tamped down his body's reaction and cursed himself. She was wilder at heart than any of the wild animals in Scotland were. Her heart was true and his was sensed by her draw. If he could save her, perhaps then... What was he thinking? Binding herself to a British Lord would not be her first act as a woman freed from her uncle's grasp. And even if he thought it a possibility, why would she bind herself to him. Her station alone would not allow a simple dalliance, plus Clive's character would always win out from his baser desires. To bed her, was to marry her, and he would be good to remember that. Perhaps that would cool his ardor.

No, the mere thought of marriage to the tenacious Louissa was not enough to make him even hesitate.

"Wonderful," he muttered as he brought the key back to the box sitting on the low table in front of the fire. He sat and looked at it for some time. Once he opened this, he would know things. Things about Louissa, he was sure that she didn't even know about herself or her family. Was it fair? Was it right? What if he found out something that would break her? He couldn't take seeing the spark of independence and defiance smudged out.

He sat back, not so intent on opening the offending item. He thought back to Pandora's Box. Some things might be best left undiscovered. Damn, this was when the legacy of his father haunted him the most. What should he do? What if he chose poorly? What could happen if he did not choose properly? Most days, that question was more trifling than anything, but this time, this was different. The contents of this box could do one of two things. It could prove her uncle did kill her parents, and potentially her brother, if Henry is not proven as the heir, or it could show that Louissa has been fighting against a falsehood and it would destroy her spirit. Neither would be good, but if he had to choose, he knew which choice he would make. Her uncle was definitely capable of the crimes of which he had been accused, and deserved a great many different punishments for how he had seen fit to care for his ward and niece these many years. Therefore, it would not diminish the world if he hanged from the noose in Clive's estimation.

The box was going to have to be opened, so without another thought, he decided knowing was better than not, and this way he might be able to ease Louissa into the truth and help her get acclimated with whatever the outcome of the information was.

With a creak and a click, the key twisted. The lid was heavier than he expected. Inside the lid was an engraving of what looked to Clive to be the Royal Crest of the British Crown, which gave him pause. What would his aunt be doing with a royal box? He wondered fleetingly about why every woman he had ever cared about was more trouble than other women were? He had gentlemen friends who spoke of their wives and female family members as docile, content, winsome. He had even heard one young gentleman speak of his wife as being too quiet and accommodating.

Inside the box were rolls of parchment and folded letters in envelopes. Not wanting to disturb too much of the contents in case it was ordered, he plucked the first scroll from the box and leaned closer to the fire as he unrolled it.

It appeared to be an order of surveillance. Whoever received this order was instructed that Gareth Adair was of the upmost import and to forgo another assignment until further notice. It said that he was being investigated on suspicion of many offenses, not the least of which was murder.

The next scroll was a bundle really, with several financial documents torn from an unnamed ledger, but mentioned the Gem, Louissa's uncle's ship, the one her parents were supposedly thrown from. Louissa's father was named with his yearly assets at the time of the mailing. Clive realized these pages were showing what Gareth would be in line to gain if Louissa's father and her brother were to die.

As he scrolled down the list, he noted a line crossed off, which just so happened to be the dowry set aside for Louissa. It was clear her father saw her worth, and it was no doubt that by modern standards, she would have had her pick of suitors once word of her dowry was out. However, Clive realized that either it was crossed off perhaps because he had planned to kill her, before he found a use for her, or, and this made Clive's skin prickle with fear and disgust, her uncle was planning on selling her and making a profit instead of having to spend any of his money on her.

Clive managed to roll the bundle back up and not crumple it in his hands as he so wanted to do at the moment to her uncle. How dare he? Clive was beginning to see that Henry's version of events was entirely more conceivable than Clive had wanted to think.

Once he worked his way through all the scrolls, which were more orders and updates on the matter of Adair that frankly didn't tell him anything he hadn't already found out himself, he moved to the letters. They were addressed to his aunt from various people, but the ones that stood out, sat on top with a red wax seal with the letter A. They were from Louissa's mother. The tone of the letter spoke of friendship and intimacy. Clive realized Louissa's mother and Aunt Margaret were close. On the surface it seemed like a letter from one friend to another who was traveling abroad, but as the letters progressed, Clive noted a desperation in the tone and by the end, Louissa's mother asked that she extend the same courtesies to her daughter upon her arrival home that had been offered to her so many years ago.

> *Tis a sad state that I am forced to call on your services, but my dear friend, I fear my husband and I will not be in a position to protect and care for our Louissa anymore. The tide has turned and I fear the worst. He has made it so the crew will not even look us in the eye. We are adrift on our own ship with a full crew. These are dark times indeed.*

Inside the envelope with the letter was the church notice of the funeral for Louissa's parents and brother. The date of death was circled and it came only a month after the letter had been dated. Clive turned the envelope around and found that the letter had been posted in Spain. He wondered if Louissa would remember her mother's condition when they landed in Spain. Would she know this was the last correspondence her mother wrote to an old friend asking to protect her daughter as much as possible?

Below that were other letters, but not from Louissa's mother. These letters were dated later, much later. At least four years after the last one. The handwriting was not neat and free, but it looked choppy and very rigid. The letters spoke of sending funds or clothing for the charge, as if his aunt was the guardian of some poor relative. He would know if that were the case, and he had not seen any such documentation. The last letter simply stated that the boy in question had been dispatched to a ship and now had her contact information and would be in touch as needed. Clive got a decidedly annoying feeling. The man, who kept breaking into his house and drinking his good liquor, was he truly Henry? He had said Lady Margaret had been helping him. Did someone reach out to her when the boy was ferreted out of the boat and away from his uncle? Had Margaret paid to have her friend's son hidden away?

He, all of a sudden, was thankful for all of the doting and kind relations in his family tree. True his tree was overrun by women, but they loved him and he them, and not a one would do harm to anyone who was considered family. He would forever count himself lucky.

An hour later, he had finished reading every note and letter in the box. No more confident in his ability to save Louissa from herself or her uncle, he was certain that her uncle needed to be stopped. The question was how could he do that without getting himself or Louissa killed and still protect Henry's identity without putting him in danger? Having figured that, he also needed to decide what to tell Louissa. That might wind up being the most dangerous decision he has made in as many months as he has been in Scotland.

The next morning broke cool with a mist covering the moors. Clive had risen early to write some correspondence, and hopefully now have enough information to write the correct questions and get the needed answers. Mary had ridden out early to meet Louissa and ride the countryside. Mary, an avid horsewoman, had never considered it an accomplished day unless she had spent no less than four hours in the saddle. Once her husband died, Clive had been told by Nettie that she had begun to spend less and less time in the stables, and that worried Clive, so to see her color high as she rode out with a groom was very promising indeed.

His good mood waned not two hours later when Mary came galloping into the courtyard yard screaming for help. Clive heard the commotion and was almost to the front door when the doorman flung open the heavy oak door and almost collided with his employer.

"Oh, yer Lordship, 'tis Lady Landsdown. She needs ye right away," the youth said, his eyes round as saucers from the screaming woman on horseback, or perhaps said woman's wild eyed brother almost bowling him over to get to her.

"Thank you, Francis. Now get out of the way if you will." Clive attempted to keep his demeanor even, but heard the edge in his voice. The footman moved as quickly as could be expected, but Clive thought not quick enough. Out in the courtyard, Mary was still on the horse circling this way and that, sensing Mary's tension and unease.

"Oh, Clive, you must come this instant!"

"What? Where..." Clive managed to get out before Mary talked over him.

"Tis Louissa. We were riding and two men rode upon us and cut me off from her, then forced her mare off the trail into the trees. I have no idea where they have taken her. You must hurry!"

The panic was clear in her voice. Mary was not privy to the drama unfolding in Louissa's life. Nettie, his mother, and he, had all decided to shield Mary as much as possible. His mother was afraid her frayed emotions could not take the stress. The groom dispatched to protect Mary dismounted and Clive swung up on the horse instructing him to bring more men and horses as quickly as possible, and then they were away. Mary was in the lead, giving no heed to safety of her or the horse. On his best day, Clive found it a trial to keep up with Mary on horseback. His instructor always bemoaned him not being as good a horseman as his father was. Today, he had his doubts about his father's ability to keep in stride with the woman in front of him. He was beginning to believe that Mary had much more fortitude than the family was giving her credit. In an attempt to protect her after the death of her husband, might they have been smothering her? He had no time to ponder any of that at the moment.

Around a copse of trees still on his property, Mary turned off the trail. Clive would have liked to turn Mary back, but she was far enough ahead that his voice would no doubt carry to wherever the bastards were with Louissa. At the thought, he gripped the reins tightly, making his horse resist the sudden change in energy. "Easy boy," Clive said and stroked the horse, but his blood was boiling. Who are these men to abduct a woman on horseback and drag her horse off into the woods? And on his property as well? Either they did not know it was his or they did not care. Either way made no consequence, because he was going to beat them within an inch of their lives if they so much as harmed one hair on her head. He heard his men thundering behind and waved for them to continue down the road that surrounded the group of trees. If they were still on his property, they would be held to task.

He came up on Mary stopped and silent. His body stilled and he could feel the blood in his body run cold. Were they hurting Louissa? Was she already hurt? Or worse? He slowed and came up beside his sister. She turned with a finger to her lips. The men and Louissa were in an opening. All were dismounted and the two men were talking in low voices to each other as Louissa looked on. She did not appear to be in danger, hurt, or even scared for that matter. Lord help her, she looked annoyed. The first man, after coming to some agreement with his partner, looked at Louissa and grabbed her by the arm. He could tell it affected her, but to his surprise, she gave no quarter. She met the man toe to toe. If she went down, it would be defending herself. No simpering miss, begging the big strong man for mercy. He bet she would get in some strategic blows before she went down, but she would go down, of that, he was certain. After a few moments, the men mounted and continued through the woods to meet the road at the other end of the forest.

Mary immediately coaxed her horse into the opening and dismounted to check on her friend. Clive would have liked to watch and see Louissa's reaction when she thought herself alone, but that was not to be, so he followed Mary into the opening. Surprise registered on her face, but it was replaced by her mask of arrogance and disdain.

"Oh, dear, are you quite all right? Did you know those men?" Mary asked as she embraced Louissa while at the same time checking her for bumps or cuts.

"I am fine, Mary, thank you," she said, all the time never losing eye contact with Clive. "I did not know them. For some odd reason, they thought I might have some knowledge about that highwayman tormenting travelers on the Milton Road."

"For the love of… whatever would they think you had such knowledge? That is simply preposterous. Tell her, dear brother, preposterous."

Clive had to pull his thoughts away from the look Louissa gave to answer his sister.

"Well, any man need just look at her and see she is not but a fair damsel, not a highwayman with some notoriety." He managed not to give away the humor as he watched Louissa scowl.

She pulled out of Mary's embrace and put some distance between them. Clive noted the fact. It said volumes about what level of intimacy Louissa was accustom to. Any sign of affection had her pulling away. "Who were they?" He asked keeping his distance. He wanted to rub his thumb along the line forming on her brow when she was in a state.

"They said interested parties, when I asked. I told them they should speak directly to my uncle…"

"Do you think that was wise?" both Clive and Mary asked at the same time, which brought Clive up short. Mary had no knowledge of what was going on, so why would she be concerned about Louissa's uncle?

"I was trying to intimidate them. If my uncle's reputation is bad for matchmaking, 'tis very good when fending off such as that," Louissa said and hitched a thumb behind her in the direction the men went.

Clive was not happy with this latest development. Either, the Lords that had hired him to take care of the situation have moved on and no longer trust him, or her blasted brother was trying to check the fact Clive so plainly stated. Worse, this could simply be another group of annoying country bucks trying to make names for themselves while passing the time in the country.

"I would feel better if you ladies did not ride anymore today. However, if you must ride, then come back to the house and I will dispatch more protection, but even then I would prefer you remained in close proximity to the manor." To his surprise, Mary did not argue but just as the sun rises every morning, Louissa opened her mouth to speak, then appeared to think better of it. "Good, it is settled. We will head back to the manor. You ladies can go to the parlor and have some tea. I will go directly to the stables and have some others ready horses."

Clive helped the ladies mount their horses and get set before swinging into the saddle and leading the solemn group back to the manor. Clive left the women at the door making sure they had help and that tea was on its way, then he headed to the stables. His hope was that the two trespassers would be waiting for him in as uncomfortable a fashion as possible.

As he had hoped, he knew from the activity that his guests were indeed present. He turned his horse to a groom and instructed him to round up no less than four others to ride out with the ladies if they still chose to do so, but was reminded his sisters would be leaving with their mother soon to visit Jane and a longer ride would not be possible. Clive continued into the dimness of the stable ready to get some answers.

An hour later, the two men were being escorted off his lands with instructions they were no longer welcome on Lady Margaret's property ever again, since they had a difficult time understanding a dirty Brit could have inherited said land, and it was not his care how they remembered, just so they did. Also, he made it clear that Lady Louissa was under his protection and anyone who acted in any fashion that could be construed as ungentlemanly, may find themselves in an undesirable situation. As for answers, he didn't get many. He did learn that the identity of the highwayman being a woman was beginning to gain traction in the area and apparently, her uncle was not doing a thing to quash the rumor. Clive found that interesting, because according to those close to the situation, they see Louissa as worth more to him alive than dead.

He made his way back to the house where a flurry of action was made apparent as he opened the side door. He remembered, again today was the day his houseguests would be traveling to visit his sister Jane and her family for a week. Jane was his third oldest sister who was happily married to Mr. Damen Alton. He sighed heavily at the thought of quiet evenings and not having to sneak in and out of his own dwelling. A maid scurried by with arms piled high with undergarments, linens, and shoes. She attempted a curtsy when she saw her employer standing in the narrow hall.

"For God's sake, gel, do not bother with such foolishness when you are so heavily laden." Sometimes, the foolish rules made not one whit of sense. He continued into the main part of the house hoping to avoid more altercations. As he walked by the small parlor in the back of the main house, he was stopped by Nettie, avoiding the melee as well, he assumed.

"Why, dear sister, are you not busy packing?" He asked as she dragged him by the arm into the room, shutting the door behind her.

"Oh, for the love of all that is good in this world, you know Mother would never allow me to choose my own apparel when going to a house party," she said with disgust and frustration in her voice. Clive knew she had given up years ago trying to fight with their mother about what she wore. "I swear, when I get married, I will have to proceed into public naked, because I apparently do not know how to dress myself."

"Well, I will count myself fortunate that you plan on waiting until you are some other poor bloke's burden before you choose to set a new fashion trend." Clive's dry comment made Nettie smile.

"You will not try to stop me?" She asked trying to provoke banter.

"Not in the least. I think once I have procured the consummate belly that comes from a Lord's time at a desk and not in the fields, I shall join you. We could attend the Duchess Dorchester's grand ball together. What would the rags say then?"

"Oh, no, you may not prance around naked for all of London to see. I have a hard enough time finding friends who have not asked me shocking questions about what might or might not be under your cravat," she said in disgust and threw herself down on the settee.

"Honestly, what is it you and your friends talk about in public? I have not heard of one conversation topic that is acceptable in a ballroom," Clive answered back, not deterred. "Perhaps, you could ask Luc his thoughts on changing current fashion to include nudes."

"And why ever would I discuss such with Luc?" Nettie asked, perplexed?

"Well, isn't that who Mother is hoping to push you at this time? He will be there I assume? He wouldn't let down Jane as a doting brother-in-law would he?" Clive knew that his sister's brother-in-law, heir to the Duke of Avenbury would be in residence, because his mother spoke of it not less than ten times at the breakfast table two mornings ago. Nettie had taken a tray in her room that morning.

Nettie smiled, but did not offer an explanation. "Did you interrogate those villains?" Nettie asked changing the subject.

"How did you know I had them captured and brought-- Never mind, I do not want to know." He stated pinching the bridge of his nose wishing the carriages were packed and ready.

"Well?"

"Yes, I spoke with them."

"And?"

"And nothing. I got very little information, but passed along that Louissa is under my protection and all who try anything will be answering to me. If nothing else, it may force people to start seeing her as something other than a local menace." The smile Nettie flashed that time unnerved Clive. "What?"

"Nothing. I am glad you are helping her," she said, but the smile never slipped from her mouth.

"No, not nothing, dearest sister. What does that smile mean?"

"There are only three reasons a man would make known to the world that a woman is under his protection. Either, he is indeed her guardian, she is his mistress, or he loves her and is intending on asking for her hand." She waited expectantly, Clive knew by her expression, for him to say something telling.

"Can a man not just want to help a woman who has no one else to speak for her?"

"Well, I am sure that is plausible, but can you give me an example in the Ton when such a thing has happened and the two haven't ended up in matrimony?" She batted her eyelashes in the most annoyingly innocent way, just as she had learned when she was but a small child. He opened his mouth, but then remembered that the couple in question was now on their third child. Then there were the Win… no, they wed by special license, or the Standtropes, wait, if he was thinking about all of his clear examples as sharing a name, then his sister clearly had a point.

"Well, regardless, we are not in town and Louissa is not your typical Ton-raised lady with a mindset to marriage."

"Poor, poor, dear brother. Every girl is equipped with a mindset toward marriage. 'Tis the only thing that can make what would otherwise be a mundane, monotonous life exciting and different. 'Tis the way of the world, the one that men just never seem to be well versed."

"Is that Mother calling? You wouldn't want to miss the carriage, love." Clive embraced his favorite sister. If he didn't leave, she would convince him a quick marriage and trip on the continent was the way to go. He was more concerned with the fact he was scared it wouldn't take that much convincing for him to talk himself into love. "Give everyone my love and show those little tyrants some better pranks. From the letter I received, they need new material," he said of his nieces, Emily eight, and twins Carolyn and Carmen, five.

Nettie squeezed him tighter than necessary and kissed his cheek. She had a look that clearly was one of pity. He was sure she believed him already in love and just denying it. Bollocks.

When his sister's carriage arrived to pick them up it came also carrying the post. Clive took the letters he had been waiting for into his study as soon as he saw his family off. The house seemed silent without his sisters and mother in residence, but he was convinced it was better that way. The first letter had no new information, but the second and third shone light on Henry and Louissa's uncle and it made his blood run cold.

CHAPTER THIRTEEN

Clair Brett

Louissa snuck past the sleeping dogs with ease. Knowing them as pups, they paid no heed to her when she was about. The youngest stirred only long enough to open one eye, stretch, yawn, and flop onto her other side and begin snoring straight away.

She smiled at the thought that Lord Breakerton was under the assumption that his holdings were protected by the beasts. She would make sure to leave the scraps she brought with her when she left.

Louissa had learned many things after her last visit to the manor. Among the most interesting and off-putting was the fact that while she was certain she could seduce the Lord in residence, she could by some fault of her true character be just as easily enamored with her prey. The other and more pressing matter tonight was currently nestled safe in the walls of the gallery, her immediate destination. She knew Lady Margaret had been protecting her family and had proof she said would save Louissa, if it came down to it, but Louissa had almost given up in the finding of the proof, until the day when Lord Breakerton had taken her on a tour. She had been to the gallery many times, but allowed him his due and obediently followed. It was there that he kissed her rather soundly, and at the same time, she noticed a painting that had been Lady Margaret's favorite. One she had commented on more than should have been considered casual, but it wasn't until Louissa's senses were otherwise occupied that she was able to put it together.

She stood now in the gallery with only the moonlight streaming in through the floor to ceiling windows as her guide. The painting hung majestic with a stray moonbeam calling attention to it. It was so obvious now that she felt foolish not thinking of it before. Walking up to the painting, she noticed what she had previously. The frame just seemed to hover a tad away from the wall, and when she tugged on the bottom corner, it smoothly swung wide. Her breath hitched a notch and her heartbeat followed.

She could still save her family name, her brother, and by doing so, herself. The painting now blocked the moonbeam leaving the indentation in the wall in the shadows, but Louissa was not frightened. She reached out into the blackness and grabbed... nothing. The space was empty. To make sure, she patted around all sides, the top, sides, and bottom. Finally, her hands landed on something soft. She pulled out a single red rose by the soft, petal flower head. She squeezed it with frustration, and the clean, sweet rose scent released into the air. She dropped it to the ground and reached way in the back, hoping to find a false back. Nothing.

Breakerton.

She knew Lady Margaret. She knew the painting of the ship would have been her hint. It had been there. She would make a wager on her life that the proof was tucked safely in there when she last visited the gallery, which meant only one thing. Breakerton found it.

"Damn," she spat carefully to keep her disgust at a whisper. Now where would he have moved it? His sisters and mother would be curious, she was certain, so he would have to squirrel it away. Her options, she decided, were very specific: his study, his private rooms, or his person. She might as well start in his study. The last option sent an involuntary shiver through her body.

The hallways were all dark, but Louissa needed no lights and hurried along the thick-carpeted corridors in near silence, only the slight shushing of her breeches as she walked. While annoying, she deduced her skirts would have been more of an impediment even if they had been quieter.

The study hovered in shadows, but Louissa quickly lit a candle to make her rounds, not as familiar with how he had transformed the space since he took up residence. Hoping luck would be with her, she began her search with his desk, but she found nothing. The top was tidy and organized. The drawers held only correspondence from London according to the envelopes and all the paper was new, not aged. She then moved to his sitting area looking in and around his books piled on the table next to the chair. Nothing. She worked her way around the room looking on the shelves. He would probably still be sorting through the find, so there would be no reason for him to put it out of reach, so she didn't bother to search the higher shelves. The ladder would have made too much noise anyway. No, it was probably in his rooms.

Yet, another shiver. She scolded herself, leaving the study as she had found it. With her candle snuffed, she made her way back up the stairs. She had searched his rooms before, but that was before. Now, the thoughts of entering his private chambers were disturbing and pleasurable at the same time. As she neared the door, her steps slowed and her breathing became faster. The one logical part of her mind that had yet to be taken over by foolhardy emotion chastised her actions. Her steps halted at the door.

"He is away visiting family. It is no different from any other time I have entered. I must gain control, this is ridiculous." She squared her shoulders, took a deep breath, and turned the knob. The door swooshed open with ease only just rubbing along the thick padded carpet. Louissa loved the feel of it under her feet. She wondered how it would feel barefoot. She had never had the luxury of carpets in her room, once her uncle took over. Uncle Gareth closed the main house and moved her into his much smaller cottage on the property. Her room had cold hard wood, which even after so many years was still jarring when getting out of bed on a cold winter morning. As she thought on the indulgences of carpeted bedchambers, she took no time to relight her candle. There were still low embers in the fire, which for a moment brought her up short, but then she decided it made more sense to keep the room at a comfortable temperature, as it would take longer to get it up to a temperature his Lordship would approve of if it were allowed to go out entirely. As she made her way from the door to his writing desk, she was hoping to locate the information and be gone. His writing desk was almost as large as the one in his study. She bent down to see if it was a box that, perhaps he might have slid underneath. That is when she heard it. All at once, she realized she had miscalculated.

"Good evening, my darling." The deep smooth as silk voice

came from the dark recesses of the huge four-poster bed, making her heart jump into her throat and seize. She was caught.

Clive knew the moment Louissa sensed she was not alone in the room. He would have liked watching her search his desk further as his vantage point from the bed was exceptional. He also decided leaving the curtains open had its advantages past helping him wake early, and while he was considering matters, he quite enjoyed the female form in breeches. Louissa's heart shaped bottom looked delectable in them, which did not help his current situation of being naked under his sheet with his dressing gown across the room. "I am afraid you have me at a clear disadvantage. I would have at least had a tray delivered." He droned more to peak her annoyance and lighten the mood for her.

While he did not mind at all having her pillage his bedchamber, he was sure she was a tad discomfited at his presence.

She popped up as if she was attached to the sky and tried to settle her hair, which was spilling from its pins and ribbons. "Oh, I-- ah-- my lord." She curtsied, but had yet to look at the bed, Clive noted with humor. "My lord, I was not aware--that is I thought--that is to say..."

"You assumed I had left to go visit my sister Jane with the others," he finished for her, with a smile in his tone. He had expected she would be back, but this particular situation had only crossed his mind several hundred times.

"Yes, yes I did, my lord. I should not be here. I--I will leave..."

In that instant, Clive was lost. His feet hit the floor before he knew what was happening. His addled brain had thought at least to drag the sheet around him. He should let her leave, right now with no hesitation. She was a gentle bred lady. An unmarried, gentle bred lady. He had boundaries. He had scruples. Virgins were *not* part of his allowable dalliances.

"You do not need to rush off, my lady." He heard the words come out his mouth, but didn't know from where they came. Before he could gather himself, he stepped so close that he could feel her breaths, quick and short on his chest. The moon shone across her face as it had the night they first met. How he had ever thought her to be a man was unfathomable now. Her tanned skin glowed and her eyes glistened, but she showed no fear. He felt his chest rise and fall, and realized his breathing was just as ragged as hers was, but he assumed for a very different reason. "If you want to leave though, I suggest you do it post haste, for in a moment, I might find it most difficult to change the direction I wish to go," he warned, in a voice much deeper and with more emotion than he intended. He stood so close, but he could not touch her, for if he did, he would be lost.

He knew where this would lead, and to his surprise, that realization did nothing to cool his ardor. In fact, it warmed him. At the same time, he willed her to leave, to run back to her uncle to the safety of her home, for he was certain she would not be so interested if she knew. They stood, held captive by the moonlight. Just when he thought he might be able to rip himself from her gaze and walk away, she stepped toward him looking into his eyes with anything but fear and trepidation. He knew at that moment, he would wake in the morning a very changed man.

Clive wrapped one arm around Louissa's waist and pulled her to him, as he lowered his head for a kiss. Their eyes never left each other. He could spend an eternity wading through the depths of those deep brandied eyes. They all but possessed him now. The first touch of their lips was slow. Not like the demanding kisses they shared on their walk, this was a kiss to last, one to help in making choices. Stay or go. When Clive could take no more, he meant to pull back out of the enchantment of her mouth, but as he pulled away, Louissa stood on her tiptoes, reached up and guided his head back into place.

The next time Clive tore himself away, he was dizzy with desire. His breathing even more ragged and he couldn't break the connection, so he leaned his forehead on hers. With his eyes closed to keep what restraint he had tethered tightly, he managed one final warning, "Love, I must know that you have a complete awareness of what will happen if you stay. With great difficulty, I am trying to remain a gentleman..."

"You speak entirely too much for my liking, my lord. I am well aware where this is going to lead. By the gods, this part of my life is one that I will not have dictated to me. Now, if you would please continue kissing, my lord, and do be quiet for the moment."

He opened his eyes then. Her smile dimmed the moonlight and his laughter filled the silence. Without one word, he scooped her up into his arms and carried her to the bed while kissing her, as she demanded. In the process, the sheet fell away and once he settled her on the bed, he heard her intake of breath. Fearing he had damaged her bravado, he quickly bent to retrieve his cover.

"No, don't," she said in a raspy voice, and then began trying to unbutton her shirt with shaking hands.

Clive sprawled out on the bed next to her on his side with his head resting on one bent arm.

"Allow me, my lady. I have some skill in this area," he said as he carefully slid his hand under hers to capture the button she was currently working on with no progress. He waggled his eyebrows to soften the moment and it worked, because she giggled nervously. With every button, Clive was more and more lost to this woman. Not as darkened by the sun, the skin of her chest and stomach was still not a porcelain white that so many women were. Louissa's skin glowed with a shimmer of light, speaking to some distant Spanish or Mediterranean heritage. Whomever was to be credited, he would build an altar to them later. Once all the buttons were freed, he exposed one side of her body by folding the shirtfront over, then the other. She was magnificent. The idea of a man, who did not see her worth in every way, did not deserve to witness what Clive was. As Louissa did in all things, she laid completely exposed from the waist up with bold dignity and courage. She had not looked away, not fluttered an eyelash. She met him as an equal. His body throbbed. This was not for him. This would be for her.

Neither knew how this was going to play out, but this one moment, this one tableau was in their control. She had chosen him and he her. He would make sure this one time she was treated as the lady and goddess she was meant to be. Clive couldn't think beyond that right now, but every fiber in his being was certain if there was a next time, it too would be with him and no other.

CHAPTER FOURTEEN

Once divested of her shirt, Clive bent to finish the job, but stopped short. He had never removed a pair of breeches from outside of them. Louissa lifted her head and gave him a quizzical look.

"It appears, my lady, you once again have me at a disadvantage. I have never removed a gentleman's breeches other than my own."

"Well, I should hope not, my lord," she said with a saucy smile playing across her lips.

"You, my dear, are a beast. Lie back and let me get to work," he said and she obliged, lifting her hips in anticipation for the removal. It didn't take him long to have them on the floor. It seemed he found what motivated him. Had his tutors only known, he might have been better at Latin. "There," he grunted as he slid up alongside of her and lazily rubbed his hand down her arm and across her belly. The hollow of her belly button was a perfect little indentation in an otherwise flawless expanse. He bent and kissed her belly button. The skin soft as silk smelled of rose water and tasted as sweet as any confection he could imagine. Her stomach firmed as she sucked in her breath and he took the opportunity of her distraction to move his hand, now at her thigh up her leg to rest on her warmth and her center. He felt the tension radiate out to her limbs and he sensed her quieting.

"I will not do anything without your consent love," he assured her and she relaxed a bit. He chose to abandon his destination for the moment and instead kissed his way up her body stopping at her breasts to give each his care and attention. For a woman yet to bare children she was surprisingly well endowed, which gave him pause, as she had been bandying around the countryside playing at being a man for months and no one had noted her chest on first inspection. Not even him. "I must ask. How have you managed to keep such glorious breasts a secret during your escapades?"

"I bind them," she said quite unemotionally.

"You what?" He asked lifting up on one elbow to see her face.

"I bind them. I wrap linen strips very tightly around my upper body and it helps to flatten them. Then, once I have all the other clothing on, they are hardly noticeable," she explained more proudly.

Clive gave her a look of what must have been absolute horror. "What?" she asked.

"It should be a crime. From this day forth, you are hereby not allowed to put such beauty through such an ordeal. I decree it."

"You decree it?" She said, laughing as she began to twirl the curls in Clive's hair. Women loved to do it and it had always rather annoyed him, but watching Louissa's face and seeing how it put her at ease, made him enjoy it now. "What are you, the magistrate now, my Lord?" She asked.

"As a matter of fact, he has deputized me in a fashion to be rid of the highwayman, so I would say it is well within my duties to decree that you cease at once." He slid his hand from her belly to her left breast. It filled his hand and he could feel when her nipple puckered at the sensation making him harder than he already had been. He rolled her nipple between two fingers until she moaned her appreciation and leaned into his hand more. Once he had her panting, he moved to the other breast already peaked and waiting for attention.

"Perhaps, for now, I could be persuaded to keep them unbound. Would that suffice?" She asked between the sounds of pleasure that Clive knew she had no more control over than he would in a while.

"Well, that will do for now, but we shall see." He acquiesced and bent to suck one full nipple into his mouth and roll it around his tongue. She arched and moaned louder. Soon Clive could move to his final destination he thought. He pulled himself away from her glorious breasts and leaned in to kiss her. It was not as gentle as before. She was hungrier and her body understood more fully the potential.

Her hands were now roaming, pawing at Clive. He reveled at the pressure on his back as she pulled him closer to her and held on.

He would never need to be held down with Louissa. He would gladly remain in bed with her forever. He needed nothing but her in his arms. Nothing.

"I need to make sure you are ready, love. I don't want to unduly hurt you," he whispered trying to prepare her for the invasion of her body. He could feel her heat before he got past her thigh. Her curls were damp and her whole body jerked at his feather light touch. As he slid his fingers past her curls into her folds, she was wet with anticipation. He took his time and slowly rubbed his hand along her opening, as Louissa relaxed and gave into the feel of him invading her. Once she parted her legs and she was lying still moaning her pleasure, he slid one finger inside her. Her body reacted with blatant passion. Her hips rose and her breathing hitched up. "Oh, God, my lord," she panted.

"Clive."

"What?" she asked in a passionate haze.

"I am not my Lord when we are in bed together. We are equals in our passion. Say it, love, say my name," he whispered in her ear as he sucked on her earlobe and nibbled slightly continuing in a rhythm with his finger.

"Clive, oh God, Clive," she cried out.

His heart slammed into his chest hearing his name. He was well and truly lost. "Louissa, love, your body is ready, but are you ready?"

"Yes," she breathed.

It was all the encouragement that he needed. He positioned himself above her and for a moment hovered to drink in this wild, untamed, woman in her glory. He bent his head and pressed his lips to hers as he glided in, taking care not to overwhelm her all at once.

Clive would never admit to, or therefore be accused of being a celibate man. He had bed some of the demimonde's most beautiful women, and many of the Ton's most accomplished widows. If pressed, he would admit there were a few that may have still been wives at the time of his bedding, so his swift and impactful reaction to Louissa must only be explained by his time spent in Scotland, where he had not sought out the company of a woman as yet. His last paramour had ended on a sour note, with the whole of the experience being lack luster at best.

As Louissa surrounded him in the most intimate of ways, he was not finding any of this lackluster, in fact, he noted nothing about his life had been quiet or uneventful, since he was thrust into Louissa's life. Her breathing hitched for a moment at first penetration, but as he stilled and tried with herculean effort not to continue, she took a few calming breaths, and then lifted herself to him, until they were touching body to body. He groaned at the slow magnificent torture of her body moving to his. Nothing about Louissa was tentative, why should this be any different?

Pulling himself onto his elbows, he looked into her face. Her eyes were closed and she was concentrating while she continued to move her hips up and down. He bent and kissed her nose. Her eyes fluttered open and he had to chuckle at her expression.

"Am I not doing it correctly?" She asked.

"Oh, my little temptress, you are, but this is one arena that I must insist I take the lead." He bent his head and put a soft, feather light kiss on the hollow of her throat. He then moved to the sensitive spot where her neck and shoulder met. She leaned into his caress.

"But I…" she began.

"No, no buts. You may be a more experienced thief-by-night and swordsman."

"Swordswoman," she corrected, which received a nip just behind her ear lobe for her troubles, and a giggle from her.

"Swordswoman," he corrected, "but I am certain I am more experienced in this vein, am I not?"

"Mmm, yes," she admitted, "'Tis not my pleasure to have, I am sorry, my lord, I forgot myself."

Her words and tone pulled him up short. He had been enjoying himself more than he had with his last two mistresses, and to hear her tone, well it would not do. He brought himself back up on his elbows, so his face filled her vision. He took her face in both of his hands and kissed her nose.

"I never have said, or even thought that making love was a one sided experience. Women, for all their frustrating and irrational behaviors were not put on this earth solely to please a man. All the women I have been with were capable of amazing pleasure. Would God have given women that capacity, if he didn't want it exploited?" Clive said with passion before he kissed his way to her breast and extracted a little mewl from Louissa.

She seemed to forget their sparing for a moment because she bent her head back and moaned as Clive laved at her breasts. With her otherwise occupied, he began moving slowly, but with more vigor as she again lifted her hips to meet his, but she allowed him to set the pace this time. There were merits to her way, which was with passion and speed, but this was Louissa and he wanted to enjoy himself. Most of their encounters had been short-lived.

This one would not.

He could get lost in her. Her heat, the feel of her around him pulling him further. He buried his head into the crook of her neck and groaned her name. "Louissa. God, Louissa."

Her movements matched his and he mused if they were on the dance floor, it would be something to behold. Her soft pants and moans vibrated his nerves as he fought for purchase to hold out, to keep her with him, to make her his as long as he could. He knew she was enjoying herself, but that wouldn't make her return. Once she left, her passion might overwhelm her so that it frightened her. His last thought before Louissa wrapped her legs around his hips and drew him into her more deeply crying out his name was that he might have to follow her about like a puppy, if she refused to be with him again. Then he was lost to the pleasure of it all, and so was she. Her cries with his name on her breath made his release so much more than ever before, Clive feared for his sanity, but then collapsed on her soft luscious body and forgot that the world outside his bed curtains existed.

An hour or so later, he finally felt like his bones had hardened enough to allow movement. He had spent some time dozing and then some time watching his vixen sleeping. She looked so young and innocent in sleep. Not at all the fierce warrior she personified in wake. He had slid enough to keep his weight off her, which gave him a perfect view of her body from the waist up, which was bared to the world. Lying against the gentle swell of her breast in the delectable space between the two was her pendant. He hadn't noticed it in their lovemaking, but honestly, if it hadn't been in his way, he doubted he would have noticed the Prime Minister of Britain had he been in the room.

He took the time to look more closely at it this time. Both pieces were ornate. One, heart shaped with a piece taken out by the looks. The second a long vial with ornate, delicate metalwork around it. He picked up the vial and turned it in his hand. It was heavy, but it seemed unevenly so. Upon further examination, it had a symbol on it that was familiar, but he couldn't place where he had seen the rose symbol before. He also noted it was a vessel of some sort and it was filled with something liquid. Clive got a very uneasy feeling.

He rose and silently got dressed. It was still early in the night so the moonlight was more than enough. He didn't bother with boots, cravat, or jacket. He padded over to the bed and as carefully as possible unlatched the pendant and slid it from the necklace, re-latching the necklace. Hopefully, it would find its way back before she knew. He covered her with the thick comforter and went to his study to think. He found that her very presence, smell, and the sexual energy still in the air was not conducive to logical discourse with himself. He needed to think, and that meant he needed to leave.

CHAPTER FIFTEEN

Clive brought the fire to a warm crackle in his study and sat, turning the pendant over and over in his hand. His body still sang with the remembered feel of her. He knew what this meant. It had to happen at some point, and he decided it was better with someone who challenged him like Louissa, instead of a simpering deb who never questioned him. He chuckled at that. All of his tutors, and his father's men would advise against such a match. It would lead to nothing but problems, they would say. She had no real connections, probably no dowry, and she would make his life difficult, as a wife should.

He smiled deeply then. Her passion during the light of day would only fuel their passion at night, and he knew having an easy life was not as it was heralded to be. His life in Scotland was easy by all accounts. It was also lamentably boring, lonely, and worthless. Until that is, Louissa came bursting into his life with her dictates, misadventure, and penchant for trouble. None of his sisters would ever be accused of making their husbands' lives easy. He was certain, easy was not on his father's list of criteria when he wed his mother.

The pendant in his hand felt warm and he looked down at the rose carving again and remembered where he had seen it. Clive jumped and one of the dogs who had settled by the rekindled fire grunted at him for his disturbance. He went to the back of the shelves and pulled the red leather bound book out of the stack. He had not read it or even opened it, but its red color and the rose emblem at the top and bottom of the spine had him looking at it every time he considered his next read. His aunt had an extensive library and his servants had simply incorporated her titles into his when he began making the room a library.

The book felt smooth in his hand as he brought it back to the fire for adequate light. He noted the lightness of the tome for its size, so he wasn't entirely surprised when he opened the cover to find a dainty pillbox with the same design as the pendant. It would have been obvious they were a matching set even without the empty space hollowed out in the shape of the vial. On the page opposite, the set-ins were instructions.

Clive's blood ran cold and any lingering sentiment from their lovemaking died a savage death.

Poison. Louissa was wearing poison around her neck, and obviously, she got it from his aunt. A niggling question was whether his aunt give it willingly or if his little thief nicked it when she saw the opportunity. Inside the pillbox, was one pill. He took the offending thing and threw it into the fire. He then uncorked the vial and poured the liquid poison in as well. He dunked it into the water pitcher to make sure no poison was left, then refilled it with brandy from his decanter and he poured the water out the closest window.

If Louissa knew, she might skin him alive, or at the very least, challenge him to a duel, but until he could get this bloody farce under control, he was not going to worry that Louissa was going to poison someone or God help him, herself. He knew how she felt about being married off to the braggart in business with her uncle, and he also knew his soon to be bride's penchant for action before logic. The thought of her being his wife, and the speed of which he settled into that idea rocked him and he took up the decanter and drew a long swig off it, without worrying about a glass.

His next order of business on the sunrise was to send word to her brother that he must speak with him. It was obvious they were cut from the same cloth, and now, Clive was actually thinking about attaching himself to their family. If Louissa bore him daughters and they too took on the traits of their mother and uncle, he would have not one wit of rest, but the vision of wild raven haired little girls bounding through the gardens playing with wooden swords, warmed him as much as the brandy. Having left the study, he stood over Louissa and just watched the moonlight play across her face and shimmer in her hair. Perhaps her brother, her, his father's solicitors, and any number of other people who compared him to his father would not believe that he would keep her safe, but in that moment, he knew without a doubt he would or die trying. She was his, though he didn't think it ever wise to tell her that.

He bent and reattached the vial to the chain, making certain it was still warm from his hand and that he set it gently back on the rise of her bosom. She never reacted, but when he had stripped down and slid back under the covers, she turned toward him, wrapped her curves around him, and settled in. He would have to wake her very soon if she was to get back to her uncle's before getting caught, but for now, she was his and he would enjoy the feel of her, the smell of her, the energy of her engulfing him and helping to buoy his resolve.

As he played with a heavy curl around his fingers, he considered life with an easy wife...easy was for fools or self-serving bastards and lucky for him, the world was in great supply of both.

Morning had broken on his way back from escorting Louissa to her house. Breakerton glanced at the bed and its still mussed sheets. When he woke Louissa well before dawn, showed her but one letter that gave proof of her uncle's plans of killing her family, it surprised him that she so easily came to tow with the idea of him keeping it until she needed it. He forced her to suffer his company back to her home. He never bothered to get back into bed. This worried him some, because he had always liked anything about his bed, sleeping in his bed, lounging in his bed, making love in his bed. Yes, that was his favorite and now that it was with Louissa, he craved it now. It would be more the pity if that hoyden of a woman spoiled such a simple pleasure for him, well, those solitary habits any way.

He had been in the stable as soon as he reached the manor to send a boy for Eric. He had been such a help thus far that Clive now depended on Eric for much of his more delicate tasks. Eric always said he was more than happy to help, but Clive made sure he was well compensated for his trouble and his continued alliance.

Eric left by half six to make his way to Henry's boat to deliver the command. It would have to be a very carefully calculated conversation. If Henry knew what Clive had been doing to keep his sister safe, well, there would be nothing for it. Both men would be fighting a duel. Breakerton admitted to himself that he deserved no less for his actions. That was why he had also sent his head solicitor for his Scottish holdings to talk with the nearest bishop in Edinburgh. He would have Louissa married long before this bastard could claim her as his own.

Clive paced back and forth, thinking of the papers he found last night with the proof Henry needed to prove who killed his parents. He also knew Louissa wanted the proof. The question was who would be better to have the information. The letters from Louissa's mother to Aunt Margaret were damning, and the stolen ledger pages made it quite obvious what her uncle stood to gain after their deaths.

Both siblings were overtly hot headed and prone to action before thought. Clive looked up into the air and took in a great suffering breath as he realized he sounded just like many of his tutors. If his actions were reckless enough to make those men so exasperated, who could blame him for such a reaction? He never put anyone in danger—well, except for Mary's husband. He thought sobering his mood more.

He knew mother's plan was to force Nettie and Luc into an accord, but he wished Mary could find happiness again. It might assuage some of the guilt he carried, and a large stick might help in the way of beating some sense into Louissa and Henry. It was not an action he would live out, but he did harbor a level of satisfaction in the vision.

He sat waiting. He had sent enough messages to make people begin wondering if he alone was the patron of the post, and still he sat waiting, so instead, he rose to check Hector and see if he knew anything, or of a way to speed things up in Scotland.

Hector was located. He had not seen the post, but Eric was

already returned and had a missive for his lordship. It had not been delivered because Hector felt it an ungodly hour to be bothering the lord, and therefore had decided to hold it and put it with the rest of the post. Clive instructed Hector that until further notice, he was to be made aware, no matter the hour, of any letters that come for him. Hector assured him it would be done, but Clive suspected Hector had not yet finished his morning meal below stairs and refused to deliver it immediately until he was done. He opened the missive from Eric, and realized he was late for a meeting in his own study.

Clair Brett

CHAPTER SIXTEEN

Clive made his way back into his study and there, in the chair he had vacated earlier, sat Louissa's brother, Henry. "It took ye long enough." He said absently, as he took a drink from the glass he had apparently poured himself.

"I assume you are not accustomed to running a house." Clive talked more to make conversation than anything. "Tis not as easy as one might think. I would assume it very similar to keeping a ship floating on the ocean." Clive poured a glass for himself and sat. "It becomes more difficult when women descend and expect things different than what the household is accustomed," he added.

"You would be surprised actually. Most say 'tis bad luck to have a female aboard ship, but with our work for the government and my own personal endeavors, we find ourselves overly burdened at times," he said with more pride than annoyance. Clive still wasn't sure how much to share, so he decided to listen for a while.

"The men were up in arms with the first girl who needed passage, until they saw the state of her. Young, no more than six and ten years, but the poor wretched lass was a sight. Saved her from a tavern keep south of Edinburgh. He had her on the menu next to the lamb stew."

Clive's throat caught at the thought. Why was it that made men feel they had such a right. The one letter he had of his father's was to one of his friends. The man sent it to Clive's mother and asked that Clive receive it when he reached his majority. It gave great insight to his father and his principles. Principles that Clive had every intention of living up to. His father had said that the law of women being property was not so much that they should have monetary worth, but that with any valuable possession, one was supposed to hold it above all else and protect it always. If only his father's interpretation was the way of it.

"I asked for two hours with her, then harried her back to my ship where the men stowed her below deck, after making sure she was bathed, fed, and dressed properly, while I returned with a couple of my larger men and made certain that the tavern owner was persuaded not to be replacing her."

Clive was impressed. "When did this happen?"

"Right after I took over the ship. I was ten and eight."

"Why?" Clive had to know what was driving this young man. Thus far, he had seen a need for revenge and a selfish need to do it himself.

"Why? You mean why save the lass?" Henry asked, his eyes flashing dark as he stared down Clive. "Why waste me time with a wretch?"

"No--I," but Clive never got the chance to explain his views on the subject before Henry was whipping him with a tirade Clive's mother would be most proud of.

"Listen here, Breakerton. I don't suffer fools, but because you claimed to be concerned about my sister, and you seemed to think your station could also aid me, I was willing, but I will not countenance an insufferable pig who believes that women are for the most part, less than chattel." He went on, not glancing at Clive, so Clive sat back to learn about this young man and wait.

"And if you think I would allow such a man to be in my sister's life..." Clive couldn't take it anymore considering the men Louissa was currently contending. He rose and got within steps of the impassioned pirate. So close that Henry stopped speaking and finally looked at Clive.

"That is quite enough," he said with no humor or quarter in his voice. "You come into my home by subterfuge in the shadows and accuse me of crimes against women, when your sister, the very woman you are accusing me of contaminating..." At that comment, Clive had to clear his throat, as visions of just hours prior shone bright in his head, making his words sour on his tongue. Collecting himself, he continued, "And putting in danger is as we speak in the very house of the man who plans to sell her to a monster that goes through wives like some men go through hunting dogs."

To his credit, Henry reddened and looked as uneasy as an insufferably stubborn green blood could, so Clive turned and walked to the window, giving him physical space, but he continued his discourse. "A man, who has blackened her eye, forced her to take on unknown travelers, alone, at night, with nothing more than a sword for protection, then expects her to play the Lady of the manor during the bright light of day. I am willing to bet the only thing that has protected her other...abuses, was what she would be worth to him pure." Clive almost choked on the last from the anger he allowed himself to own.

"Well, I—I..."

"I am s-o-r-r-y," Clive chided. "The word is sorry. You can do it lad. It won't kill you."

Henry bristled, but nodded once. "I am sorry. I am used to men being very closed minded, especially men of power."

"Yes, well, as I mentioned, I am notably blessed with sisters, nieces, and female cousins, etcetera. I was taught at a young age, being the youngest as well, that women could very well rule the world if they so desired, but it was more entertaining and diverting to orchestrate the men to think they were in charge, or so my sisters say." Clive smiled at the thought of his sisters, and it was enough for Henry to relax his shoulders and settle back down.

"You said you had news?" Henry asked, dismissing the last twenty minutes as men were wont to do. When an issue had been dealt with, it was forgotten.

"As a matter of fact, I do," Clive responded, letting the argument go, and moved to his desk to procure the one letter he was willing to share. The rest of the documents were safe and they would remain that way, but he knew Henry would need something physical. He handed Henry the envelope as he walked past to regain his seat.

He sat while the younger man read its contents. He paused a couple of times looking up at Clive with an expression mixed with well-fueled anger, and surprise. Clive simply nodded each time and motioned for him to continue reading with his hand.

When Henry was finished, he laid the letter in his lap and sat in silence, taking in all he had just read. Clive could see the emotion on the younger man's face, just before Henry cleared his throat and schooled his features. "Was there more?" he asked with a hard edge to his voice.

"Letters? Yes, there are, but this was the most damning of the lot. I am not ready to break out all the evidence just yet." Breakerton put up a staying hand to be allowed to finish. "I do not yet know who I can and cannot trust, including you. My priority is Louissa, as I have said in the past. You see, I have enough to at least warrant an investigation, perhaps actual proof to gain a conviction, but right this moment, Louissa is more important than your title," he said the last as a reminder to a man who had, for the majority of his life, not had to think about someone else above his own agenda. He might save damsels in distress, but only as it suited his schedule. Louissa was not an inconvenience, and he would make certain everyone knew that.

"What do you suggest?" Henry asked after a moment.

"I have connections that reach farther afield than the local magistrate, and I assume your dealings with the British government have given you the ear to some influential people. I have reached out via private courier, and I suggest you do the same. Once we have them all accounted for here at the manor, we can show them what we have. I do not trust that your uncle's reach doesn't go deep into the local gentry and magistrate's office, or perhaps further."

Henry nodded, but sat quietly for a moment, "Thank you," he finally said. "Thank you for stepping in. I don't know that I could have gotten past my need for vengeance, before it was too late. I do not normally admit such to anyone, you know," he said with a crooked smile.

Clive was touched and he knew what it took for a man like Henry to thank someone. He made to take some of the burden from Henry. "Well, I have done nothing for you. It is Louissa I am concerned about."

Henry nodded again, then sat back looking at Clive in a way

that a brother would look at a suitor calling on a sister. The place was not one that Breakerton had ever been, and as he decided, not a place he cared to be. Then Henry made a decision. Clive could see it in his eyes, and he relaxed his tensed muscles and moved forward. "Now what?"

"Well, we need to find a way to stop, or at the very least slow the progression of this marriage your uncle has planned for your sister," Clive said, not able to take the disgust from his voice. Henry's expression became closed and guarded. "I have an appointment with your uncle this afternoon. I plan on asking for Louissa's hand and offering a bride price no sane man could refuse."

Henry looked up and studied Clive, but to his surprise, the younger man did not argue. He only pointed out, "If you offer for her hand and he accepts, once this is all over, she will be ruined if you back out on the arrangement."

Henry's protective streak could be prodded to life when the time was upon them, Clive thought. He attempted to hide his smile. "If, after we are rid of your nefarious uncle and Louissa is amiable to the match, I will not withdraw," Clive conceded. "However, if Louissa is against such a union, I will withdraw as quietly and with as little attention to the matter as possible." At the thought, Clive felt cold and empty. He would make damn sure his little highwaywoman did not protest to the match.

His word seemed to be enough for Henry, which took Clive back, because not a month ago, this man would not have taken him at his word, or anyone else's for that matter.

"You know my uncle will see your offer as an impertinence to his status in the area. He will likely throw you out on your ear. Moreover, he has already made a deal for her hand. It is not to his benefit to go back on that agreement. In fact, it could prove downright dangerous."

"I have considered that, but the amount I have in mind will make your uncle consider his options. Plus, if it were to get circulated about that Lady Louissa had another suitor who was in negotiations with her uncle, well, that would make things much more interesting wouldn't it?"

Clive did not want to tell Henry of his sister's plan, which in truth was still not overtly clear to him, but felt he needed to impress upon Henry just how desperate Louissa was to have this over. "I am not sharing this with you to alarm you as much as to press upon you how very dire this situation is to your sister. In fact, I do not know the whole of what she has planned, but I have it on good authority that she wears around her neck a vial filled with poison. I believe that it is in wait for the outcome of this farce. I am not aware, however, if she plans on using it on herself if she is forced to go through with the marriage, or if she plans on murdering her new husband."

Henry blanched. He apparently had no words or was unable to make the idea straight in his mind. Finally, after a long pause, "Damn."

"Exactly, my boy. We can't have her running about the countryside ready to commit murder, or worse, suicide. The first would only be added to her long list of crimes, if it is ever exposed that she is the highwayman, but the last, well..." Clive couldn't finish.

"Yes, well," agreed Henry.

Clive chose not to share with the younger man that he had access long enough to take the poison out. That was something he planned not to share for the remainder of his breathing moments, if he was able.

"So, what is next for you?" Breakerton asked Henry.

"I am meeting a contact this evening who may have some more proof of my uncle's murderous ways, and then we will need to compile everything to bring before-- Well, before someone."

"I will have a name sooner rather than later, I hope so hold out as long as possible until I contact you again. Have you given anymore thought about making yourself known to Louissa?"

"No, right now it is still safer for her if she has no idea I am alive and so close."

Clive didn't like to admit it, but Henry was probably right. He just knew how much she wanted to see her brother alive, and hated keeping such a thing from her.

Henry stood and drew the last of his drink down, "Well, I am off. Good luck with my uncle. I am sure I will hear of your visit from my man. Just take care, for once you become known to my uncle, you could put yourself, Louissa, and your whole family in danger," he warned before the men shook hands and made his way back the way he came.

Clive sat and checked the clock. He still had three hours yet before he was to meet with the man in question. He had the paperwork all ready with the offer. He thought about what Henry said about his family's safety. They were aware of the dangers and had instructed him to take whatever course of action he needed, but right now, he wished they had no plans of returning from his sister's.

He honestly wasn't as worried about the reaction of her uncle, but Louissa's reaction if she was made aware of his offer, considering last night's events. Henry was correct. He was in danger, just not as much from their uncle, as he was from Louissa.

Clair Brett

CHAPTER SEVENTEEN

Exhaustion tugged on Louissa. She had no idea her body could be so tired and energized at the same time. The burn of embarrassment and remembered embraces battered her like waves on the rocks. Her face had been hot all day. It was a wonder Cook hadn't made her take to bed for fear of a fever.

Growing up with her uncle and his crew, she was not cloistered from the ways of men and women, but she had assumed the act did not change one. That in the light of day, life would be as it always was. She had been wrong. She was not the same person who left home last evening. The world knew it too. The flowers were brighter, the sun warmer.

Louissa shook herself out of her woolgathering. She was behaving as the enamored schoolgirl, not a world wise, knowledgeable woman. She was certain that was the type of fare Lord Breakerton was used to. Women who could do the things they did under cover of dark, and not spout poetry in the light of day. It was good that she would not be seeing him anytime in the near future. She needed the time to become more unaffected. It couldn't be that difficult.

She had chosen to spend the day helping with the laundry. Good labor is what would help her expel her nervous energy. She thought about other ways to dispel it and shivered at ideas she had never had before, but couldn't seem to get rid of now.

What if Breakerton had cursed her, or put some spell on her? That would be most helpful, because then she wouldn't have to admit to the churning in her stomach or the lightheadedness, when a flash of last night filled her vision. She gathered the laundry in a basket and headed for the manor. She never liked coming inside after being out in the warm sun. The house was dark and cold in comparison. As she made her way down the servant's hall toward the kitchens, she felt it before her ears pricked with remembrance. Clive's voice vibrated down the hall, slamming into her chest. Her entire body heated and hummed with energy.

Just as his voice made it to her ears, she had tried to

convince herself she was imagining, but when her uncle's voice raced through her with an angry growl, she knew she wasn't mistaken.

"Fool Englishman," Louissa spat as she hurried to get rid of the basket. Then she could get back to the servant's entry to her uncle's study to decide if she needed to intervene.

As she made her way back to the door, she considered the reasons Clive could be in her uncle's study only hours after he led her back under cover of darkness directly from his bed.

It was a possibility he had local or government business with her uncle. They were both men who held great power in the area. It was also possible that Clive decided to bring his proof that he showed her last night to confront her uncle. Once at the door, she knelt down to look through the crack.

Clive stood on one side of her uncle's desk and her uncle sat on the other. To the unfamiliar eye, it looked like two men of import having discourse about anything from business to the sport of the day. Louissa, however, knew differently.

Her uncle sat straight, his arms braced on the desk, his hands in fists. His expression was that of pure defiance. However, Clive stood with calm confidence. He didn't appear intimidated at all by her fearsome uncle. Louissa's heart swelled at the thought. She knew he was brave, but she also had been around men long enough to know there was a fine line between bravery and stupidity, when a man's ego was in play.

They were now speaking at normal levels, making it difficult to hear, but they were discussing a business deal of some sort. There was money involved, and a great deal of it, but she had missed the beginning of the discussion. This seemed to be a discussion about the details of the agreement.

Why was Clive doing business with her uncle?

Hadn't he said he would never do business with someone who treated his charges as badly as they treated her?

What changed?

As quickly as Louissa's heart had risen at hearing his voice, it sank to the pit of her stomach. What had changed was last night. She was no longer a maiden. Perhaps Clive's propensity for protecting damsels in distress was limited to chaste damsels, and he of all people would know how unchaste Louissa now was.

Now, the hair on the back of her neck rose and prickled. What if in the light of day, he was disgusted with how loose she appeared that he was here to sell the evidence he found to her uncle after she entrusted him with keeping it safe?

Breakerton knew full well that she had nothing to bargain with. The one thing she did have... Well, after last night's adventures she no longer had that bargaining chip.

"How dare you come into my house with such…" Louissa's uncle bellowed and thumped his fist on the desk as he rose to his full height. Louissa didn't hear the rest of his rant, as panic rose and rushed into her ears. Clive didn't seem at all impressed and pointed to the papers on the desk.

"My Lord," he said, "if you look at what the offer includes, you will see that it will more than double any reasonable offer you would have on the table. I highly suggest you consider my offer."

What was Louissa to do? She slid the rest of the way to the floor and leaned her back against the hallway wall. If she bolted into her uncle's study, she might very well endanger her own plans, not to mention her own health and safety. The voices had died down again, and Louissa had to rise back up to listen through the crack. It would not be wise even to consider rising to his aid. She had too much at stake. More than she had admitted to him. If her uncle realized what she had been doing right under his nose, well, the timeline would be moved up and her chances of finding her brother and getting her uncle convicted of murder would be lost.

Louissa chose to watch and wait. The men bent to the papers on the desk, Clive pointing to different places and her uncle getting an inquisitive look. She hated that look. Chills snaked down her neck, arms, and back. Her uncle only got that look when it was in his benefit. That never bode well for anyone in his path.

The two men spoke a bit more, but then her uncle nodded as did Lord Breakerton, then he was gone. Her uncle remained, looking again at the papers and sitting back in his chair full of thought. Louissa wanted to see what the paperwork said, but she knew she couldn't risk getting caught, when she was well and deep into a plan that required her freedom for the next few nights. After that, if all went well, she would be able to spy on her uncle, so she watched and waited to see where he put the papers.

A few minutes later, her uncle rolled the sheets up and tied them together. He then rose with them under his left arm and made his way out of the room. Damn. Louissa knew what this meant. He was going to hide them in his rooms. She also knew that meant they were of the upmost import to him. Her curiosity was peaked again, but she held to her earlier estimation that they did not concern her and would only prove to endanger her plan or they were the papers Clive refused to let Louissa see, and they were the evidence she needed to prove her uncle's crimes.

Damn and hell.

The knot forming in her stomach snaked up and stilled her breathing. It also took capture of her heart where a dull ache formed. She did not want to consider that Breakerton would do such a thing, but how well did she know him? How much time had they spent together having meaningful discord? Their last engagement required very few words at all. No, she needed to see what those papers were. She hoped she was wrong. She needed to be wrong, and it scared her at the forcefulness that those five words settled on her. It should not matter if he is a good man or nay. Likely, she would not have an opportunity to be in his company ever again, but it did. She would see those papers before night fell.

Then she would move on to her next task. She had heard rumors of a young man in the area that might have information on her brother. She intended to search him out. Her resolve set, a calm washed over her at her decision. She had no time for men and their games. If Clive was selling her evidence because he no longer cared to protect her as a fallen woman, there was naught to do about it. She knew last night might be a fleeting enjoyment, so best not to get despondent over such a trivial encounter. If her plan played out, in less than a fortnight, she would be freed or she would be dead. With that in her future, it tended to put things in perspective.

With that decision and the knowledge her uncle would be busy for the remainder of the day, Louissa set out to the tiny fishing village only an hour's ride from her. She had reason to think her brother was possibly raised on a small farm, owned by Cook's family. It would also give her the opportunity to go by way of the wharf and see if the man with the information might be found. This would help her not to think on the recent events that could do nothing, but add to her distress.

Four hours later, Louissa returned home just in time for dinner, as not to be missed, but with nothing to further her inquiries. The man with possible information was nothing more than a drunken deck hand with a sketchy description of a young boy, half-starved and wretched who might or might not be her brother.

The fishing village was not entirely a waste. Cook's family denied raising any such boy on the farm, and only admitted to a teenaged lad who was being paid to help support his family, but in town, shopkeepers seemed to remember a younger boy with the family. One that matched her brother's description. It gave her hope that he at least was rescued from the ship. From there, what happened to him was still a mystery.

Louissa managed a quick change and made it to the dinner table only to find one place set.

"Where is Uncle tonight? I thought he said he would be at dinner?" Louissa asked one of the footmen as they brought her meal.

"He 'ad ta leave for a meeting. Won't be back 'til morn, I 'spect," he answered and left her to eat alone.

Eating alone was the loneliest thing, Louissa thought. She

hated her uncle, but at least when they sat in silence at the dinner table, she could pretend they were a family. Sitting in silence alone at the dinner table was a stark reminder of her reality.

Once finished, she made her way to her uncle's bedchamber. Louissa would be able to see those papers without fear of being caught, and there was still enough light that she wouldn't have to light a candle. Her uncle's door loomed at the end of the hall. She didn't love Breakerton, no fool would fall in love after one intimate encounter, so whatever deal they made would not hurt her in the least.

As she neared the door, she was certain repeating it like a prayer would make it so. Or so she hoped.

CHAPTER EIGHTEEN

Breakerton made it back to the stables and no less than ten of his men, various male servants, were gathered.

"What's the occasion?" Clive asked dismounting and giving the reigns over to a young stable boy. Eric stepped up to speak for the group.

"Weel, Milord, we heard you were goin' to Loc Landon and we were waitin' to see ye back safe." He had an odd expression on his face that pricked at Clive's curiosity.

"Ah, I see, and what is it you all thought I was doing at Adair's home today?" It would not serve his purpose to have Louissa aware of his reason for being there, not that he ran into her. It bothered him that in the entire time he was at her home, he never even heard her, and he would have to admit that he was listening for any indication she was about.

"No idea, Milord. Jus' know he's a dangerous man, and well, we were worried," Eric answered straight. "Not to mention, if me Penny found out you disappeared to that man's house and I didn't do anythin' to rescue you…" he included.

The local baker, Penny, was very protective of Clive, and he knew it. Ever since he helped her previous employer reunite with her estranged husband, Penny had had a bit of a liking for Clive. Not to mention a protective streak.

"Well, I appreciate the concern and the obvious preparedness to send in troops, but it was an amicable enough meeting," Clive assured.

The men nodded and grumbled among themselves as they cleared the stables. Some seemed relieved, others disappointed at the word of no rescue attempt. Clive thanked them all for their concern, and then turned back to Eric who was waiting patiently, leaned up against a stable door.

"So, are congratulations in order?" He asked with a crooked smile. Clive had taken time to pen a note to Eric about speeding up his other assignments and letting him know what was about to transpire. He felt another person, apart from Henry should know what was going on in case Clive had disappeared. He doubted Henry would take the time to search.

"Ah, no," Clive responded dryly, "but he did not kick me out all together. I think he is considering how to exploit this new option on the table, so as to benefit from all his choices." What bothered Clive was how it would affect Louissa. He was not sure if Gareth would bother to inform her of a new suitor or not.

Eric pushed from his position, and both men walked into the late afternoon sun toward the apple orchard and subsequent privacy.

"Any news?" Clive asked.

"Once I got your note, I rode out t' check on the inquiries I 'ad made. The chief magistrate from Edinburgh will be arriving at your door in two days' time and he was able t' contact the naval commander in charge of the coastline following the Milton Road. Both men are familiar with Gareth Adair and 'ave an interest in seein' 'im dealt with."

"Are you sure?" Clive asked, because he could not take a chance of allowing one of Louissa's uncle's confidantes in the house.

"Of the chief magistrate I am certain. He actually 'ad ta look up who the magistrate was for the area, afore he spoke with me. I got the impression, they 'ave had dealins with McFee afore and they were not of the jovial kind." Eric assured Clive. "As for the commander, I 'ave a message ta pass along, which I was assured would be helpful in determining his loyalties."

Clive turned and quirked a brow, now he was interested. "What is the message?"

"Tis only this, tell your man that he 'as been workin' with one of our agents, who is currently workin' to ferret out a man or group of men responsible for a long list of missin' women in the whole of Scotland, among other traffickin' and smugglin' charges."

Clive was surprised that the government would acknowledge their dealings with a privateer, but the facts could be easily checked, so he just nodded.

"What else can I do?" Eric asked.

Clive had been thinking all day about how to try to keep Louissa busy to slow her progress down a bit longer. Things would be coming to a head shortly, but he would like it very much if Louissa were nowhere close. "Would Penny be interested in doing a very large delivery to the poor? I am feeling charitable and was hoping that Penny, Bethany, and my sisters, once they return, could rally Louissa to help make mass baskets to the poor of our great community. I would be the benefactor."

Eric's smile widened and he slapped Breakerton on the back. "Tis, an outstandin' idea! I'll go right now and talk t' Penny, then she can press t' Bethany how important 'tis would be, and then Bethany can ask Louissa for assistance. Brilliant, Milord."

"Good. My sisters should be returning in a few days from my sister's and I will speak with them as well." The two men shook hands and headed in opposite directions. Clive would need to have the staff prepare two rooms. As much as he would prefer them to remain at Jane's, it was better that he orchestrated when his family traveled so he would pen a note and send a courier asking for them to return and let his mother and sister's know they would be entertaining and helping with baskets for the poor. He would also need to get word to Henry by way of Nicholas, so perhaps that is where he should start. He turned and headed back to the stables.

A sense of purpose hummed through his body. He now felt like a man of action. Adair would, at the very least have to consider his offer. The price was too outlandish not to, and he now would have the ear of some men of influence outside the blackguard's web. He was sure the exhaustion of not sleeping last night would soon begin to take its toll, so he must act while he still had the energy. However, if Louissa were to be waiting on him in his bed, well, he was certain he would muster the energy from somewhere. He knew it would not happen again tonight, but just the thought seemed to buoy his resolve.

By the end of the next day, the rooms for his soon to arrive guests were readied. Because of his family's haste in returning to residence the same night as they received the request, a new menu was set thanks to his mother and Mary. Nettie had taken the lead on the community baskets for the poor, and she was busy emptying his larder for the cause, not yet out of their traveling clothes. They all understood the import of the next few days. They also understood the possible danger. For safety sake, the rooms of the visiting magistrate and the commander were put as far away from the private wing as possible, in case of any attempt. Clive also arranged for armed guards of his choosing to be stationed around the house, and in the corridors of the guests' rooms. It was decided the men would come by the south, avoiding the Milton Road all together. There had been no word of another highwayman attack, but being so close to an end mark, Breakerton would not take unnecessary chances.

The candles had burned low in the hallway as he used the moonlight from the windows to his right to make his way to his chambers. He had considered moving his room for the time being as well, and then thought better of it, from a concern of leaving his female relations without protection on this side of the house. As he stepped past Nettie and Mary's adjoined suite, he could hear them chatting, as a maid hummed a gentle tune. They were bloody good sports, he knew. Most women would have nothing to do with such a nasty business, but not his ladies.

As he made his way down the hall, he could hear his mother's lilting voice coming from her rooms, as she sang a lovely song he remembered her singing when he was a boy. For a man being overrun by the fairer sex, he was genuinely lucky. Louissa would fit quite nicely into the fold. His feet scuffed to a halt on the thick carpet. He straightened and found his chest too heavy to drag in a full breath. Where had that thought come from? He shook the feeling of surprise from his entire body and hurried on to his room. The exhaustion had finally had its way with his already addled brain he supposed. A long night of dreamless sleep would no doubt fix it.

He turned the knob on his bedchamber door and took a step in as something came shooting from out of the darkness spiraling through the air toward his head. He only just managed step back and close the door before whatever it was smashed against it, and it fell to the ground.

"Ye, come in here, ye lout and face me!" Louissa growled. Standing in the room, waiting on the coward finally to seek out his own bed was exasperating. She had not meant to let the large bookend she had been admiring go flying across the room, but she had.

"Louissa? What in hell?" She heard Breakerton from outside the door hiss in an attempt to whisper, as not to sound an alarm. "I am going to open the door. Please, do not attempt to sever my head. Please."

Louissa balled her hands into fists to try to acquiesce to his request. She also dug her heels into the soft carpet to stop from rushing at him. Knocking the idiot out would not advance her cause in a timely manner.

The door made no noise save a quiet swoosh, as it swung open and glided on the carpeted floor. Clive stood in the doorway, visibly cautious. She was certain he was lithe enough to be able to turn and run if needed. They stood staring off in the dim light of the room. The candlelight from the hall shone from behind Clive, giving him an ethereal visage. At the same time, it accentuated his broad strong shoulders and trim waist. He was not wearing a jacket, probably left behind in his study after dinner. This made the distinct V shape of his upper body visible, and it also gave her a very pleasant view of his muscular thighs and calves. Her heart hammered against her breast, and she actually looked to see if the fire had begun to blaze, as she felt heat fill her face and then travel like a warm scotch on a cold night down her body. All of a sudden, a vision of Clive naked and lying above her appeared. She felt her knees begin to give way, so she took a step to the side to steady herself.

"May I come in?" He asked with a quiet, calming voice.

"Tis your room and your peril, so do as you must," she answered with clipped tones. She was mad at this man. She needed to remember she was mad at him.

He entered and turned to close the door quietly. She heard the lock turn as well. He then turned back at her as someone would a rabid animal. "Good eve, Louissa. I wasn't expecting a visit from you tonight, but it is always a pleasure…"

"Oh, shut up."

"As you wish."

"Oh, now ye are all kind and accommodating," she spat, annoyed at his compliance. He was supposed to be all arrogant male, that would make this easier.

"Pardon? I am afraid you have me at a loss, my Lady," he drawled stepping toward the fire to stoke it, which Louissa didn't think was required as warm as the room was already.

"Perhaps, if I bring up your visit to my uncle's yesterday, it will jog your memory," she offered.

"Yes, I did in fact visit your uncle. I was hoping to bump into you, but I dare say you were otherwise occupied," he said casually as he continued to play with the fire.

When Louissa had been able to get into her uncle's room and find the papers in his hidden shelves, she was expecting her heart to be broken into a thousand pieces when she saw that Breakerton had not sold her evidence to the man who was trying to sell her off to a murderer. Instead, she had decided it was worse as she read the marriage contract and the outrageous bride price that Clive had offered. She all but felt her heart stop before it attempted to pound out of her chest. All the air fled from her body and she got the oddest feeling of her brain being emptied of all air and thought.

He hadn't been there to trade her life for riches. He had been there to trade her. At first, she felt light. He didn't hate her and he still wanted to protect her. Their night together had meant something to him. She felt the prick and sting of tears as she had then, but this time she would not allow them purchase. Once the initial schoolgirl emotions settled, she then realized that this was no different from her other engagement. It would not lead to her death, but she was still being sold. The price shocked her. She was not worth such a sum. Even if she were skinned and sold by weight, she would not be worth such an outrageous amount, but she was still being sold.

"I cannot imagine, my lord, why you would have wanted to see me. 'Tis not like your business had anything at all to do with me," she answered with a sticky sweet voice, laced with just enough bitterness to have him turning to see her face. "So, tell me, Milord, if that is how shrewd you are when buying chattel, how is it that you are not a pauper yet?"

He rose with a fluid masculine movement that spoke of power and elegance. He took care to replace the poker quietly into the rack and then straightened to study her. He stepped away from the fire, but kept a respectable distance. Had they been in her room, they would have needed to be uncomfortably close, but here in his grand suite, there was plenty of space between them. Still it wasn't enough, or it was too much, Louissa wasn't sure.

Damn him.

"I am sorry for not speaking with you. When I first arrived, I did ask if you could be present and I was informed by your uncle that nothing of import had to be discussed with his charge and he would send me away if I insisted."

"Why?" She asked, and she knew he understood by how the plains of his face became rigid.

"Louissa, I could not in good conscience, after... I had to do the right thing by you, or at least try," he pleaded.

"Is that how you will settle Nettie when the time comes?"

She could Clive taking care with his next statement. Since growing up with only women, it was obvious he knew when to take heed when dealing with a woman.

Clive looked everywhere but directly at her. He couldn't

even make eye contact. Louissa noted an odd expression on his face, and the muscles in his shoulders and arms were taut. He had no right to be angry with her. She was the one being bartered for, not him.

"Well?" she brought him back to the fact she was waiting.

"I-- no. What I mean to say is that Nettie has yet to express an interest in a husband."

"And I 'ave?" She threw back. "And what is tha' foolish look on your face?" She added. He looked between a laugh and a scowl.

His expression shifted, sending chills along Louissa's arms. She knew the moment he had made some private decision and it unsettled her. "What are ye smilin' like a fool for?" she asked.

"I am just thinking about Nettie getting married. I would not make the poor bastard pay, because he will pay with his very life. I am certain of that." He smiled that crooked smile Louissa both loved and hated.

How in bloody hell was she supposed to defend her honor and her freedoms to a man she was so susceptible to? Louissa straightened her spine and drew in a deep breath. Being raised on ships, she was surrounded by men and she knew exactly how to deal with them, but this man, this was an anomaly. No matter how hard she tried to keep her guard high, she found herself fighting a smile or quelling a shiver.

Her first plan was to wait until he was asleep, then douse him with cold water and beat him about his head. She should have kept with that plan, because the only part of her still contemplating bashing his head was her brain. That stupid grin made her knees weak and her heart pound. Her mouth was dry and her hands were sweaty. Cook would have her in bed with a hot poultice if she knew her symptoms. She was certain at least the bed would help to assuage her feelings, if not exacerbate them for a while beforehand.

She caught sight of the intimidating four-poster bed to her left and her cheeks flamed. Glancing back at her nemesis, she saw that he was fully aware of her thoughts and that would not do. He had no right to try to purchase her as one does a piece of art. She hated that the world was as it was, and her decision was still either to be left alone or to kill herself. It was the only way. Her brother would understand. She knew it. Why wasn't Breakerton different? She needed him to be different, to understand. She had no idea why, but she did.

"I was not raised as a conventional woman. Society does not dictate who I am or what I can be. It doesn't get that privilege, because of what it took away from me. Just like my uncle doesn't get to profit from what he believes is my virginity." The tears stung before they dropped hot onto her cheeks, but there was no pulling them back. She was tired. So, so, tired.

"Louissa, I…" She held up a staying hand, when he would have crossed to her and took a step back to be more in the shadows. She did not allow anyone to see her cry. Not many things were in her life that she didn't owe someone else, but her tears were the one thing she owed no one. Her uncle did not deserve to see her tears of fear, frustration, or mourning. Her brother would never know how many nights she soaked her pillow wishing he would come to save her. No, her tears were her own. A tight knot of disappointment in her only made them flow faster. She took a deep calming breath and tried to ignore the streams dripping onto her chest.

"What do you think I owe society? Where was society when my parents were being killed or when my brother was being taken from me? Where was society when my uncle made me clean the deck of the ship in torn rags? Where were they when he had me be the one who emptied the buckets from the men who didn't have their sea legs? What about when my uncle decided to dress me as a man and stick me on the Milton Road to keep people away while he unloaded his smuggling boats?" She watched as he looked nervously at the door, and she realized her voice had risen. She cleared her throat and looked down at the rug, because if she made eye contact with Breakerton, she couldn't trust that she wouldn't throw herself into his arms. She continued at a much quieter tone, and she still would not look at him. "I do not believe I owe anyone any part of me. Not my uncle, not society, and not you."

At that, she did look up and catch his gaze. What she did, she did because she wanted to. She would not have it appear anything more than it was. "You also do not owe me anything. I had no expectation…"

When he crossed the space, she didn't know. She had seen him, hadn't she? Perhaps she glanced away for a moment to collect herself, but just a moment. Regardless, he was there, staring down at her, taking her hand in his. How could a man be so warm and soft to the touch? Her insides felt hot and swirly the same way it did on the rare occasions that she was able to indulge in a cup of drinking chocolate. "Neither of us had any expectations. That was part of the enjoyment," he assured her. To her credit, she did not let on that her mouth was dry. "Society is a fickle wench for sure and you of all do not owe anyone anything, but all I wanted was for you to see you have options above what you may have already considered."

He was rubbing his thumb in troublesome little circles on the back of her hand. It was disturbingly distracting, making her the heat in her burn.

Perhaps, Louissa thought at that moment she might have had an inflated perception of her own ability to give this man a proper dressing down when what she wanted was to undress him and feel his skin on hers. However, if she gave in, would he pursue his marriage suit?

"Louissa." Her name sounded exotic and sensual coming from him. It didn't seem to be a question as much as it was a plea. A plea she wanted to answer with one of her own. She wanted to forget her uncle, her brother, her parents, and her life in general. She wanted to be this woman in this moment with this man. The fire light filled the room giving it a golden hue. The dark wood seemed to shimmer in the flickering rays. For its size, the room was very cozy and inviting, making her desire to remain rooted all the more strong.

     In this room, Louissa felt like she was in a velvet lined jewelry box safe from the world. It no longer existed. It was only this one room and this one man. He continued his assault on her senses by moving his caress up her arm and tenderly squeezing her shoulder, then moving to cup her neck while rubbing little circles, again in the hollow of her throat. His eyes made their jewelry box fall away and pulled her into their depths. She hadn't noticed before, but the blue changed with his moods. Tonight they were the color of the Mediterranean Sea on a bright sunny day, and just like that, she fell, lost in this man come champion. Lord help her or forgive her, but for the sake of her heart, she hoped God would not let her hurt too much when he was gone.

CHAPTER NINETEEN

Before she could put too much thought into such a sad affair, she was lifted off her feet. She knew if she protested, he would not force her. He was the first man in her life since her father who would consider her wants and needs before their own, at least in the physical realm. The shock of the mattress under her brought her back from the depths of his eyes. He splayed her out on the massive bed. Her clothes felt heavy and constricting on her body. He bent over her and continued his assault on her neck making her concerns about her clothing unimportant.

"Breakerton…"

"Clive," he gruffly interrupted her plea. "In this room, you will call me Clive."

He wasn't looking at her, so Louissa could not read his face, but was not sure why a particular moniker was important over another, "My lord, I…"

"And you will never call me that when we are in bed together." This time, he stopped his ministrations and stared hard at her. The scrutiny was uncomfortable. She tried to squirm, but her skirts and his legs proved effective shackles. "My titles are meant to show superiority in society. My Lord is what a lesser calls his better. When we are here, when you are here," he kissed her neck and pressed one hand around her breast and squeezed in a delectable fashion, "we are equals. One not being more important than the other is. I will not allow it. I want to hear it,t Louissa. I want to hear you say my Christian name." He bent and put his hot mouth over her nipple that he had managed to coax to life through the bodice of her dress and squeezed with his teeth, ripping an intake of breath from her, and on that breath, his name.

"Clive, for the love of God, Clive." She hardly recognized her own voice. It was a low, husky groan, more than actual words. She wound her hand into his curls and held him to her breast. She didn't know the feel of her dress, being heated by her lover's breath and rubbing against her skin could cause such a reaction. The sensation shot straight to her belly and then lower. She wanted to squeeze her legs together causing friction there, and Clive being more experienced, freed her legs from his stronger ones to allow the movement.

His name on her lips caused him to growl and move to her other breast, but he moved his free hand over to continue the onslaught on her already sensitive nipple. Her body seemed to want to go in all directions at once. Her hips lifted toward his body, but she wanted to continue the pressure of her legs in her most private place. Then there was her chest that she wanted to lift so he would take more of her into his mouth, and force more pressure from his hand.

Clive must have realized her dilemma, because he adjusted his hips and legs so she had room to buck her hips. Then he moved his leg between hers rubbing his knee or thigh, really she didn't care, against the spot she was trying to satisfy. She moaned her approval. She found as he applied pressure and she rubbed against him, the need was not slacking, but becoming more urgent. Before she could cry out his name, her world burst into a million pieces and she was floating. The heaviness of her body before was gone, the need for pressure no longer in the forefront. She felt her whole body relax into Clive's arms and just settle in like a leaf being set down in the warm sundrenched grass by the breeze that had carried it there.

When she opened her eyes, he was all she could see. His softened expression made her warm inside again, and the smile he blessed her with told her he knew it. "Welcome back, I was hoping we could rid you of your excess clothing, so that I might join you."

Louissa felt her lips curve into a sleepy smile with her skin pulling at the corners of her mouth. "What a beautiful idea," she agreed and allowed him to divest her of her attire. She tried not to think about how adept he was at such ministrations, but before she could think on it too much, he too was naked and once again lying next to her, but partially on top of her, skin to skin. She didn't think feeling him so close his warmth seep into her would ever be old. The light dusting of hair on his chest, belly, and legs added another layer of sensation to his otherwise smooth skin. She liked it very much, she thought. This time, when he slid his bare leg between hers, she needed no coaxing and before she knew what was happening, he was fully above her. She could feel his erection lying heavy on her patch of hair between her legs. "Mmm, Clive, Clive..." she didn't know what to say or verbalize what she wanted.

"What love? Say it, what do you want?" He asked her, as he continued to rub his whole body over hers.

"I-- I don't know, I just want you," she ground out, as she kissed his chest and neck and pulled his body closer to her, if that were possible, she felt like he would envelope her and absorb her very being if she could get him close enough. "Now, Clive. Now," she demanded.

"Yes, love," was his response as he bent and kissed the top of her nose while he adjusted and slid deep inside her in one slow deliberate motion, stopping once he was fully seated, but again, she wanted more of him. She felt as if she would die of thirst if he didn't get closer. She lifted her hips and lowered her hands to his tight buttocks, as she drew him even closer.

"Easy love, unless you want this to end much sooner than I had planned." He moaned and buried his head in her neck, making her squeal and bend her head, lessening her grip on his arse. "A man with more resolve than I could not resist your sweetness, so you must allow me time to marshal my strength, or I will embarrass myself like a green school lad."

"I 'ave no idea what in the bloody world you are talking about," she said with laughter in her voice.

He held himself up on his elbows and lowered his forehead to hers. She could feel the corded muscles in his back and shoulders stiffen and slightly vibrate from the effort. "On that morning in the field near the stream, you forced me to have a reaction from half the field away. If I give into my reaction to being inside of and on top of you, I will no doubt lose my seed, before we both can come to enjoyment again."

"Oh," she said feeling her cheeks burn understanding what he was saying. "Tis sorry…"

"There is no apologizing in this bed, Louissa," he said with a serious tone to his voice. "You are new to love making, and don't understand, I assume that my lack of control at this moment, is a compliment to your allure, and the power you hold over me," he said the last with a grin, waggling his eyebrows with humor. "I am your lap dog, my lady," and covered her mouth with his before she could comment. At the same time, he began moving, slowly pulling out, only to return in an even more agonizingly slow motion. Her hips rose to meet him. He only managed this pace for a few strokes, before he lowered himself on her and they began moving as one in a steady dance that Louissa in her desire, pleasure filled haze, acknowledged it was similar to a sword fight, but with a much more pleasurable outcome.

After what seemed like an eternity, yet only a too short moment, both collapsed on the bed floating back to Earth. Louissa looked up at the canopy and mused that if not for that they both might have floated right out of the room and into eternity.

Clive pulled her limp body close to him, and pulled the disheveled covers over them. She lay in his arms, spent from only their second love making session, and at that moment, she realized she had done what she feared. She had fallen into her own trap.

She loved this man.

Her last thought, before his gentle swirls with his finger on her bare belly, and his breath, warm, and brandy kiss in her ear made her finally fall asleep, was that she was well and truly in trouble.

When Louissa woke, it was to Clive's soothing voice, "Such a serious expression, Love." Reaching up, Clive rubbed Louissa's forehead to ease the creases there. After they finished making love, he had wrapped her in his arms and drawn the covers over their heated but cooling bodies to keep out the chill of the room. He didn't force any conversation, and if Louissa was right, he had dozed too for a while. He had skillfully tucked her in the crook of his arm, making it difficult to see his face unless she made enough commotion to wake him so she remained, head resting on his chest with his heart steadily drumming an even tap in her ear.

She shouldn't have come here tonight. She knew that before she left, but she was unable to stop herself. Had she known they would end up making love again? Probably. This bothered Louissa, because she could see a life here. Waking up each morning in this bed, with this man. If circumstances were different, if she wasn't being sold in less than a fortnight, if her brother wasn't still missing, the only one who could save her.

"I was just thinking," she admitted, closing her eyes to the stroking finger on her forehead. It reminded her of when her mother would comfort her. It felt good.

"Heavy thoughts or light thoughts?" Breakerton asked, as he bent and smelled her hair with a deep breath.

"Both, I guess," she admitted, never having before thought about it. "I have been thinking what it would have been like to have been introduced to you in a conventional manner. If my life had been different."

"Hmm," he thought aloud stretching more onto his back and putting one of his arms behind his head. She turned to prop her chin on his chest and look at his face. "What would it have been like to enter a ballroom with only a mind for drink and cards, but to look up and see the likes of a wild one such as yourself across the room?" He quirked a brow in concentration. The giggle bubbled up into her throat before she could stop it. "Shh, minx. I am considering your effect on such an unsuspecting assembly."

"Oh, and what is it you think I would do? I 'ave been in an assembly before."

"Really, and were there any survivors?" He jested, and kissed the top of her head lessening the accusation. "I cannot say I would have been able to control myself. I probably would have shocked many a maiden, not to mention their chaperones."

"Whatever for?" she asked with mock shock.

"I would have taken one look at you with your wild hair, sun-kissed skin, and perfectly sinful body, and would have crossed the floor and taken you on the orchestra stage."

Louissa felt the blush burn to the roots of her hair. She buried her face in his chest and poked her finger into his side making him squirm. After a moment, she managed to regroup. "That is not what I meant, you horrible man," she assured him with a smile. "I meant if I had been brought up a lady, if you had been introduced properly, if you..." She trailed off not wanting to put voice to such nonsense.

"If I had been able to court you?" Clive finished for her.

"Yes."

"Well, I assure you, we would have ended up right where we are now." He drew her up his body and planted a gentle kiss on her lips. "I am sure, when you are not dressed like a deck hand or stable boy, or household maid, I will find you just as intoxicating. In fact, now that I know what you look like sans any clothing, I am sure I will hardly notice your attire at all."

She loved his humor. It made her feel things she shouldn't, as if there would be a time when he saw her dressed for a ball. She knew that would not happen in her reality.

Louissa drew in a breath. If she remained in this bed and in his arms, she would begin to second-guess her plan, and it was not a plan she could go back on. She pulled away from Breakerton's warm embrace and rose. She began to find her clothing strewn around the side of the bed in silence. She noted her bed partner did nothing to stop her, or question her actions. She stole a glance as she bent to retrieve a boot and saw him propped up against the pillows with the sheet lying across his lap, his bare chest and arms glowing in the moonlight. Her breath caught. He looked very intensely at her.

After another minute of silence, he finally spoke, "You are angry that I did not ask you first, before I spoke with your uncle."

"Yes," she agreed, pulling the simple and serviceable gown over her head.

"I knew you would not accept my offer, for no other reason than you think you must go through this nonsense alone."

"Nonsense?" She asked. Her limbs turned hot, then cold in an instant. So, her life or death struggle was nothing but nonsense to this man? "I found out just today that because of your generous offer, my uncle has notified my affianced, and instructed him to come post haste. Now, the sennight I had left to find Henry is no longer within my grasp," she said with panic flowing like waves through her body.

"Louissa, I..."

She cut him off. "No, nothing you can say will make any difference. I know to you, I am nothing but a dalliance, a silly girl playing at being a boy. I wish it were different."

"You wish what was different?" He had left the bed and he was next to her in an instant. Louissa stepped away from him for fear she would reach for his steady embrace. She couldn't lose herself in that again.

"Everything," she stated with more vehemence than necessary. "I wish my uncle had not killed my parents and left my brother, Lord knows where. I wish my uncle cared for me as a niece, not as chattel. I wish I were not put in the position that I have been put in. I wish I did not have to follow through with..." She stopped. Shock filling her. It would not do to let her secret out so close to time. Not to a man with such a penchant for playing the hero.

"Following through with what?" He asked, the deadly edge to his voice making the fine hairs on her arms and her neck stand up.

"Nothing."

He was there, with a manacle of a hand around her arm in a blink. He wasn't hurting her, but she also understood he was not letting her go, until he got an answer.

"Clive, I cannot…"

"You will, not cannot, you will. I will keep you hostage until you tell me what it is you are planning."

She sighed, but before she could pull the words back, she began to tell him of her plan.

"So, to summarize," Clive said in a dull, annoyed tone, "if you have not found your brother, of whom you have no solid proof whether he is even alive or that he is even on this side of the world, you intend to either poison your new husband. If you find you cannot do so before he tries to consummate, you will drink the poison yourself before he has the chance?"

"Yes," she stated, hitching her chin up as much as a woman standing in her lover's bedchamber with an unfashionable dress only partially secured and her stockings in her hand could.

"And this you consider a good plan?" He asked, again with that deadly edge.

"Clive, I am alone. I have no one to help."

"What? You are alone? You have no one? Poor Louissa, always abandoned, has no one she could possibly reach out to for aid against her corrupt uncle?"

Louissa didn't like his tone. It made her want to slap him, but good.

"What about Bethany or the vicar? Nettie and Mary would put their fool selves in danger for a half-drowned kitten, so they would be up for the task as well. Hell, you have the majority of my servants so in love with you that they leave doors unlocked so you may come and go as you please in my home. Or, oh, I don't know, what about me?" His stare coupled with the gravelly voice made him look the deadly lord, not the man who had been so tender only thirty minutes ago in bed. His grip had tightened with every word and she tried not to show her the effect it had on her.

"I will not put people I care about in danger. I have always known how my life would end. It was apparent that if I did live long enough to be married off, then it was my destiny. My only hope was to find Henry. When I am gone, I can no longer protect those I care about from my uncle. I would never do that to them."

"You don't have to do this," Clive said with a wave of emotion following his words. She could feel it wash over her. "Any of it. There are people who would protect you. Or is it because you don't want to say you have experienced enough? Perhaps you uncle has made you come to believe in his plans." Her heart exploded into a thousand pieces in her chest.

"I do," she said. "Please let me go, Clive." She asked quietly. This would be the last time she saw him, and was almost being taken away by the tide of regret, love, and fear she had buried for so long.

He did as she asked and stepped away. "What are you scared of, Louissa?"

That one question was all it took. Before she could pull it back and bury it deep, the fear of her entire life came spewing out like the waves crashing against the rocks.

"How dare ye ask such a question of me or even think to accuse me of working with him! What am I frightened of? Everything, you daft, idiotic fool. I do not remember a time anymore when fear didn't drive my every action or word. You have no idea what 'tis like trying to navigate life with a man who makes every day seem like a typhoon on a ship."

"Then there is the fear of never seeing my brother again, or the fear of never knowing love, or never having a family. Or what about the fear of having a foolish Lord come and try to apprehend me as I am pretending to be a highwayman in the dregs of the night, alone on a road with no one close to rescue me. The one thing I am not afraid of is my own death."

CHAPTER TWENTY

Clive had not had as many lovers as many in the Ton would have thought, but even for him, last night did not end as he had hoped. Once Louissa told him of her plan and her vehemence that she was not afraid to die, she proceeded to tell him he was an cad and she would never see him again. She also mentioned that she was no longer in need of the evidence he still held at bay. She said once her uncle captured the man he had been following all would be done. She didn't stay long enough for Clive to question her. In fact, she threatened to wake the entire household if he did not allow her to leave.

Now, in the light of day, he did not feel any more at ease with the situation. He took no time once she left to pen a note to Henry about what he had heard. His suspicion that Henry was the target was strong. The biggest question in his mind was what Louissa actually knew.

Word had come early that his guests from Edinburgh would be arriving early afternoon, so Clive decided to go riding before to try to puzzle his way through the dark thoughts churning within him.

Everything he knew of Louissa, everything he had heard, experienced, and just plain felt, told him she was an innocent, being taken along on a dangerous run by her uncle. When she was afoot, his protective senses flung into action. Until last night.

Something she said, or the way she said it had him questioning her motives. When she said that once her uncle had captured the man he was following, it would be done and she no longer needed the evidence he had to prove everything her uncle had done. Also, he hadn't questioned it at the time, but thinking back he wasn't so sure. Did she know her brother was alive? Did she know that was who her uncle wanted dead? Was she helping him?

Clive was aware of stories of kidnap victims who began to sympathize with their captors. Perhaps Louissa had been brainwashed by her guardian. If that was so, he might very well have unwittingly put Henry in danger. He had yet to hear back from the young Lord, but hoped that was a good sign that he was at sea at the moment.

He had an idea of how he could prove to himself if Louissa was duping him or not. However, he would need Henry to play along, and to this point, Henry had not been overly willing to go along with any of Clive's plans.

His ride had brought him to Nicholas's house, which was a bit of a surprise to Clive because he had not been planning a visit, but what he heard from his friend made him even more upset than he had been upon rising from bed this morning. It seemed that, with all of Clive's work to prove Louissa's uncle the dangerous man that he was that he had not done his due diligence in keeping the other Lords and the local magistrate at bay against Louissa. It seemed that Nicholas had heard the magistrate was closing in on Louissa and would soon have enough to arrest her. Perhaps a prison cell was the safest place for the minx right now, either to protect her from her uncle, would be fiancé, herself, or him, and to also protect Henry. On the other hand, Clive had an idea that, once she was arrested, the trial would be shortened, and they would be frantic to get her head in a noose.

Rounding the bend of the west barn, he saw the carriage in the drive. His guests had arrived. After he left his horse in the stable to be groomed and watered, he made his way to his study. It would be polite of him to allow his guests time to freshen up after their journey, but he was never accused of being a gracious host.

The darkness of the old castle was a contrast to the bight spring day and Clive's eyes needed adjusting as he entered the house. He heard voices coming from his study before he could focus on them, but knew one of them was Nettie and the other a deep unfamiliar male voice.

"Oh Breakerton, there you are," Nettie greeted when he made his way into the room. "I suggested that your guests take time to freshen up after their trip, but they felt you would want to get to work immediately."

"Ah, yes gentlemen, thank you for your consideration. Thank you, Nettie, for keeping my guests company until I arrived." She curtsied, bid good-bye to the men and left the room.

"Lord Breakerton, thank you for notifying us of your concern. We were more than willing to come to your assistance," said the man who had been speaking with Nettie. He rose and extended his hand. "I am the Lord Advocate, Sir William Rae, and this," he motioned as the other man rose to extend a hand, "is the Lord Justice Clerk, Lord Boyle."

Clive blinked and then blinked again. He had been hoping to see the men above the local magistrate. He had not been expecting to entertain those at the top of the judiciary chain in Scotland. "I am sorry. You will forgive my pause. I was not expecting…"

"Ah, yes, we assumed our appearance would be a bit of a surprise," Sir William Rae, the top legal officer in all of Scotland, assured Clive.

"You see, my lord," explained Lord Boyle, the judge second only to the Lord President of the Court of Sessions, "when it became known to us of your situation…" he was cut off by Sir Rae.

"We felt it imperative to come with all urgency, and not leave this matter to someone not as versed in the law and its limitations. We have been trying to find a way to prosecute Adair for quite some time."

Clive motioned for the men to resume their seats, just as a maid entered with a serving tray of tea and a selection of cold meats and cheese with bread. The two men were very grateful for the sustenance, and it gave Clive time to process this news. This was very good indeed, but he had to be sure these men were whom they said.

As they filled their plates and mouths with the offerings, Clive cleared his throat and dove right in. "I am very grateful of the government's interest in my predicament, and while I mean no disrespect, I am afraid I will need to ask for some proof you are who you say. Also, I was expecting the naval commander in charge of the coastline in this area."

"Mmm." The Lord Advocate nodded, while chewing a large piece of roast goose. Once he swallowed, he continued, "Yes, we expected you would be skeptical, as would we. Here." He dug around in his satchel until he came up with a folded piece of parchment and handed it to Clive. The seal was that of the Scottish government and it had not been thus tampered with. He opened it and read its contents. Once satisfied these men were who they said they were, Breakerton nodded and handed the note back to Rae.

"Thank you."

"We would have thought you daft had you not questioned. The Naval Commander spoke with us for counsel. It was decided that Lord Boyle come instead of him due to the enormity of this matter," Boyle added, as he cut a hunk of hard cheese and popped it in his mouth. "I guess you should bring us up to date with what has been going on and what you have for evidence."

Clive sat back, wistfully eyeing the decanter across the room, wishing his teacup were a brandy glass. Instead, he recounted all of the events leading up to these men taking in his hospitality, leaving out his two nights with Louissa. Once finished, he noted that both men sat with their mouths in a flat line, lips drawn together. "Where is Master Henry now?" The Lord Advocate asked with concern.

"I am unaware. I sent a messenger with a note to his known colleague, but I have heard no word back. I am hoping he is off shore, but he has not been a trusting bloke, as I am sure you can understand." Both men agreed with gruff acknowledgments.

Before Clive could continue, a crisp rap at the door had them all looking up. "Enter," Clive directed and a footman walked in carrying a note, and handed it to Clive.

"This was just delivered by private messenger."

"Thank you, Thomas." Clive took it and didn't look up as the servant left. The seal was of the local magistrate. A chill pulsed down his back. This was not good. He knew he had not made an update of the local Lords and the magistrate, except to send a note stating he was dealing with the situation.

As expected, it was a note telling him that the Lords were not wont to wait any longer, and the magistrate felt he had ample evidence to apprehend the subject, who happened to be a local lady named Lady Louissa Adair. The note was terse, with a heavy bit of reproach and scolding included between the words. He must not have done well schooling his features, because the Lord Advocate spoke up. "Is that missive of a personal nature, or one you would care to share?"

Breakerton chuckled at the question, because at this point, how was he to answer? "Both, actually. It seems Lady Louissa, the woman I have pitched my hat toward is to be arrested and tried for the crime of armed thefts, and summarily hanged by the local magistrate." He handed over the note and stood. That glass of brandy was no longer a distant desire. As he poured, he lifted the decanter to his guests in offering. They both nodded. He poured a hearty splash in his glass, drained it, and filled it again, then proceeded to fill two more and brought the tray over to replace the teapot. Clive wisely left the decanter across the room. If closer, it would be in danger of being drained.

All three men sat in silence considering all their options. The Lord Advocate spoke first and said what they all had been thinking, "I could pay a visit to the magistrate and encourage him to exercise extreme caution in this matter. However, I would be afraid that my involvement would jeopardize our purpose for being here."

"No, no you are most assuredly correct," Clive agreed. "If you were to step in, it would raise eyebrows and hackles, I am afraid. This community is filled with gentry who would prefer the wheels of higher justice turned more slowly, allowing them to handle it as they think appropriate."

"According this missive," Boyle added, "he would not be acting on this until two days from now. Do you not think that strange that he would divulge when he would be apprehending Lady

Louissa, and also waiting two whole days before doing so?"

Clive agreed. There were a few possibilities, and as Clive's luck was currently on holiday, he leaned toward the lesser of the two options. "Either the magistrate is secretly rooting for Louissa's escape, or he is in her uncle's pocket and is waiting until whatever plans are afoot have played out. I am tending toward the latter, as the man does not appear the romantic sort," Clive scoffed.

"What plans?" Both men asked at the same time.

"Louissa spoke about one last job her uncle had for her, before she was to be carted off by her affianced. She did not give any details, and I have been pondering the possibilities since." Clive downed his drink and immediately wished he had brought the decanter with him. The men sat waiting for Clive to expound. However, if Clive put his fears to voice, would that make them so?

Scrubbing his hand over his face and through his hair, he stood and walked to the mantle. With his back turned, he continued, "As she was talking last night, I got a bad feeling. I began to think what if she was working with her uncle by choice? What if she knew her brother was alive, and she had been searching for his whereabouts so she could help her uncle bait a trap? She could have even used me as a means to an end." Saying the words out loud made his mouth taste vile. He didn't want to believe it, but if he didn't consider it, a young man could be in danger.

"Do you actually think it possible?" Rae asked.

"I have read accounts of men held hostage in the war, actually beginning to relate to their captors and switching sides. I can't assume a fragile young girl could not be persuaded," Clive explained.

Boyle stood and went to the mantle next to Clive, lit a cigarillo, throwing the match into the ashes of the fireplace, and clapped Clive on the shoulder. "What, my boy, does your gut and heart tell you?" He asked with concern in his voice.

"Best not to muddy the waters with emotion, wouldn't you agree?" Clive asked. If he had to dwell too much, he would easily talk himself out of thinking her capable of such. Would his father have eschewed facts and logic or emotion, and instinct?

"I would say, we have a young girl who has been forced most of her life to be stronger than most boys attending Eaton and she is owed a champion by now," Boyle answered.

"Breakerton," the Lord Advocate chimed in, "let us weed out the facts and legalities of it all. That is why we are here. We know you want justice served, and if we find that your Louissa is part and parcel of the matter, we will follow through, but until then, I would suggest you follow the course you started."

The vast library opened up and widened at his words. The very rafters, which only moments ago were so low they were weighing him down, soared skyward, and took with them the weight he had been carrying. They were correct. He could not be a champion for Louissa and try to ferret out the what and who of the treachery. "Thank you, gentlemen. In that case, no, I do not want to believe she is an accomplice for her uncle, but I do feel responsible for pulling Henry in closer to this than he was. But, if you are going to handle the details, I will be able to try to keep them both alive."

Clive made his way to his desk and opened the secret bottom pulling out all the evidence his aunt had collected and turned it over. The men moved to the large round worktable and settled in to study it. Clive excused himself to send another missive to Henry.

It was fortunate Louissa wasn't scared of her own death. It would be unfortunate for them both to feel as Clive did about the whole mess, blasted girl.

After much effort to concentrate, he could not get the magistrate's note out of his head. Something was not right. Clive found Nettie in the salon working on her embroidery, and hiding from their mother.

"I need you to visit Louissa and see that she is all right." Clive had been thinking about Louissa in between every other thought he had experienced. He made the decision that he had entirely too many thoughts throughout the day.

"I would love to call on Louissa. I was feeling the need to get some air. Have you found something that would tell you she was in danger?" Nettie looked up from her embroidery, concern clearly in her bright eyes. He loved that all his sisters were so magnanimous and would rather put others before their own needs. However, he would not pass along his message from the magistrate. He had begun to think that if orchestrated correctly, being incarcerated could very well save Louissa from herself.

"No, nothing of that sort," he hated admitting his argument, but knew Nettie would not let up. "We had a bit of a difference in opinion, so I fear she is not speaking with me currently."

The look Nettie gave him was one of complete exasperation. "What on Earth did you do now?"

"Why, dear sister, do you just assume it was I who misspoke?" He glared at her annoyed stare. She just remained silent, and continued to look at him as his nurse used to after some grand prank that ended badly. "You know that look is why you are yet to be married," he jested to his sister, still not wanting to admit anything.

"Really? And here I was sure it was the fact that there hasn't been a Lord worthy of all my best bits for the past two seasons. I should have conferred with you sooner. I might be in wedded bliss as we speak." He couldn't help but smile at his sister's cynical nature.

"Will you go?" He asked, hoping she would stop asking questions he didn't want to answer, because he wasn't sure how to respond. *Well my dear sister, you see when she left my bed last night, I tried to talk her out of committing suicide, but not before I accused her of working alongside her uncle and being a willing party to all that has conspired.*

"Yes, of course."

"Will you take Mary?" Clive asked, just realizing that he had not seen Mary all day. He would usually see her in the gardens wandering about the flowers, but not today.

"I will search for her, but I do not believe she is back yet," Nettie said offhandedly, finishing the row of delicate stitches on the piece she was working on.

"Back? Back from where?" Clive got an uneasy feeling. His neck prickled and a chill snaked down his spine.

"She and one of the maids went to the village early this morning to do some shopping. Mary was in need of some ribbons, and she wanted to find a new shawl. I am so happy she is finally shedding her widow's weeds. They were dreadfully depressing." She looked at Clive expectantly, but he only barely registered her words.

"Yes, fabulous. Do you know when she had planned on returning?"

"No, perhaps Mother knows."

"Fine, when will you leave to call on Louissa? It needs to be soon, Nettie."

"Within the hour. If you call for the carriage, it will be sooner." She set her needlework down and walked to him. She reached up on tiptoes and kissed him on the cheek, then left the room. Clive followed, giving a doorman the instruction to call for the carriage and headed back to his study where his guests had made themselves comfortable, complete with divesting themselves of their coats and cravats. As long as they were going to help solve this mess, they could work in the nude.

"Any luck?" Asked Clive as he made his way to the decanter and splashed a moderate amount into a glass. He was trying not to be concerned about Mary being missing. After all, there was no reason to be. Who would target a widow and her maid shopping for ribbons? He took a sip. Standing by the window, he waited for the heavy unease to shed like a heavy cloak, but it remained.

"Yes, as a matter of fact, these documents are just what we have been looking for. Who was it you said held them safe all this time?" Lord Boyle asked, looking at Clive over his spectacles with an almost cross-eyed stare.

"My Aunt Margaret," Clive answered.

"Margaret? Margaret of Loc Moore?" The Lord Advocate clarified.

"Yes. Were you familiar with her?" Clive asked, more to keep the conversation going than real interest. Most days, he would be happy to chat about his aunt's escapades, but today his mind overflowed with more pressing matters.

"Only her legacy," the Lord Advocate chuckled.

"So, what is our next move?" Clive asked hoping to move this along.

"Well, with what we have here, it would be well within our right to apprehend him and take him back to Edinburgh for arrest. Many of these charges go well beyond the bounds of the local magistrate. However, we do not have a large guard here and I believe it would be difficult to find men willing to stand against him."

The last of the statement was obvious and he couldn't blame them. The people in this area had to take care not to put their families in danger, but if the three of them were to ride up the drive and bang on the door, they were more than likely going to be killed for their efforts. "Wait, what if we found Henry and his ship? He has a full crew. Could you use them?"

"Well, yes that would work fine, but you don't have any idea where he is," reminded Lord Boyle.

"No, but in an emergency, I think I know where I can ask. It will take a bit. It is going to require a note sent, and then another note passed that." For once today, Clive set his glass down before it was empty. He went to his desk and scribbled a quick note to Nicholas. He would know how to find Henry. If he stressed the urgency, it might get back to them before nightfall. He folded and sealed the note, then called for the doorman to get a messenger.

After deciding there was nothing more the men could

Clair Brett

do, Clive put the papers back in the hiding place while his guests retired to their rooms to rest and freshen up.

There was a pressure swirling around Clive, taking the air from his lungs. He had once been swimming in the sea as a child, where he found a cave. He spent over an hour exploring, until all of a sudden the tides came in and water gushed unheeded into the space. Clive feared he would be crushed by the rushing water. Funny how this waiting swirls and thrashes him just as the waves did years ago.

CHAPTER TWENTY-ONE

"Are you chilled?" Louissa asked Nettie as they sat in the parlor with a tea tray between them, only the sound of the cups on the saucers breaking the silence. It had been obvious Clive sent his sister to--to do what? Check she was safe? Check she had not killed herself or possibly to check to see if she was planning his death? The latter had crossed her mind on her way home last night, but there wasn't enough poison for three of them, so she decided to spare the fool his life.

"No, I am perfectly comfortable. Are you chilled?" Nettie asked with her usual direct, but kind nature.

"I have been cold since I rose this morning. Perhaps I am coming down with something," Louissa said offhandedly, but the truth was she had gone cold when Breakerton had all but accused her of working willingly with her uncle, and it had yet to pass. The cold was one that is felt deep in the bones.

"Oh, I hate that feeling. I hate being cold. I often wish we lived in a more tepid clime, but alas, even London winters are frightfully chilly," Nettie agreed, obviously grabbing onto the only topic that had continued past one comment and one response.

Louissa sipped her tea, and couldn't help but drift again back to Clive with his sad accusing eyes, then to her uncle who informed her the job had been moved up to tonight, and then it would be over. His words not hers, but they were very apropos to what she knew to be true. Now the time had come, and she knew she would never again see her brother, and that her uncle would in all reason go unpunished for the crimes he committed against her family--his family. Louissa was so deep in thought, she hadn't realized the conversation fell off again, until Nettie put down her cup, leaned forward, and spoke.

"My dear, my brother is terribly worried over something, and I am prone to believe it has to do with you," she said leaning in to whisper, but Louissa scanned the room just in case there was a servant lurking about.

"He should have no reason to worry for me," Louissa

scoffed. She knew what they had was not something either of them planned to make permanent. He had asked for her hand, yes, but in truth, he hadn't actually meant it. It was playing at being the hero and they both knew it.

"I beg your pardon, but my brother is in love with you," Nettie said flatly, and Louissa couldn't catch the nervous laugh before it spilled out of her mouth.

"I know for certain that statement could not be further from the truth," she explained.

"Did he tell you he was not in love with you?" Nettie asked, then included, "In those words?"

Louissa opened her mouth to protest and say that yes, but then she realized they had never discussed his feelings, beyond his anger. "I am sure a man as important as your brother has more important matters than worrying about me. I am capable of tending to my own, Nettie."

Before Louissa could finish her statement, Nettie was laughing. So much so, she had to set her teacup on the table so not to spill. "My apologies, but my brother is not any more important than any other man, and to hear him labeled as such is almost farcical." She smiled and smoothed her skirt a bit reclaiming her calm. "I mean really, my brother as wonderful as he is, does little from what I can see on a day to day basis."

"Your brother is a very powerful man, Nettie." Louissa's cheeks burned at the declaration. Why did she care if Nettie felt her brother was less than important? It was nothing to her. But it was. Her need to come to Breakerton's defense churned in her chest. "My uncle feels threatened by him, and let me assure you that does not happen often. And, the Lords of the area have gone to him to protect them from the highwayman in the area. And, my uncle's man, Darius, told me that your brother had some very important guests who arrived this morning. He maintains his land holdings here in Scotland and his estates in England. Many people depend on your brother..." Louissa stopped in mid-sentence. She did not like the twinkle in her guest's eyes. "What?" She asked, not wanting an answer she would likely be embarrassed by.

"My dear, my brother loves you, because he sent me to check on you, and his only concern at the moment is your safety, and you love him, because when presented a less than complementary assessment of my brother, you were most ardent in your defense of him." Nettie held up a hand that lodged Louissa's protest in her throat, along with the thudding of her heart. "Whatever fool plan you have, please remember that you hold a more prized possession than any pirate could hope to obtain, my brother's heart." She reached across the table and took Louissa's hand in her own. It was warm and comforting. "It is the one thing my brother has never given to anyone."

"I..." Louissa was about to say that she would love to have the luxury of worrying about Clive's heart, but a commotion in the entry hall killed her excuse. Her uncle was home and not happy by the sound.

"Where in the bloody hell is Darius? Go find him!" Her uncle burst through the door after shouting his orders to whoever had had the misfortune of being in his view. This was not good. Louissa rose, knocking her teacup on the floor with a clank.

"Uncle, how are you? I believe you have met Lady Nettie, Lord Breakerton's sister?" She prompted, hoping to curb the full extent of her uncle's anger for the moment.

Her uncle harrumphed, but it came out more as a growl. Nettie, to her credit rose and walked over to Louissa's uncle, and curtsied. "Good afternoon, my lord. I hope you don't mind, I needed to take some air, and I just adore your niece, so I wandered here for some conversation."

Louissa stifled the giggle that rose and sat in her mouth. Her uncle was used to people scurrying and avoiding him, especially women. He was not accustomed to a woman like Nettie who seemed fearless in her demeanor and discourse. He took the hand that Nettie proffered and bowed slightly, then Louissa saw him think better of it, and he dropped her hand.

"Yes, well, 'tis time you leave. Louissa has duties she must attend. You may return at another time." His gruff stilted words showed a long unused civil behavior that Louissa felt took much from him to use.

"Oh, of course, my lord. It is no doubt time I returned. Breakerton will be wondering why I have been so long." She curtsied again, and bustled over to grab her shawl and reticule. She leaned in and hugged Louissa. The hug lasted a bit longer than necessary, because Louissa did not want to let her go. In her ear, Nettie whispered, "All will be well. Clive will see to it." With that, she breezed out of the room. Louissa's heart wanted to soar out of her chest forcing her to fight down a frustrated cry and bite back tears. She so wanted Nettie's words to be true, but--

"What in bloody hell is going on around here?" Her uncle bellowed once Nettie was gone disturbing Louissa's dangerous train of thought. "Doesn't everyone understand tonight is what we have all been working toward?"

"Sorry," she apologized to her uncle, not wanting to increase his ire, "but I felt it would have been foolish to turn her away. No need to bring more suspicion to us than necessary. Correct?" She had not been expecting Nettie, so she wasn't lying. Her uncle must have agreed, because he just grunted and walked to the other end of the room to a servant's door and opened it, as he bellowed again for Darius. "Where is that idiot?"

He turned then, all eyes on Louissa. "You need to get ready. Are you packed?" He barked at her.

"Yes."

"Then get suited up. I'll have someone grab your trunk and bring it to the ship," he continued with no emotion at all.

She knew it would do her no good, but she had to make one last plea, "Uncle, please, I don't…"

"Quiet Lass. Now is not the time to be whining about what you want. You are my property, and 'tis time I am well rid of you.

Now, Ewin Dermit's debt will be paid, and I will get rid of you at the same time. 'Tis about time."

"He is dangerous," she protested.

"Aye, I know. 'Tis why I want to be rid of him." He made no connection to the fact to get himself out of danger that he was throwing her into it.

"He will kill me."

"Well, then I would suggest trying to be the meek wife, better than you were the agreeable niece. If he forgets ye are afoot, until he wants to remember ye twill go better for ye."

And that was all the advice she was going to get from her uncle. He rose and made his way back into the hall where he again yelled for Darius. She listened to his footsteps recede. She remained on the settee, considering what her uncle said. She was certain that was not the advice Clive would give Nettie on her wedding day. That one sentence from her uncle summed up her entire relationship with the man. Louissa brushed unshed tears from her eyes. She would not allow this man to take what dignity she had. She would not cry for a family that was never destined to be.

She would don her highwayman garb one more time. Ride to the Milton Road one more time. Fight for herself one more time. Then she would die. That had been her destiny all along. She silently made her way to her room to dress--one last time.

CHAPTER TWENTY-TWO

Clive was not a patient man on a good day. One trait his father's solicitors liked to use as an example of his many shortcomings when it came to reflecting his father's greatness. If there was, a time that was appropriate for not having patience, Clive was certain today was the day. After speaking candidly with his mother, or more aptly, being spoken to by his mother, he was feeling more comfortable with the idea that his father was just a man doing the best he could, which according to his mother was not perfect consistently. And, considering Breakerton was certain he was treading in unfamiliar water for most Lords of the realm, he decided he was doing as expected.

Before the doorman could open the front door fully, Clive was out of his chair and into the foyer when the rap came. He was certain it would be a missive from Henry, stating all was well and he would be at the manor post haste.

It was not.

Instead, a bevy of grumbling, graying, Scottish Lairds with their various hats, walking sticks, coats, etc., all demanding attentions from the one sorry doorman, who looked as confused and perplexed as any Clive had seen.

"Gentlemen, I will have to stop you there. I have guests and am not able to attend you at this time." Clive's attempt at keeping his temper seemed to be working, until one of the more overbearing and underwhelming men stepped up and poked a finger at Clive.

"See here, Breakerton, we will not be ignored. You were given a job to do and you failed miserably. We demand recompense for your inability to produce."

Clive drew in a deep breath and made another attempt at being civil. "Ah, Laird McKinley, I can see you are shaken. Can I have a maid bring you a chair and some tepid tea? That always aids my mother in calming her nerves when they get the better of her." *Well, perhaps civil was a bit out of his reach at the moment.*

Just as Clive thought Laird McKinley would turn more of a puce than a red color, before he exploded, Laird Westmont spoke up. "We are not here for a social call, as I am sure you are aware, Lord Breakerton. We have stopped by on our way to Loc Landon manor to witness the apprehension of Louissa Adair."

"That is Lady Louissa to you," Clive reminded them.

Westmont continued unaware of the dangerous tone in Clive's voice. "She has been proven to be the criminal whose apprehension you were put to ascertain, of which you were not able to complete and therefore failed."

"You are aware, are you not, that the young woman in question is an heiress?" Clive asked, with barely restrained brutality in his voice. He knew it, because three of the other men stepped back, closer to the door.

"We are aware that she is nothing more than a criminal, who was raised in such an unseemly situation that no one could expect her to be anything but a thief or a harlot," the man continued, obviously unaware of the danger he was in.

"She is an heiress, nonetheless, and must be given the protection under the law as such." Clive hoped his goading would force the man to say something, without realizing who Clive's guests were.

The sound the man made was of utter disgust and sent spittle spraying through the air. "She does not deserve any such protection, and since our magistrate is paid very well to mete out the law as we see fit, I would predict she will see the gallows by sunrise, if not earlier."

Westmont's face fell a fraction, when he saw the smile cut across the stark plains of Clive's face. Clive was sure the poor bastard had no idea what he had just done.

"Very interesting," came a voice from just inside the study, and then a body appeared to prove that Clive had done the right thing. "Now, tell me again, sir, how the law in this region works? We would not want to be traveling home and find ourselves in a mess, now would we?"

"That is Laird. Laird Westmont, and I'll ask who in bloody

hell are you?"

"Oh, no one of consequence, my laird," Rae, Lord Advocate answered.

"Well, then I would suggest you travel very carefully. Our laws are strict and punishments are harsh and quick in being dealt."

"Is that so?" Rae prompted.

Clive noted that the men in the back, those who had yet to speak were having quite a lively discussion. One of the men kept pointing toward Rae and gesturing. Clive took a step back, leaning against the wall. He wanted to give the scene plenty of breathing room, and he didn't want to miss a single second. Just as Westmont would have opened his mouth to speak again, the man who had obviously recognized Sir Rae, put a staying hand on Westmont, and stepped forward.

"I may be mistaken, but aren't you the Lord Advocate, Sir Rae?" He asked.

Rae swept into an elegant bow. "Why, yes I am, My Laird. And you would be?"

"Lakey, Laird Lakey," he introduced himself and bowed as well.

Clive could see Westmont turning the same puce color that McKinley currently was.

"Have we been introduced?" Sir Rae asked, shaking Lakey's hand.

"Yes, yes we were. Last year, I was in Edinburgh on business and was invited to a dinner party that you attended as well."

"Right, right. Lord Ashby's dinner. Now I remember," Rae said jovially, ignoring Westmont and McKinley for the moment. "Good chap, Ashby."

"Yes, very personable fellow I found," Lakey agreed. Clive loved the peevish expression on the man. The two still in the back of the crowd inched again closer to the door, and refused to make eye contact with Clive or the Lord Advocate.

"Well, very nice to make your acquaintance again," Rae said, and turned once more toward Westmont.

"Laird Westmont, I am intrigued about this alternative form of justice, where a Lady can be arrested on the order of a group of lairds and hung without due process. I am riveted."

Clive could not stifle a cough to mask his need to bark with laughter. One thing his father's men always told him about his father was that he surrounded himself with powerful people. Perhaps he was not so far removed from the paragon that was his father after all. Westmont sputtered and backtracked, trying to find a way out. When no apparent answer came to him, he puffed up to his entire six feet, considering Clive in all his years of coming to the country to visit his aunt could not remember a time the man didn't hunch over leaning on his cane, Clive thought it a grand effort.

All of a sudden, Clive could feel the small foyer closing around the men who invaded his home to gloat about killing a woman who needed saving instead. Clive mused as he tuned out Westmont and McKinley, as he had begun an attempt to bully Scotland's highest judicial official, he had considered remodeling the front of the manor to accommodate a larger more grand entrance. After today, he quite liked the cozy feel of the entry, and he would elect to keep it small and cramped as to trap dirty vermin such as these men when they attempted to overtake his home.

"I have sent a letter to your magistrate ordering him to collect Lady Louissa, but to hold her safe until such time I can see the claims against her and I will decide on a course of action, gentlemen, not you. I also think it is time that I send some people down to look into how Scottish law is being handled in this community. I have a feeling you in particular, will not like what we uncover."

"Now, see here," bolstered McKinley, "you have no right speaking to us as you are. We are lairds!" He bellowed, hinting at the fact that Rae had only the title of Sir and was much lower on the social ladder.

Clair Brett

"Laird McKinley, I will be sure to remember my place, if we ever attend a ball together, which I do not believe I will have to worry about that, but right here, right now, my position gives me the right to apprehend you and have you shipped to Edinburgh for further questioning. So you should take care."

At that point, Lord Boyle made his presence known as he stepped into the smallish space next to his counterpart.

"Good afternoon gentlemen, I would like to introduce myself. I am Lord Boyle, the Lord Justice Clerk," he intoned with all the respect he would demand. "Is there a problem?"

These men, Clive would be inviting back, perhaps for the hunt in the fall. Clive noted the man, still holding silent in the back, turned and simply left. As if sensing the air circulation, or the fact that their support had just thinned, McKinley turned in time to see their backs and coat tails. He blanched.

"I am certain Sir Rae and I will be able to sort this all out without difficulty. I am also certain that you men, men of honor no doubt, would not want a lady to be unjustly punished for a crime." None of the three left spoke. They clearly understood the threat in the words.

"Tis out of our hands, Boyle. The order has been sent and the magistrate has already left to see the deed done," Westmont said, with a bit too much pompous air for Clive. He pushed from the wall, and was toe to toe with Westmont before the air could change.

"Westmont, I want you to understand exactly what I mean from what I am about to say. If something happens to Lady Louissa, you will for the rest of your life have to know that I will not cease until you are adequately punished for the harm you have caused. That goes for all of you." He made a point to look each man in the eye. "Also, you should be aware that Henry Adair is alive. Once he claims his inheritance, I will be happy to have long discourse with him to explain how the lairds in the community were less than protective of one of their own. I will also let them know that they were in a way responsible for all Lady Louissa has had to endure, considering none had a strong enough constitution to speak on her behalf to her uncle."

If Westmont could go from puce to white any quicker, Clive doubted he would survive the act.

"Now, Get. Out. Of. My. House," Clive ground out, showing how tightly wound his control was. He would love to call to the dogs and have them give chase, but didn't want them eating tainted meat. The men bowed to the two most powerful men in the Scottish judicial system, eyed Clive with a good amount of fear, and left without a word.

Clive's arm clenched around his scar, making him realize he had been clenching his fists so tightly it was causing cramps. In the last couple of days, he had almost forgotten his injury. He absently massaged the ache.

"Now, what?" Asked Boyle.

"We do what I have been doing for the past month or more. Save a damsel in distress, who doesn't wish to be rescued." The bitterness of it burned his tongue, but regardless of her desire to die, he left to dress for a battle. It was at this moment that he realized when he died, it would be because of a woman. Lord help him.

As Clive and the officials rode up to the manor not an hour later, he knew immediately that he would not find Louissa there. As they knocked on the door and waited, there was no sign of the magistrate, but the drive was littered with horse hooves and carriage tracks, so it was impossible to tell. After an eternity, the door was opened by a woman, whose eyes were ringed red with shed tears. Panic raced up his spine and squeezed his brain. "Is Lady Louissa at home?" He asked with as much calm as he could muster.

"Lady Louissa rode out some time ago, Milord, just as I told the magistrate when he come lookin' for her," she said, and then hiccuped a sob.

"Her uncle, is he about? Did he know the magistrate was here?"

She shook her head almost losing her cap. She was unable to speak now.

"Thank you." Clive made his way back to the horses and the officials.

"She had ridden out before he got here." His words were forced, as his lungs had constricted. The magistrate would have known where to look, and she would be like a rose bush on the cliffs. Exposed and very visible.

"We must go," he said as he mounted and tore out of the yard. There would be no reason to think they would be there in time to save her, but he had to try. The Lord Advocate's men had arrived not long after the lairds' visit, and they were back at Clive's awaiting instructions. If they were not able to stop the arrest, they would go back and mount a prison break. It still bothered him that he had not gotten word from Henry. That left a very dangerous feeling that Clive could not fully grasp, but his attention had to be on Louissa at present. Henry was a grown man, and admittedly had dealt with more in life than Clive's sheltered upbringing would have allowed, so whatever mess he was embroiled, Clive had to believe he was equipped to handle it.

At the Milton Road, where he first encountered a plucky, brave, highwaywoman, the open space was empty. Clive dismounted, walked to the center of the road and listened. Waves, trees rustling in the sea breeze, a horse snorting. "She was here," he said and bolted for the trees, where she would have tied her horse, and sure enough, the beast stood, tied to the tree she used as a hitching post. He was not happy if his head shaking and hoof stomping were any indication. Then he saw a spot close by, trampled down and disturbed. They had her, but it appeared she put up a fight. Damn it. Was it too much to have one thing go right for him in this whole bloody mess. He unhitched the horse and led it back to the road. He would tie it to his and bring it back to the manor with him.

Just as the men were readying to turn and leave, a whistle

came from the other side of the road. Clive recognized the sound as the signal Louissa gave the night she was being overtaken and no one came. Clive dismounted and handed the reins to Lord Boyle. "I'll be but a moment."

In the thicker, denser side of the road as soon as Clive stepped into the bushes, his visibility became poor. He listened again for the whistle and followed the sound. Darius stood in a small opening. Clive knew Gareth's man from his few encounters. His guard went up even more.

"Darius, what are you playing at?" Clive asked, unsure at this point, who was on which side. It seemed to him that the local law enforcement were the bad guys and the guardian was the evil villain. The only trustworthy lot were the sidekicks and the privateers.

"I know you have every belief that I am for Laird Gareth, but in reality, I work for Henry. I am sure he said he had an inside man. Well, I am that man."

Clive was impressed. To have someone inside and as close to Gareth as Darius seemed, it was a good trick, if he were telling truth. "And what of it? I have to find Louissa—"

"Louissa has been taken to the magistrate's private home. I heard him say he would put her in a shed under lock and key, but I was not in a position to help her right now, and felt if she was not about, it would be safer in the end for her. I have to worry about Henry. He has been taken by his uncle."

"Balls!" Clive ground out. "When?"

"This morning. He snuck into the village to meet..."

"To meet who?" Clive did not like the feeling he was getting, not one bit, but he knew what Darius was going to say, before he said it.

"Your sister, Lady Landsdown."

"Mary," her name escaped Clive's lips with an exasperation and tiredness that settled on him

"Yes, they have been meeting often. Never in the same place

or at the same time, but Gareth had gotten wind that Henry was close."

"Where?"

"On Henry's ship. Gareth took it over as soon as Henry was out of sight of the vessel this morning. He has also found out that Ewin Dermit is actually Henry."

"Louissa's betrothed?" Clive knew Henry said he had things well in hand, and it appeared he did, until he began smelling around Mary's skirts and got careless. Little did he know, his sister had plans to kill him once he took her, until Clive warned him earlier. "How do we rescue them?"

Darius's jaw clenched and made the shadows take on a stark impression on his face. "I am not sure. His men are in the hold and Laird Gareth moved his crew onto the ship. I would assume Mary and Henry are in one of the quarters, but it is impossible to know which one. Then there is Louissa. If someone doesn't keep watch, that fool could hang her before a judge can be summoned."

"Does Gareth suspect you or are you still trusted?"

"He has no idea. He is too pompous even to consider such a thing."

"Good." Clive began pacing, trying to put the pieces together. "We need to know where they are. Can you get on the ship and signal us about where they are being held? You could hang a rope to either the left or right of the boarding plank. To the left means they are on the dock side, and to the right means on the water's side."

"That sounds doable. There are three quarters running the length of each side. Two smaller ones for the officers on each side and a larger one for the crew. The captain's quarter is in the bow of the vessel, but Gareth will be in there searching for anything that could incriminate him."

"Good, meanwhile, I need to get to Louissa and get her somewhere safe. For a woman who doesn't need protecting, she seems to have a lot of men who want her dead."

Darius laughed. "Was a good day when I saw you step up. She is not an easy lass to look out for that is true. I have told Henry on more than one occasion, she was just a version of him, all be it a much prettier one."

Clive smiled at that. He was beginning to think he was the only one trying to protect someone who did not want protection. It was refreshing to know he was not alone in his frustrations. The men finalized their plan and parted ways. As Clive made his way back to the horses, he had a plan in place.

They rode back to his manor to brief the men waiting, and then sent the officials ahead to keep the magistrate busy with a laundry list of allegations he would have to answer. A handful of the men would accompany Boyle and Rae, and for back up, the rest would make their way to the wharf. Clive was thankful that Henry did not lay anchor near the beach, as he would have when it was time to meet with his uncle as his alternate self, Dermit. Storming the ship would have been infinitely more difficult. They would wait for Darius's signal and hopefully liberate the ship with few casualties. Clive was happy with the plan. It was a solid plan. However, he had come to learn where Louissa and her brother were concerned, there was no such thing as easy. He decided, as he rode to free the woman he now could not deny that he loved, he planned to keep her tied to his bed for at least a fortnight once this was over, and he would like nothing better than to imprison Mary and Henry in a turret somewhere. He was afraid Mary would enjoy that too much however. Blasted women.

CHAPTER TWENTY-THREE

The magistrate's home was a well-kept modest brick manor with three stories and a gate out front. He noted that Rae and Boyle had tied their horses to the gate, and one of their men stood at the front door. He couldn't see the other men, but knew they were close at hand.

He turned down the lane running along the property border, until he spotted the back of the shed in question. It looked damp, dirty, and dark. The horse shook his head to protest Clive's tensing muscles. Perhaps the magistrate should be housed in that blasted pit while waiting for his trial, Clive thought.

He dismounted and moved his horse out of sight. Careful not to be seen from the house, he skirted the perimeter of the property in the trees and behind the shrubs, until he was next to the out building. He was very glad that the door had been placed facing away from the house, because he would be able to work the lock and argue with Louissa about her ideas of not needing rescuing as he did so without being spotted.

He broke out of his cover right in front of the wide open door. Louissa was gone, if she had ever been in the shed to begin with. What if that was just a story the magistrate let out to keep others from freeing her, or what if he did as Darius said and dispatched her without calling for a judge.

Clive's vision shifted and blurred. He saw red. This woman had become part of him in the last month. No way was she was allowed to die, and may the gods help the man who attempted to take her from him. With no concern about being seen, Clive prowled up the lawn directly for the house. Two men stepped out of the trees as he neared, but one staying hand from Clive put them back into their hiding places.

The door was not locked and Clive had no patience for knocking, so he stalked through the house following the raised voices. The cook peeked out of a doorway, squeaked at the sight of Clive and scurried back into the room. If he looked on the outside the way he felt on the inside, he would scare small children and animals he was certain. Lord help him if he got hold of this fool and found out he killed Louissa. He would not be seeing jail time, because he would break the man in half with his bare hands, then hand each of the highest officials in Scotland a piece of the bastard.

"Where is she?" He bellowed as he erupted into the small parlor. He saw nothing but the magistrate and was on him before the man could take a step out of the way. "Where is she? You have one opportunity to speak, before I rip out your tongue," Clive ground out, pinning the man by the throat against a desk that was set against the wall. Clive was certain a month ago, he would have lost an honest fight to this larger more experienced man, but today, his fear and rage made him a more formidable enemy. He watched the man open his mouth, and then close it repeatedly.

He felt a hand on his shoulder and Boyle's voice in his ear. "He cannot speak with you crushing his windpipe." He felt Boyle gently pull his arm away as the magistrate slid to the floor. He allowed Boyle to guide him back, but only far enough to allow the magistrate room to sit up, but not stand.

"I—I left her," his eyes darted from Boyle and Rae to Clive and back, obviously looking for an ally in the room. Clive grabbed the man under the chin and forced his head back to him.

"I am not a man with an abundance of patience on a good day. Today is not playing out to be a good day for either of us."

The man sputtered and looked like he might be sick, but rallied and dug out an answer. "The shed. I—I left her in the shed, out back."

"Yes, that is the story I was told. However, the shed is empty."

The man paled and might have fallen to the ground, if there had been enough room between Clive and the desk. "No, no that is impossible. When I returned to the house after locking the door, she was shouting some very foul things at me. There is no way she could get to the lock to open it. No way."

The fool was stammering, but correct. Clive was well aware Louissa could not have freed herself. So the question was if he did in fact put her there, who took her out? He leaned into the magistrate so close he could smell the man's breath, which was laced with strong Scottish Whiskey. He was certain they would be drunker than he was before nightfall. "If anything happens to that girl, anything that I feel would have not happened had she not been taken by you, I will be back. Know this, if I come back, there is nothing these men or the whole weight of the Scottish government can do to protect you."

He gave the man one last shove, then turned to Boyle and Rae. "I agree she is crafty, but there was no way she would be able to get to the lock. Someone either freed her or took her."

"What can we do?" Rae asked, concern clear in his voice.

"I am going back to her house to see if she may have fled there. I doubt it though. Then, I will head to the ship."

"I agree," said Boyle. "Right now, we must deal with what is in front of us, and perhaps rescuing her brother will give us an advantage when we do find her."

Clive agreed, but didn't like his options. Every nerve in his body screamed to find Louissa, but he had to think about Mary. His sister had seen so much death in her life. Part of his guilt with Mary is that he was not honest with her about Henry. She had asked, and Clive simply dictated that she was to stay away from him. Thinking back, Clive could see what his ego would not allow him to then. She had been married. She was a grown woman, a widow. She had no intention of following orders from her little brother. She was a woman grown, but she was his sister, and she now needed her little brother to be the man he needed to be and set aside a foolish hunt for the woman he loved, when he had no place to start.

He felt a stinging behind his eyes, but held the tears at bay. When all this began, he promised himself he would be her champion, but feared his responsibility to keep his family safe would threaten his promise. He sorely hoped this was not the case.

He left the men to finish with the magistrate and headed back the way he came. His heartbeat pounded in his ears in time with the galloping strides of the horse. Once in the yard, he didn't even wait for the horse to come to a complete stop, before he was off and running to the door. The same maid looked shocked and a bit scared when she opened the door to Clive, but said that no one had returned to the manor.

He left without a word, because the only words he could muster were not meant for mixed company. Back on his horse, he turned toward the wooded trail leading to the main road and then to the wharf in the village. As he crested the knoll of the road looking down at the wharf, he saw the ship with a piece of rope dangling from the right side of the gangplank. They were on the waterside of the ship.

He made his way to the appointed overlook spot and found all of the men waiting, plus every single one of the males in his employ. All of them. The emotion almost rose forth without control. Then a lucid thought. It was a very good thing he had taken the time to send his mother and Nettie back to his sister's home when Nettie returned earlier, as there would be no one at his manor to serve as protectors for them.

One of the men from Boyle's group came to him and began updating him. "Milord, I hope you don't mind, but your own men were not standing down."

"No, no that is fine. I had not intended to put them in harm's way however."

"It is my experience that when men are loyal to their employer they willingly put themselves there anyway," the man said. He appeared to be of a similar age to Clive, but his eyes showed that he had witnessed that of a man twice their age.

"And you are?" Breakerton asked, not able to keep his eyes off the ship.

"Daniel, Milord."

"Daniel? Daniel what?" Clive asked.

"All you need to know is Daniel, my lord," he answered with a comforting smile that held an edge.

"Very well, Daniel, what are we looking at?" Clive moved on.

"There appears to be a full crew on board, but they all seem to be loyal to Laird Gareth. The real crew is most likely in the hold as your friend said, or dead. It has been very calm and quiet since we arrived. However, about an hour and a half ago, two men brought in a woman bound at the ankles and wrists, and gagged."

"Louissa." Clive wasn't sure if he should be happy she had been located, or utterly broken with fear that she was in the thick of it. "Was she unconscious?"

The man laughed, "Ah, not in the least. I wasn't close enough to make out what she was trying to say, but she was managing to yell at them even through the gag, and she thrashed enough that she kicked the one carrying her legs off balance enough that he dropped her and stumbled. She was not making their job easy."

"Good." He felt the band constricting his lungs and heart ease a bit. She was hale enough only an hour and a half ago to still fight. "We add her to our list of people to rescue." It wasn't a question and Daniel understood that. "Do we have enough to take the ship?" Clive asked looking at the small sea of men hunkered down around him.

"Bodies, yes, fighting ability, I am not sure," the man admitted.

Clive did not want to sit by and wait for Gareth to make a move. If he already knew Dermit was actually Henry and his deal would go south, he would not react well to that news. However, if he had not made the connection yet, they might have a chance when he moved out for his meeting. "Do we wait and hope he isn't wise to Henry's duplicity, or do we move soon?" Clive asked Daniel.

"I would like to send someone closer, perhaps to over hear any discussions."

"How?"

"Well, we have a young man in our company that has in the past served in the capacity of beggar or street vendor. He is willing to approach the ship with a tray of food for sale. He feels that they would allow him on board."

"What if they choose not to allow him to leave?"

Daniel smiled a very sinister smile, "Well, then I will feel sorry for them if they try to keep him there. He is much more than he appears."

"Where again, did Sir Rae and Lord Boyle find you?" Clive had a feeling it was not from a tavern or boxing establishment.

"If they did not tell you, my lord, I am not at my leisure to divulge such information." He clapped Clive on the back and made his way over to a man, boy really, of no more than ten and seven if Clive could make that assumption. When Daniel gave him the news, his smile stretched across his face and widened. He jumped up and disappeared down the road.

Clive settled in, watching the ship for any signs of life. There were a few men cleaning the deck and keeping guard, but no signs of anyone of import. Mary would be beside herself, he figured, in a strange place, with no one to look out for her. She was never put in such a predicament. She was a lady bred and raised after all. Then, his thoughts went to Louissa. She was angry with him, and she had good reason to be. He accused her of working with her uncle to find and kill her brother and that was after he had bedded her. She made it clear she wanted nothing more to do with him, and as much as it pained him to think about it, even if he saved her, she might still harbor hatred toward him. It would be well deserved.

He loved her. He knew that now, and frankly, wasn't sure why it took him so long to understand that. He probably decided she was the love of his life on the ride home after she stabbed him with her sword, but it took until now. All his sisters and even his mother at times had made it clear to him that men could be addled in the head and worthless. Now he believed he understood, and he agreed.

He would save Louissa. He owed her that, and if it were entirely possible, he would see to it that her brother was saved as well, and given his rightful place as head of the family with her uncle led away to the gallows. He would see her an heiress by midnight, if that was the last act of love he showed her. Even if she chose to walk away after that, he would learn to live without her. He would have to.

Clive and the others watched as the young man that they sent to find information made his way onto the ship and began conversing and milling about the deck. After a time, he left with a big wave and smile to the men. Now, it was just the waiting. Clive hated the waiting. He wanted to act.

Once back, the boy came straight to Daniel, who was with Clive.

"Not the brightest lot." The boy went on, "I was able to overhear they are getting ready to move at dusk. One said something about needing to bring the carriage around. There was also talk of the brat."

"They must be referring to your Louissa," Daniel pointed out. Clive nodded, not liking that they called her a brat, or that Daniel was so quick to pick up on it, but if he were having to contend with Louissa in a fit of anger, that might be a word to consider.

"I assumed as much. I could hear someone screaming insults from below deck. Some, I will be honest, were a bit colored even for me." He smiled, obviously impressed by Louissa's extended vocabulary.

"Any word of the others?" Clive asked needing a full breakdown, so to make a plan for all those involved.

"Yes, I overheard someone ask. The plan is to dispatch them once at sea and dump the bodies, but they said Gareth would be doing it to make sure it was done this time."

"How many will be left when Gareth disembarks for his

meeting?" Daniel asked.

"I didn't hear the exact number, but got the impression that most of the men would be leaving with Gareth and they would come back later to set sail with Henry's ship."

Daniel thanked the boy and sent him to get some food and drink. Clive sat back against the tree he had claimed and waited for Daniel to speak. He did seem to have more experience than Clive did about executing such endeavors.

"Well, I am concerned about what will happen with Louissa when her uncle gets to his designated meeting and there is no Dermit to be found. If as you say, Dermit is actually Henry, then the meeting cannot take place."

"Correct," Clive agreed.

"Our men should easily be able to overtake those left on the ship and rescue Henry and your sister. I am not so sure how to proceed with Louissa. If we allow them to get there, she will be in danger."

"She will no longer have any worth," Clive stated what Daniel was trying to ease into.

"Yes."

"Also, we are not familiar with the terrain of that area. We would be at a disadvantage."

"What if we waited to attack once they brought Louissa above deck and off the ship? The men would be divided, plus any men left to guard Henry and Mary would no doubt be called up to help the rest, leaving Mary and Henry alone."

"Promising."

"If we had a small dinghy, would it be feasible to send a couple of men to the starboard side to climb up and free them?"

"This could work. How delicate is your sister's constitution?"

"What do you mean?"

"I am going to assume that Henry, being a captain of the ship is not adverse to heights or water, so climbing out of the window and down a rope would not bother him, but is your sister able?"

Clive thought about Mary. Poor fragile, delicate Mary. Had she always been that way? No, she was just as reckless as the rest of his sisters when she was young. Clive guessed he had begun to see her as fragile after the funeral of her husband. Perhaps she had not changed, but he made her into something that had to be taken care of in order to do penitence for what he felt was his part in her husband's death. "No, I think Mary will be fine. She is a very strong girl."

"Good, now the only question, where do you wish to be? In the boat or at the carriage?" Clive was grateful to Daniel for not barking orders at him. He had a heavy stake in both operations, but since he had not grown up climbing ropes as much as he had reading about sums and figures, and how to conjugate Latin verbs, he would be best suited at the carriage.

"I will be in the way on the dinghy. Not to mention, if I get my hands near Henry, I just might kill him myself for getting my sister involved in this," he pointed out.

"Very well, I will man the dinghy and take one other man with me. You will lead the charge at the carriage."

It was also decided that Phillip, Clive's driver and a handful of his livery would waylay the carriage and put Phillip as the driver. The plan was to try to wait until they put Louissa inside, then to drive the horses, getting her out of danger as quickly as possible. It would also stop her from wanting to jump into the fray as soon as she was rescued. Clive personally instructed Phillip not to stop said carriage until he was at the front door of his manor.

Clive's group of men made their way about thirty minutes until dusk toward the wharf. They would hang back in the shadows or behind crates until Clive gave the call. Clive donned a cape and wide brimmed hat taken from one of the houses close to the look out. With a disuse, it would allow him to get much closer to the carriage before he was recognized. He was looking forward to feeling Laird Gareth's jaw crack against the force of his fist. He flexed his fingers and tightened his hand into a fist just for practice.

Clive now appreciated all those fool theatricals his sisters forced him to partake in as a defenseless lad in a house filled with women. He meandered toward the ship in a lazy, drunken fashion, planting himself just left of the gangplank. As the sun began to dip below the horizon, a carriage came rambling up the alongside the ship. Clive held his breath. If Phillip and his livery were unsuccessful in taking the rig, then their plan would not work and they would be found out. He managed a surpassed glance toward the carriage acting the unaware drunkard, and there in the driver's seat was Phillip, a broad smile on his face and a large bruise beginning to color his right eye. Just then, the ship seemed to come alive.

"Unhand me, ye idiot!" He heard Louissa's voice rise above the creak of the ship and guide ropes. Her voice was that of an angel, "Untie me, or I'll knock ye on yer arse." A fowl mouthed one, but still an angel.

"Will ye get her in the carriage before she does escape," barked Gareth as he too made his way on deck. "Tie her to the grab bar inside. We wouldn't want her falling out on her way to meet her fiancé," he joked, and all the other men laughed. As the man roughly handed Louissa down the gangplank, he could see in her face that the events of the day were taking a toll. She was pale. She probably paled more at the mention of her fiancé, of whom she was petrified.

No one bothered to take any notice of a drunkard in the middle of such a scene, so Clive made his way closer to the horses with the carriage. It took the man some time to force Louissa into the carriage. Clive was certain that the doorway could not have been big enough for the man, as he pushed and twisted trying to get her through the door. Finally, with a loud grunt, he muscled her in. A moment later, a bellow of pain could be heard from within the carriage and the young man came out holding the side of his head.

"She bit me ear!" he yelped. "When I bent ta tie her hands to the bar, she bit me ear. She's a witch I tell ye!" Clive tried to stifle a laugh. Even tied she was unruly.

The moment the man shut the door and took a step toward the ship, Phillip lashed the reins and yelled, while Clive helped by slapping the lead horse in the arse. The carriage bolted forward and out of sight in a moment. Clive took no time in getting back to the gangplank. He reached it in time to reach out his arm tripping Gareth as he ran down to try to stop the carriage. He went down with the thud and a curse. By the time he was able to lift his head, which was bleeding from a healthy cut above his right eye, Clive had divested himself of his disguise.

"You." Laird Gareth recognized him and the game was on.

All around Clive, fists flew. He had not heard any gunshots, and for that, he was thankful. Gareth bounded down the ramp, but Clive was ready and landed the first blow, sending his opponent back a few steps. Clive knew he was not fully invested in the fight, because he kept trying to spy a boat with Mary and Henry. The first blow, he didn't see coming, connected with his right eye, sending shards of sharp pain to the center of his skull. His vision blurred, as to be expected and his hearing actually dulled as well.

He was able to hear a loud hurrah as he assumed Henry's men had been freed from the hold and they were mixing into the fray. How they would know whom they should fight was beyond Clive's capacity to logic out at that point. He danced around and delivered another solid blow to Gareth's chest making him gasp for air.

From the corner of his eye, he thought he saw the dinghy round the bow of the ship, but he was distracted as one of Gareth's men jumped in where his employer had stepped aside. The blighter had a sword and went at Clive's mid-section. Clive stumbled back, tripped over a rock and went down with a grunt. The man was on him before he could get up. The tussle was not one Clive would lose, but if he could tire the man a bit, it would be better when he rolled him. Just as Clive would have lunged up and overtaken the bastard, a swish of skirt and something yelled about a baby brother and the man was gone.

Clive looked around and realized his delicate sister, the widow, had landed a sound kick to the middle of his attacker and was now the one on top of him hitting him about the head. Her victim, too disorientated to fight back, tried to cover his skull to save it from being beaten.

"Mary!" Clive yelled, but to no avail. So instead, he looked around for Henry as he made his way to his feet. Henry soon came running past, tipping his hat to Clive on the way, and with no words, lifted Mary off her battered assailant, and began to carry her off.

"Hey," Clive yelled to stop Henry. Mary was squirming and protesting, but would not find a quarter in Henry's strong hold. "Get her out of here! She needs to be safe!" He demanded, not even looking at Mary.

His lack of acknowledgment did not stop her from speaking directly to her brother, however, "I am a woman grown. I am a widow, and therefore responsible for my own life now. You," she squirmed more and set deadly serious eyes on Clive as well, "have no right to demand I leave anywhere."

"You are correct, and you have my permission to be angry with me from now until eternity, but my motive is to have you alive so that you might make my life rather difficult in retribution for my sins. So you will be leaving, or I will have you locked up in the hold again," he said, making sure Henry understood, which he indicated with a nod. Then he went back to try to find Gareth who had disappeared.

The fighting had lessened and with the added manpower of Henry's crew, they were collecting what few men of Gareth's employ were still standing and seen in the growing darkness. It appeared the battle had been won, but Clive was not satisfied. What had seemed like minutes had been hours in truth, as the moon shone well into the sky. Laird Gareth had been glimpsed only briefly, and then was gone, but where? Then at the top of the trail, he saw him. For only a brief moment, but it was enough. He had stolen a horse and he was headed away from the fray.

Clive's next thought froze him with a terror so fierce he thought he might never move again.

Louissa.

The bellow came from his body. The force of it knocked him into motion, running toward Henry, but keeping his head turned to make sure he knew the direction the braggart was heading, not that he needed visual confirmation. "He's fled. Your uncle has fled. He's going for Louissa!"

Henry, handed Mary off to a man, gave some directions and ran to Clive.

"How do you know?" Henry asked, showing how young and unknowledgeable of men like his uncle he actually was. He might have helped the Crown round up smugglers all along the coast, but he never spent time trying to understand them.

"He will see her as the cause of this, because of me, and because he has blamed her for some time of being a burden he wished to be rid of. He knows he's lost by our hands, but in order to punish us, he is going to take the one thing we have both been fighting for. Louissa.

"Bloody hell," Henry said and picked up speed. They mounted the hill and grabbed the closest two horses. They had no chance of catching him before he got to the manor. Clive knew that, but he just hoped that Phillip and his men would have her protected enough to hold him off until they could get there. He was again very happy he sent his sister and mother away. They were the last people he wanted to have to worry about. He only wanted to concentrate on Louissa.

CHAPTER TWENTY-FOUR

The clock chimed eleven o'clock. It had been dark for hours and still no signs. Louissa had spent the first couple of hours looking for an escape, but Phillip proved a worthy kidnapper. He mentioned that Laird Margaret had been a solid teacher and she couldn't argue that. She had expected them to dump her in the study. She knew several ways to escape there, but alas, so did the servants. Instead, they put her in a small room with shelves covering the walls and no windows. It was off the study and she assumed it was some kind of butler's pantry. They placed a chair in there for her with a blanket and water jug for her comfort.

When her uncle had appeared at the shed, her skin crawled at her reaction. She was so afraid of the idea of being hanged as the magistrate had explained that she was more than willing, happy even to see her uncle. When he put her in the carriage and then dragged her onto a strange ship, however, her feelings were less than familial. She chastised herself that her plan for the day, which was to kill or commit suicide or both, was not any better than getting abducted and imprisoned, then abducted from her abductor and imprisoned again, only to get abducted a third time, and again imprisoned, but this had not been her plan.

She had not been privy to any foolhardy notion of overtaking her uncle and his crew, so was not hoping for good news when it did finally come. She sat from the weight of it all, Tried to the bone and sick of fighting. Louissa had been fighting since she was eight years old, and what did she have to show for it? Her brother was still not found, if he was even still alive. She would never be the heiress to her father's legacy. She was beyond saving her reputation for a good match in marriage, and now would be a fugitive for the rest of her life, if she were able to escape. However, the worst part of this whole mess was Clive. How in the world could he be the best thing that ever happened to her and the worst thing all at the same time?

She felt an invisible band tighten around her chest, so hard she began to gasp for air. The idea of living the rest of her life without him made it not worth living. Her hand shot to her pendant. She just might have a use for the poison inside it after all. She would wait for word of the outcome, and then if he had not survived, she would take it. If in fact he was as skilled as she hoped and he made his way back to her, she could still take the draught if he set her aside and turned her out. In her mind that would be the only logical outcome. If she were not capable of being his wife, she would be a pariah, a fallen woman. She supposed he could suggest she stay on as his mistress, but she could not. She loved the fool.

That admission wretched a sob from somewhere deep inside her that was loud enough to bring Phillip to the door. "Lady Louissa? Are ye quite awright in there?" He asked concern deep in his voice.

She cleared her throat and put on a big smile, because she had learned by smiling, your voice wouldn't sound as unhappy. Her uncle did not like it when Louissa sounded unhappy as a child. He akinned it to being ungrateful. She had not liked the outcome of such encounters and learned how to hide her emotions. "Thank you, Phillip, I am fine," she replied. He was a good captor, but an awful judge of women.

When had she let her guard down enough to fall in love? She began to sweat and feel chilled at the same time. She couldn't put her finger on a moment directly after their first encounter that she didn't feel strange around him. She had loved Breakerton from the moment she met him. Again, the blow of the realization took her breath. Now, she was going to lose him, actually had already lost him, or never had him to begin with.

The weight of her life caved in on her like an ocean wave in a mammoth storm. The grief of all she has lost bore down and the tears streamed uncontrollably. Gone was her ability to be the strong little sailor or the tough highwayman. She slid from the chair and curled up on the floor. With her back against a wall of shelves, she pulled her legs into her chest and wrapped herself with her arms. The only type of hug she had ever gotten once her parents and brother died, and the only kind of hug she could trust as an adult. Still the tears drained from her body, taking her resolve and all of her fight. Everything and everyone she touched with even an ounce of hope in her heart was killed or taken from her. She had been so angry for so long, it fueled her, kept her going. She did not allow herself to feel past the anger. The anger was solid. It would protect her. Beyond the anger was nothing she could use to protect herself. Now, though the anger was gone like the sea mist on a warm day. One minute she felt it hard and safe around her body, the next gone. She was exposed and raw.

Alone.

She buried her face into her knees, as another sob wracked her body and a cry so old, so heavily laden with all her fears and losses that it might rip her in half if she allowed it to be heard. So she pressed her mouth closed biting the inside of both cheeks, and pushed it with all her might into her knee until she could swallow it and put it back into the darkest parts of her.

She lay in that position letting her body drain itself. When finally, she felt like a wineskin that had bled out its contents, she brought herself to a sitting position, still with her knees tight to her chest and just sat in the darkness. To her surprise, she felt nothing. Gone was the hot anger that kept her warm on Scottish nights and fueled her daily thoughts. She was empty. She wondered a bit wistfully if Clive were alive and would have her. If perhaps, she wasn't so broken that he could fill her back up. She knew it would take a lifetime, and one that would be riddled with her instinct to protect and fight, but without the hate and fear, there was room.

"Hey, ye ain't supposed to be ere!" She heard Phillip yell, just before she saw the light streaming from under the door begin to shift and dance, as the sounds of a struggle met her ears. Her uncle. Every muscle in her body tensed and coiled, ready to defend herself. She bolted upright, the fragile shell of a girl gone and the warrior standing guard. She felt around the shelves for a weapon, and then drew her hand over a mortar and pestle. It had a huge mortar for soap making she thought. Made out of solid stone, it would make a worthy weapon. She would have to be close, as it was not long by design. Louissa was sure the inventors of such an object did not take into consideration how it would fare as an object used for defensive purposes. She made herself as small as she could against the shelves and waited in the shadows. Louissa knew how far the stream of light would reach into the room, because when she was brought food, she had metered her chances of hiding and getting free. She had not had the chance, because that had been the last time the door was opened.

Careful not to call out or make a noise, she knew that now was the time to see if her theory was correct. Better yet, her uncle didn't know for certain that Louissa was the one being held in here. For all he knew, he came upon Phillip just walking past the room. If she could remain unknown, she might have a chance. More footsteps could be heard coming to the poor man's rescue. At the same time, she heard what she knew was Phillip hitting the floor in a heap. She bit back her groan. She hoped he was not dead. She liked the man.

After more shouting, and more men hitting the floor, the corridor outside her prison went silent. Then after what seemed a lifetime, "Louissa?" Her uncle said in a lyrical tone, meant to call a wayward child back to you with the promise of no retribution. "Louissa, I know yer in there. I'm a comin' in and 'tis time ye met up with ye mother and fither. It 'tis."

She felt the tremor start at her ankles and shoot up to her knees, which she locked in place so they would not collapse. Her stomach tightened and twisted. The mortar in her hands felt like it weighed 50 stone as her muscles tightened then slacked with the fear. This was it. She was the last vestige of her family. If he killed her, he won. He would get everything and her branch of the family would be forgotten. Her back stiffened as if an invisible rod slid down and locked into place. It pulled her head back and her chin up and gave support to her arms to wield her weapon. The ocean, which had been the only constant in her life roared in her ears as she barely heard the lock slowly slide out of its cradle. Then she saw the beam of light stretch into the room, stopping just before the tips of her boots.

Her uncle stood in the doorway, sword drawn, the light fighting for purchase into the room around his huge barreling form. In her mind, she thought she could hear banging and more voices yelling, but she had already thrown herself into motion and the world ceased to exist, save for her and her uncle.

"ARRRRRRRR," she exploded from the shadows more beast than human flailing her stone club at her surprised uncle. Before he was able to raise his sword, Louissa had made contact, sending the man backward, tripping over unconscious men as he went. From behind her, she heard voices, but did not or could not care enough to stop. They might well kill her, but she was bringing her uncle to the gates of hell before she continued on to heaven. Again, she swung, and again, she made contact. She heard the cracking of bone as the man who had tormented her for most of her childhood and all of her adult life raised his arms to protect himself. She heard her name again from behind, but it didn't matter.

"Louissa! Bloody hell cease, you're going to kill him." Clive's voice rang in her ears, as she felt herself being lifted in the air, her mortar falling from her hands with a thud. She realized her vision was gone. She could smell blood, the metallic scent making the air taste funny on her tongue. She could hear people around her, men's voices, grunts, furniture being pushed or moved. And Clive. She was engulfed by his strong arms pulling her rigid body to his chest. Her ankles vibrated from kicking back against his legs vying for purchase to free herself to continue… Oh God. She went limp in his arms. Slowly, her vision cleared a bit, but remained hazy with unshed tears.

She looked up into his face. "Look at me. Louissa, do you hear me? Don't look behind you, look right at me." He cupped her cheek with one hand, but continued to move into the parlor where he finally put her down on her own feet. Her legs though, promptly gave out and he grabbed her before she dissolved into the puddle she felt like.

He set her on the long stuffed sofa and sat at her feet, cataloguing every inch of her. "What are you doing?" She asked, still trying to get her bearings about what had happened.

"I am counting every scratch and nick on your person, so that once your uncle has healed from your beating, I can then do what I told him I would, which was beat him for every mark he left on you." His face was like marble, the plains of his jaw tight and clenched. His brow was knit together in anger and his eyes were dark and ominous. He had a large cut under his left eye and a bruise spreading up his forehead and down to the cheek. She couldn't help, but reach out and touch a curl that was determined to defy its brethren and remain on his forehead.

"You're alive," she whispered, needing to fill her renewed vision with his image.

He looked up then and his expression softened. "I had no other choice, my lady. You were in a rage at me, and you needed me alive, so as to continue your tirade. I would never leave a lady unable to play out a good row."

"You saved me." Again, it wasn't a question or a statement, but more an astonished realization put to voice.

"I promised myself, my lady, that you would be made the heiress that you are. I couldn't very well go back on my own honor now, could I?" He smiled then and ran a feather light finger from her hairline, down the side of her face, and under her chin.

"I didn't ask you to." She still had the need not to be a burden to anyone.

"No, you didn't," he answered.

"Is she going to be well?" a deep unfamiliar voice behind her brought her out of a trance that surrounded them.

"A bit weathered and worse for wear, but with some food and a bath, and a good solid night's sleep, I think she will be fine. I will call the surgeon to make it official though."

Louissa turned toward the person Clive was speaking to. A man, younger than Clive, but just as broad shouldered and well-built with thick black hair stood in the doorway. He looked over much concerned, Louissa thought for someone she didn't know. Her muscles were beginning to tighten up from her exertions, both physical and emotional she assumed, so she turned back and gave Clive a look of question.

Clive motioned for the man to come into the room and he strode in, standing in front of Louissa, silent.

"Louissa, I would like to introduce you to your brother, Henry."

The sun shone bright. Louissa knew this only because through her eyelids, she could see a kaleidoscope of colors and her face was warm. She never allowed herself to be a lag about and lounge longer than necessary, but she was not in a hurry to get up. Her bed was too comfortable, too luxurious. Wait, luxurious? Nothing about her bed was luxurious. The events of the previous day flooded her making fear follow. Her eyes shot open, taking in her surroundings, but not registering, only knowing she was not at home. She sat up, and sitting by the fire, reading a book was Lady Mary, who looked up when Louissa shuffled the sheets around.

"Oh, good, you are finally awake. We were beginning to worry," Mary said as she set down her book and came to sit on the edge of the huge bed Louissa was currently occupying. Her confusion must have been clear, because Mary laid a hand on hers and patted it gently, "You are safe, my dear. Perfectly, safe."

"Thank you—I…"

"Shh, Breakerton will want to know that you are awake, and I am sure you would rather pepper him with questions." She smiled kindly. "I will call for a tray of light fare to be brought up and tea.

Everything is better with tea. I would assume you are hungry?" She questioned.

To answer her, Louissa's stomach groaned and echoed because it was so empty. "Famished actually. How long was I asleep?" Louissa asked.

"Two days."

"Two—"

"And they were two days fraught with over bearing men used to being able to dictate all that happened in their world. They were most put out that they could not simply demand that you wake." Mary's smile belayed her annoyance.

"Men? Someone other than Lord Breakerton?"

Mary chuckled. "My dear, after watching my brother dote over you for the past two days, I am wont to believe you have spent some time in this bed quite awake. I am certain you call him Clive by now."

Louissa was already a bit lightheaded, so the blush that burned hot up to her hairline didn't help. Mary didn't expect an answer, but just continued to pat her hand. "As for your questions, the doctor has advised that we go slowly with any new information as not to disrupt your female constitution any more than it already has been."

At that, Louissa sat up again and meant to protest, but Mary held up a hand to stay her argument. "My brother has spent his life around strong-willed women, raised by most of them actually since he is the baby, so he is well aware of what a woman's constitution can handle, but he has asked that he be the one to speak with you. So, with that, I will make my absence and get your food, and send Clive your way."

"Thank you, again," Louissa said lying back on the bank of pillows. She was beginning to realize that she hurt. She hurt everywhere. Her eyes burned, and felt like sand had been rubbed into them. Her cheeks were raw and chaffed, and every muscle required to do, well anything, screamed its reticence to move ever again. Once Mary quit the room, Louissa attempted to stretch out, groaning audibly as she tried. So intent was she on trying to make her muscles move that she didn't notice Clive enter, but when he was at her bedside forcibly laying her back on the mattress, she became aware.

"You are hurt, don't move," he commanded. His face was a stark contrast to the jovial, devil may care man she was used to seeing. He looked haggard. Gone was the usual healthy color in his cheeks. Instead, it was replaced by an almost gray pallor. His beard was at least three days thick, and his eyes lacked the usual intelligent spark that spoke of wit and humor. His hair had been as many days untouched. She reached up, tugged on a curl hanging over his forehead, and immediately had Deja vu. He was without a coat or cravat, and his shirt looked as if he had slept in it. Repeatedly.

"You need water," he said with concern when she didn't speak. She watched as he crossed the room to fill a glass with the pitcher. She couldn't help but notice his muscles coiled and taut, ready to fight. Was she still in danger? Where was her uncle? What about Dermit? Would he still be seeking her out as his fiancé? Her breathing hitched up a notch, and the room began to spin. "Hold, what in—" She heard Clive sputter as she also heard the glass hit the floor and spill onto the expensive rug. She had her head down, trying to stave off the panic rising in her. She felt the mattress give under his weight, then his arm was around her, and she was being pulled to him. "Shh, Shh, love. I've got you. You are safe, shh."

"My uncle?" She managed to bite out in between gasping breaths.

"He is well in hand, that is after he heals from the injuries you inflicted, and I may have gotten in a few blows myself before he was taken away."

She looked up to see the truth of it in his face. Still stark, but his smile helped to ease the hardness in the plains of his face.

"Dermit?" She asked with even more fear, "I won't go, he

can't make me."

"Shh, there is no Dermit, Louissa, there never was."

"Yes—"

"No." He stroked her hair in a slow, consistent movement making her relax a fraction. "Dermit was a spy. He was a made up character—"

"But, I saw women be taken by my uncle and brought to him," she demanded. She hadn't imagined it and he had to believe her. He had to understand the danger she was in, the danger they both were in. "Those women were taken as his brides, and then he would return for another and another. He would kill them." Again the panic rose and with it bile, burning her throat.

"No, love, they were not killed." His voice was low and comforting, the kind she could listen to and fall asleep. "They were taken to a safe place in America. They were rescued."

"Rescued?" Louissa rubber her forehead, trying to piece together the reality out of what she knew to be true.

"Perhaps this is too much—" Clive made to rise.

"No." Louissa reached out to stop him and regretted it. Her arms felt like strands of rope on a ship, when they were beyond saving. "Why in bloody hell am I so sore?"

"You beat your uncle, repeatedly, with a stone mortar weighing at least half a stone, sweeting. Do you remember?" He still rubbed her head with one hand, and rubbed tender circles on her palm. She thought quietly about what she remembered last.

She went through the day. Being arrested, being taken by her uncle, then being brought here, then… "Oh God. Clive, I didn't kill him?" She asked, feeling all the blood draining from her limbs and a coldness seeping in.

"No, love. You gave it a good go, but you only broke his arms, and bloodied his face and head. He will survive," he reassured her.

"I—I heard him outside the room beating those men, and I knew if he got to me, I would have no one to protect me. I had to defend myself. I just knew he would kill me if I didn't." She leaned into his chest, hiding her face, waiting for the tears, but she had drained them in her tiny prison. She had no more tears for him, or for what he did to her family.

"You did just right, love," he assured her. "He will be going straight to Edinburgh and face charges, which includes the murder of your parents and the attempted murder of your brother."

Louissa nodded, then stopped as the words sank in. "What do you mean attempted murder? Are they trying him based on my hearsay?"

"No love."

"Then—" She didn't dare say the words allowed.

"I was beginning to think ye would lie abed for eternity and never wake to kiss your brother." Louissa looked toward the voice, which was deep, but not as velvety as Clive's was. In the doorway stood a man. She remembered seeing him before she lost consciousness the night of the attack. She took a long moment. He was tall, at least as tall as her father, perhaps taller. He was well built, not as well as Clive, but he was also younger than Clive was. His hair was as black as her own was, but what drew her to him and tugged at her memory was the crooked smile which went to his eyes and lit them like a candle.

"Henry? Henry, is that truly you?" She looked to Clive, then back at the unknown man. Both men were nodding and smiling. At that, Louissa rose to her knees on the bed, not caring that she still donned a night rail, or that her muscles had ached just moments earlier. He was in the room and at her side before she could scurry off the bed. Clive had made his way back to the dropped glass to make space for the reunion.

That was when Louissa felt the tears. Hot and fast traveling down her cheeks, but these were tears of joy, not sorrow. She knew now that her life would be filled with a lot more tears, but all would be of joy. Henry kissed her and promised he would be back later, but the Lord Advocate and the Lord Justice Clerk were waiting to take his statement. They had given him time while Louissa had not awoken out of respect, but they were now ready to proceed and get the nasty business over.

"Promise?" She asked again, before letting him go.

"I promise, dear sister. We have much to catch up on."

"Wait," looking to Clive and back to Henry, "how do I know 'tis truly you? I have not seen you since you were a lad." She needed proof, because she would not let her heart free until she had proof.

"Let me see your locket," Henry instructed.

Louissa's hope soared, as she pulled the locket from under her night rail and let Henry take the heart shaped pendant in his large hand. He turned it until the missing piece was on top. He then drew a large signet ring, her father's ring off his little finger. It was the ring that Gareth had turned her family's home upside down looking for, until finally deciding it went overboard with her father.

Henry placed the raised ruby into the spot on the ruby in the heart and they all heard a click. The locket opened and inside were two silhouettes of their parents and the words *love family* etched around the bends of the heart. It was he.

"How?" Louissa didn't have to finish her question.

"Cook told me that father went to him two days before they were killed. He gave Cook the ring and a letter to be delivered to Lady Margaret, and he asked Cook to protect you and me." Clive rubbed her back and Henry planted a long missed kiss on her cheek. "I have to go, but we will have all the time you want to talk when I am finished. Rest."

She nodded and allowed him to leave. He shut the door quietly behind him.

Louissa laid back on the bed, her physical pain forgotten, and her past however many years, behind her. She couldn't believe she slept through two whole days of her new life. It seemed such a waste.

"Why the big frown?" Clive asked as he came back to his

spot on the bed and rubbed the furrow between her brows.

"I just realized I have been a free woman for two days, with my brother returned to me, and I have wasted the first two."

Clive chuckled deep in his chest. She liked how the rumble felt next to her. Then she remembered their last interaction. She had told him she never wanted to see him again, and that she would never want to be with someone like him, but she also remembered her declaration in the locked room, and the reality of their situation. What could she say? He felt the shift in her body, because he put his finger under her chin and lifted her face so he could study it.

"What now, sweeting? What is it?"

"We. You. Us." She began three times, because she could not figure out how one tells someone that they love them, but also know that person could never act on that statement.

This time, it was Clive's turn to shift uncomfortably. The pang in her heart had the capability to destroy her, she knew. She only got her brother back and that would have to be enough. She knew that. "'Tis all right. I understand," she said, trying to sound unnerved, but didn't think she did it well.

"What do you think you understand?" He asked with a soft concerned voice.

"You, you have done more than any sane man would be expected to do, my lord. I will forever be in your debt for bringing my brother back to me. I do not know how you managed it, but I could never repay such a gift." She was prattling and she knew it. However, what does one say in such a situation. Perhaps if she had been raised a lady, she would be able to comport herself in a more appropriate manner.

"I can think of one way and only one way for you to repay such a gift," Hhe said to her with cold steel replacing the calm quiet voice.

Louissa thought him a bit conceited in already having thought of recompense, but she would do anything to show him her gratitude. If she could not show him her love, then her gratitude would have to be enough.

"What is that?"

"Marry me, Louissa."

She sat in stunned silence, but managed to rally and get her addled mind to work. "Whatever for?" she asked, true confusion showing on her face she was certain.

"Why do people get married, Louissa?" He asked a bit exasperated.

"Well, well, there are many reasons why people get married. They get married to create alliances. They get married to pay a debt. They, they get married when a woman has been compromised— oh, oh no," she stammered. He must be offering, because he ruined her. "I will nay marry you, ye fool. Ye bedded me thinkin' I was being sent to a horrible man and that I would most likely die. I cannae hold ye to such a standard. Plus, I seduced you."

"Wait, what? You think you seduced me?" He said the humor back in his eyes and voice.

"Aye," she said a bit annoyed at him finding such humor in it.

"Do you know you do a remarkably good job at keeping your Scottish accent at bay, until you get a bee in your bonnet?"

"I—what? Did ye— ah, you get your head beaten?" She asked, but allowed him to pull her down into the warm circle of his arms.

"Yes, as a matter of fact I did, repeatedly, but that is neither here nor there." He kissed the top of her head, "You, my Lady Heiress, forgot a most inviting reason people get married."

She looked at him, not daring to try to finish his sentence.

"People get married because they love each other. And I, Lady Louissa, have been in love with you since the night you almost severed my arm from my person."

"I did no such thing. 'Tis but a scratch," she protested, but with very little bluster. He reached around her and rubbed his wounded arm. "I am glad though that it was not severed. I quite like it as my pillow."

"You do, do you?" He asked snaking his hand down from around her head, toward her breast, which was easily accessible in the untied night rail.

"MmHmm," she agreed and snuggled in more.

"I love you, Louissa, and I know I do not deserve such a prize after the things I have said and done, but—"

"Shut up. Have any of your sisters ever told you that you talk too much?"

"Very often, in fact," he assured her.

She slid out of the safe circle of his arm to get into a kneeling position. He continued to lie on the edge of the bed, his long, muscled legs outstretched with his ankles resting one on top the other. "Well, ye do talk too much. Ye need a bath and a shave. Ye look like hell, but nothing you could say or do to make me not want to marry you, Lord Breakerton. I was too busy trying to fight the tide to realize just how much I love you, until I thought I had lost you."

Clive smiled, showing his dimples. He pulled her back into his arms, but this time, he flipped and was on top of her, kissing her until he rolled back to her side. She wriggled and giggled until her ribs hurt, and then she got serious. Talking about marriage and living it were vastly different things.

"Clive—"

"Yes, love," he asked languidly, content with his eyes closed trying to doze next to her.

"Talking about marriage is lovely, but I am ruined. Not to mention, I was not raised to be a lady. I would no doubt bring more scandal on your family than you realize."

"Now, who is talking too much?" he asked with one raised brow.

"But, I…"

"Hush. Not one person in London knows one wit about your upbringing, and to be honest, once you talk with your brother, you will see that he is a hero to the Crown of England. You, my dear, would be the toast of the Ton. I will have my sisters and mother tell everyone you are my wild Scottish love and that you stole my heart like a highwayman." He had risen up on his elbow and looked at her with love. She could see it now.

"You love me? You truly, truly, love me?" She asked, the astonishment tinging her voice.

"Yes, my dear, I do, and I promise you that just a month in London, and every man married or no, will be in love with you as well. I may very well come to me death in a duel after all, just not with you, but defending my right to you."

He bent and kissed her nose.

"I love you too, darling. And don't worry, I will be happy to be your second in any duel you have to fight in my honor."

"Perhaps, you should fight the duels and I'll be your second," Clive suggested.

"As you wish," Louissa said and cuddled in next to the man she loved, allowing those tears of joy to soak his dirty shirt and she didn't care one wit who saw. She decided her time as a highwayman was well spent, because this man was her greatest spoil and she would enjoy him forever.

Epilogue

Clair Brett

London, September 1, 1817

"Scared?" Breakerton asked, standing in line to be introduced at The Duchess Colebrook's late season ball.

"Would ye think less a me if I said yes?" Louissa answered with a bit of a shake and a lot of a lilt in her voice.

"No, but you have nothing to worry about. Look around you. There is a veritable army of the most powerful women of the Ton in your service, love." He squeezed her hand for reassurance. He could only imagine what Louissa was thinking. A girl raised on a ship, or in the wilds of Scotland. The glitz and glamour of a Duchess's ballroom would be more threatening to Louissa than a gale wind and twenty-foot waves.

They waited as the couples ahead of them were introduced. He only vaguely remembered the last time he entered a London ballroom, and it was as he had explained to Louissa, it was only for the card room and drink. Now, it was to introduce the world to his wife. Thankfully, the special license came in handy once Louissa was feeling more herself. It was not a grand affair. Just his mother, Nettie, Mary, Henry, and Bethany, with Nicholas performing the vows, but it was perfection. Mother and his sisters left not long after to ready the house in town for the Earl and his new wife. Louissa and Henry spent many days together, until he had to go to sea to finish his agreement with the Crown and tie up many loose ends of various jobs he had been working on. However, Louissa's nights had been all for Clive.

He looked down at his wife, a bit pale and that worry line he had become so familiar with was marring her otherwise perfect countenance. He would not be surprised if she carried his child even now. She was not aware of the changes yet, but he had noted things. With sisters to spare, he was aware of the signs. He would not tell her, but let her figure out on her own, then come to him with the news, and he would be excited, twirl her around, and treat her like the most precious of treasures, which would inadvertently perplex and frustrate her. He smiled as they moved up in line closer to their introduction.

"Twill be fine," came a soft calming voice from behind them. Lady Renwick had put a hand on Louissa's shoulder in comfort. "We have practiced almost all the social situations you might encounter and you did perfectly well."

"Tis the ones we didn't practice that worry me," Louissa admitted. Clive rubbed the hand that rested on his coat sleeve.

"You will not be left alone. You have enough ready to come to your aid, my lady."

Nettie piped up down the row of waiting guests. "Don't worry, dearest sister. I will steer you clear of any younger ladies we should be cautious of." For her efforts, her mother covertly jabbed her in the ribs. "Of course, I am sure no such ladies would dare attend the Duchess's ball," Nettie corrected, rubbing her side.

Clive was prepared for the reaction of the Ton, when at last they stepped up to the top of the stairs. Louissa had been sequestered away from all but only the most influential of the Ladies in society. The idea had been according to his mother to keep the mystery buzzing so to make her the talk of the entertainment they chose to have her presented at. Looking out at the sea of feathers, jewels, lace, and silk his mother should be in charge of the Scottish Tattoo. To Clive's frustration, but not his surprise, the men were as interested as the women were.

"What is it?" Louissa asked with concern. She must have felt him tense.

"Nothing."

"No, not nothing," she pressed. Clive wished it didn't take an elderly woman so blasted long to get to the bottom of the staircase.

"Do you remember those duels I mentioned having to fight?"

"Yes," she answered.

"Well, I have begun my list. Do you not see every man in the damned room not ogling you? I'll kill them all."

Louissa smiled brightly at him. "Thank you."

He didn't have time to ask what for as the butler cleared his throat to present them as the room for the first time in the evening fell silent.

"The Earl and Countess of Breakerton."

Clive led Louissa down the stairs to silence that turned into a wave of whispers. He could not remember a moment in his life of being so proud. The woman on his arm was the love of his life. These people's opinions didn't mean anything really. He would love her regardless, but at this moment, he was the Earl of Breakerton, and his wife the countess, would take on the Ton as she did everything else in her life. He almost felt bad for the few women in the group who could not hide the contempt, because if Louissa and the rest of the women in his life couldn't bring them into the fold, they would bring them to their social end.

As soon as Louissa's slippered foot hit the ballroom floor, they were flooded by women wanting an introduction. Clive held forth, until his mother, sisters, and Lady Renwick were there, then he stepped back, but never leaving her proximity. More to fend off the circling foxes than to help Louissa maneuver socially.

He listened as a break in the introductions allowed Lady Renwick to help Louissa with names. "Over there is Lady Grant. Her husband, Viscount Grant, are neighbors of ours at the country manor. Quite nice. I shall introduce you. And that, is Lady Vanessa, their daughter. She came out last year. It was quite successful, but nothing quite stuck. She has many choice prospects this year. Over by the potted palm is Lady Gwendaline-Alise. She is the daughter of the Duke and Duchess of Colebrook. You will see her at every ball, but rarely will she mingle. Painfully quiet. I have spoken with her on a few occasions in the ladies retiring room, but not in public."

"Could she be her?" Louissa asked. Clive had not one whit what they were talking about?

"Could she be who?" he asked.

"Lady A," both women answered at the same time.

"She is on my list of possibilities, yes, but I am not sure. Then, over with that group of young gentlemen is Lady Amelia Strafford. She is a widow to the late Earl of Strafford. Her infant son now holds the title. She is my prime guess. She is well situated with a son who will not be in his majority for many years, which leaves her relatively free to live as she pleases. She is also as well connected as any other to hear gossip.

"Who is this Lady A?" Clive prodded, very curious. He noted the look of frustration on Louissa's face and the smile of pity on Ella's.

"Lady A writes a social column in the times which chronicles the whereabouts and doings of the Ton's most eligible bachelors for any given season. Renwick was featured, along with the sad news that he had found his wife and was bringing her back from Scotland with him," Ella explained.

"You were in it. I have it at home. I shall read it to you. It also mentions the possibility of you being abducted by a highwayman." She smiled.

"It also has anecdotes from some of the Ton's most secretive and quick of weddings, including yours. And, I was told only recently that Renwick's and mine was featured so many years ago. I have not found a copy though."

"So, why the desire to know who she is?" Clive asked still perplexed at time by the female mind.

"Because," continued Ella, "if we do not know who she is, how are we to school our features and count our words when around her. At any time her column could move from bachelor's to any number of topics that could be damaging to many."

"I am not nearly as worried, I just find it fascinating that a woman can walk among such a group without being known,"

Louissa added.

"But, my dear, you did that for quite a long time yourself," Clive reminded her.

"Oh, I did, did I not?" she remembered.

"Well then, perhaps it will be our own wolf in sheep's clothing that will help us to ferret out Lady A," Ella stated, just before a bevy of ladies descended, including the evening's hostess, The Duchess of Colebrook.

Everyone bowed and curtsied. Clive did the honors, but knew she had already attended at least two teas at the Duchess bequest. "Your Grace, may I introduce my wife, Lady Breakerton."

She looked up at Clive with sharp, penetrating eyes. "Yes, you may, then be gone. You are hovering like a veritable hound following a juicy pork chop. You may have her to yourself later. Now, she is ours. Go find the card room. That is what it is for. So that besotted young husbands will have a place to be until they are needed for a dance. Now go." And with that, she banged her cane on the floor as to punctuate her decree. The other women around the group twittered with giggles as Clive left to find a corner. No way was he leaving all together. As luck would have it, they were already standing quite close to another potted palm. He made his way around the room, and then rested on the other side of the plant.

"My dear, I hope you are finding your way," the Duchess said.

"Yes, Your Grace. It has been a bit intimidating, like walking into a foreign land, and having to learn the customs and the language at the same time. I am lucky to have my new family and friends to help."

"Of course dear. Your upbringing did nothing to prepare you, but as many in the Ton believe, good blood will always rule out in the end, of which you have an abundance I have heard. I do not think bloodline has much to do with how a person will be in society. The best bloodlines of England hold some of the biggest idiots."

Louissa apparently didn't know what to say, because there was a bit of a pause, and then the Duchess continued, "Breakerton, is he being a good husband?" she asked.

"Yes, Your Grace. He is the best husband."

"Well, why on earth would you think he is the best?" The Duchess asked.

"Because he is my husband, Your Grace. I wouldn't have married him had he not been my perfect husband."

Breakerton held his breath hoping her enthusiasm wouldn't be seen as impertinence. There was a bit more silence, then laughter, and the Duchess's voice over the giggles.

"I am sure you have the right of it, Lady Breakerton. We all were sure whoever snagged him, he would be suited well to the task."

He saw across the room his mother giving him a wave. Time to go. They had decided to stay only long enough to give them a taste, and then house visits come on the morrow. His mother had come to him with her concerns about Louissa's condition the week before and decided to limit her time in the throngs.

He gathered his mother, sisters, and Renwick, who were all in close range and went to steal his wife back from the Grand Dames.

"Your Grace, I hate to, but I must take my beautiful wife from you and call it a night."

"Nonsense, you haven't even danced yet," the Duchess protested.

"I am terribly sorry, but my mother has a headache and as we all came together, it would not do for us to send her home alone."

"Of course, you are correct. Please tell Lady Breakerton to feel better, and I will expect her to call on me this week."

Clive bowed over the Duchess's hand. "Of course, Your Grace."

They made their goodbyes to the others and found their way

out of the crush to the waiting carriages. Once ensconced in their own, Louissa laid her head back and closed her eyes.

"Tired sweeting?" Clive asked.

"Overwhelmed. So many names, and who is connected to whom. How do you and your sister's manage?" she asked, laying her hand on his thigh, causing a reaction that after a whole carriage ride from Scotland should not have the reaction it did.

"We were raised with most of these people. You'll get it."

"Yes, I suppose I will," she said.

"Are you terribly tired?" he asked again.

"Why, are you?" she asked.

"Not in the least love," Clive said with a growl to his answer.

"Why Lord Breakerton, did you lie about our mother's headache?"

"Yes."

"Am I being abducted?" She asked with sensual interest in her voice.

"Have you unpacked your highwayman garb?" He asked nuzzling her neck.

"Mmm, yes, but they won't fit you."

"They don't need to fit you either, for I will have them off you in a shorter time than it takes you to put them on, but that is not the point is it, Lady Breakerton?" He said pulling her over on to his lap and shaking the pins free of her hair.

"I suppose not, dear husband, but we should take care to watch Lady A's next post to see that she isn't aware that there is a highwayman among the Ton," she joked.

"That will be the second thing I do in the morning," he promised.

"What is the first?"

"This," he said, and the noise she made could not be mistaken for anything but pleasure. Clive dearly hoped this mysterious Lady A had heard that.

Clair Brett

About the Author

  Ex-Dragon keeper and historical romance author of two published novels, Clair Brett lives in NH with her hard working husband, and a senior in high school. Her office staff during the day consists of Cinta, a black cat and the matriarch of the fur babies, Mojo, a yellow kitten who spends his day holding Clair down in her seat to get her word count in, and a boxer/beagle mix puppy named Willow, who sleeps next to her chair to make it hard to do an Oreo run without doing a pee run as well.

  A former middle and high school English teacher, Clair has had a lifetime love affair with reading. Once she read Pride and Prejudice as an extra read in high school, she was hooked. Clair began pursuit of publication when she was a new mother in need of a hobby. Her oldest daughter and mama to the bearded dragon grand pet is off to serve in the Air National Guard as a medic and no longer in the nest, so you do the math. Clair is a firm believer that a reader finds a piece of who they are or learns something about the world with every book they read. She wants her readers to be empowered and to have a refreshed belief in the goodness of people and the power of love after reading her work.

Contact Clair

Website: www.clairbrett.com
Facebook: http://facebook.com/@AuthorClairBrett
Twitter: http://twitter.com/@clairbrett
Goodreads: https://www.goodreads.com/clairbrett
Amazon Author page: http://amzn.to/2fhSrm4
Pinterest: www.pinterest.com/clairbrett

Also Available from Clair
<u>*BUY NOW*</u>

After making a wager of marriage to settle her father's gambling debts, Ella Bowen-Thorn Renwick escaped the husband she foolishly began to fall for and disappeared into the Scottish countryside carrying a secret. Four years later, and the owner of her own bakery, she is still not free of the demands of men when a violent and anonymous blackmailer threatens her, her livelihood...and her daughter. And then, there is him...

Viscount Renwick still mourns the wife he began to love before her untimely death--that is until he discovers her alive and well living in Scotland. Now, Devon's face to face with the wife he thought he'd buried and the daughter he never knew existed. He'd like nothing more than to welcome Ella back into his arms, but mysterious and troubling incidents and a history with an unloving father have Ella trusting no one.

But, if Renwick convinces his wife he's the husband she always dreamed of and the father their daughter deserves, will the scandalous secret the blackmailer is holding threaten their future together once more?

Upcoming Release from Clair Brett

Marked for Love

Coming in Late 2017

www.ingramcontent.com/pod-product-compliance
Lightning Source LLC
Chambersburg PA
CBHW050722180626
46814CB00002B/558